DARKIN

A Journey East

By

Joseph A. Turkot

Cover Art by Joseph A. Turkot

www.novelfantasy.com

ADACON'S JOURNEY

PREFACE

This is a work inspired in no small part by Tolkien—at a young age he took me from my world and placed me firmly in his. In pursuit of creating a similar sensation of wonder and awe I continue to write today. This work began when I was fourteen years old: I wrote the first two chapters, after which it lay dormant for many years thereafter. I would go back often times and wish to complete the work, but it wasn't until seven years later that I set to the task earnestly. Now you hold in your hands the definitive edition of the first story in the Darkin saga. May it enchant you, take you on a journey, and give you many strange new acquaintances.

ACKNOWLEDGEMENTS

Thanks to Paul and Lauren—two who read this novel to its completion when I thrust it upon their busy lives. Thanks to Jeff, who did so in one sitting. Thanks to all who encourage my writing.

I would also like to dedicate this book to my loving and caring family: to my mom, Mary, Tom, Karl, and Paul—thanks for your constant support.

Contents

PROLOGUE

I sicken of burning flesh. Freedom rots here, persists as a parasite of the mind. A withered dream. The lords oppress us forever—no one fights. We are scum to them.

Why don't we fight back? Why don't we believe life can be better, or imagine a way to survive without them? We depend on them for all things—they understand this. There is no questioning their control. We must need them, we must love them. Hope is lost, freedom forgotten. Tales of old, whispers, rumors—they serve only to pain my heart now. To hang, or toil away in the confines of hell, which choice better serves me now?

~ excerpted from Remtall's diary

I: BREAKING THE FARM

Something snapped inside Adacon. He sat in his wooden hut, late at night by a glowing fire. Scraps of bread had served as dinner, along with saved wine. It had been a long and hard day on the farm, but no harder than usual: of all things, he knew he should feel happy, for today was the first of the month—the day he received his meager allowance of bread and water. But something stirred inside him, like a flame igniting, and he stood from his rotting stool, filled with defiance. He stared into the burning embers of the hearth; the fire returned his gaze. Something inside him fought to get out—a feeling he had ignored since childhood, something he always felt buried deep within his soul.

He was barely twenty years of age, a muscular young man. He pushed his fingers through maple-bark hair, staring with granite eyes, set into a face sharply featured and mature. He had no family, nor recollection of one; time clouded his earliest memories, though he could at times recall pieces of life spent in a dirty boarding hall where farm slaves were trained. The lords crammed more orphans there than the dwelling could house. Veteran slaves taught him skills for farm work, and everyone whispered that the lords saw all things. Swordladen guards maintained order at the hall, proving the existence of the lords' power over all men that lived upon Darkin. When he matured to his earliest manhood, they sent him to the farm he lived on until present; he worked as an earthtender on the seasonal harvests. Slaves spread tales of farms abroad, far across the wilds unknown; a great many farms existed, each meant to fulfill some desire of the lords. The crop work was grueling, and the labor unending.

He once had a friend, a fellow farm hand, who was hanged for defiant behavior. The young man, named Remtall, had spoken boldly about the despotism of the lords. The day of Remtall's death had burned itself into his mind, buried into his heart. He could remember some of the things that Remtall had told him: freedom was a thing worth having, and without it, life was not. He told other slaves that life was better than what they knew it as; he claimed a rebellion was needed. He said that life on the farm ought not be called life at all. Remtall's ideas roused the guards, and proved worthy of an unusual length of torture. The slaves gathered round to see his last moments before he hanged, so that they would know the price of insurrection.

Adacon knew his friend was under suspicion for some time, for he had talked of freedom too often, and too many times to the wrong slaves—for that, he had died. Adacon continued to labor, companionless, paralyzed by what had happened, until this moment: a strange force had taken hold of him this night. Death, it seemed suddenly, was no worse than the tireless slavery he endured each day. Something snapped in his head: he could no longer deny the fire Remtall had lit in his spirit; instead he would tend it, help it grow, until it consumed him, even if to his death.

The bravest of slaves stole literature from passing wagons, and learned to read what words they could by poring over the forbidden tomes at night. Rumors abounded that all the parchments ever written were to be burned at the bidding of the lords, and that each passing wagon was journeying toward a great fire in the West, where flames would consume all the knowledge of the world. Some books described a better age, a brighter time in Darkin's history. The books told of a time before slavery and oppression, a time when all who lived possessed a right to craft their own fate. The lost ideas of peace and happiness found in those yellowed scrolls had always meant a great deal to him, but harsh reality pushed such fantasies to a dark recess of his mind.

To be aware of his slavery was to suffer, and life was easier when he ignored the literature; but something inside him had broken this night, something that could not be mended. The fire was now lit, and Remtall's death no longer lingered purposeless in his mind. Life in its current mode seemed unimportant now. His life as a slave appeared without value. The idea of being free forsook his better judgment, and grew more powerful in him than the fear of death. And feeling so completed with his old mode of life, he planned a course of action.

Sentries watched over both exits of the farm; indeed the knowledge of slaves told that all the face of Darkin was covered by the mighty guards of the lords. Some slaves spun lore of rogue settlements, far to the east, where natives lived of their own accord, separate from lordship, but such people were only myth to Adacon. Elders taught those who were young in their labor that the lords kept a close eye on slaves all hours of each day, and that there existed no unseen patch of land before the guards of the lords.

He would take the northeast gate. Armed sentries stood guard there; swordsmen stalked the ground and archers stood atop wooden towers. The guards monitored all travel in or out of the farm, and any suspicious presences were taken captive; slaves whispered that the malodorous stench of burning that permeated the farm came from the bodies of those taken hostage at the gates. The elder slaves taught that it was through constant surveillance that the lords maintained order on their farms, and kept themselves in power above all others. Before his death, Remtall spoke of the arrogance of the lords: "They think themselves an undying legacy of power, that we cannot thwart them, but their sway does not darken the whole of this world yet, nor the hearts of all its creatures" he had pleaded. The very heart of Darkin's structure, it seemed, was fixed to keep the lords in power.

And a slave would always be a slave—he knew there was no chance to rise in the eyes of the lords. Elders preached that a good slave should value every opportunity he is given to work for the benefit of the powerful: a slave should always follow his superior's orders without question, and a slave should always be happy with his condition of living. The lords *made sure* that the slaves were happy, at any rate.

A tall, grisly man came each month, and stood coldly upon the step of his hut. He would ask the same questions—are you happy with how life is on the farm? Adacon was *always* happy. The dark man carried a spiked club at his side—if a slave voiced a grievance, doubted the satisfaction of slavery, the spiked club might find its way into the hands of the scary man. The *visitor* restored balance by any means necessary, even if it meant death. The whole structure of the world seemed unbreakable, just as Remtall had preached.

But something had snapped inside of him. Remtall's silenced yearning for a revolution grew anew in his own heart; it seemed the soil itself sent him courage, so that he might enact some bloody escape. As a young man he had stolen a sword from a wagon, and long kept it hidden under his cot. Nicks in the blade betrayed any look of sharpness, but it was a sword nonetheless. Adacon grimaced into the dying fire and almost smiled. He sat down on his creaky bed, tucked away in the corner of the small hut, and pulled on his boots. The embers in the hearth flickered out a slow death, and the air grew cold. His boots were sturdy, made of leather, and a rarity for slaves to have; his dedicated slavery had earned his right to them. He buckled them tight. It was night, nearly an hour from dawn; no slave was permitted out onto the fertile earth until sunrise, lest they sought a swift execution. He took his sword from its hiding and fastened it to his hip, and then he opened his door and stepped outside, breaking the law of the lords.

*   *   *

The farm covered many acres, but Adacon knew his way around it by heart, with or without sunlight. He did not know the wilds beyond; he hadn't set foot outside the gates since before his manhood. Sentry towers rose from two corners on the farm, one to the northeast, and one southwest. Each was built next to an exit gate that led away and across the countryside by way of small dirt roads.

His hut was located nearest to the northeast tower, and from his door he began a slow pace north along the dirt path that ran the length of the farm. The sky was blackened grey, without stars, and the night wind carried a pungent odor of burnt flesh—the ever-present stench of the farm. Time had dulled his repulsion to the rotten air. Slave lore told of large incinerators hidden inside the restricted building, wherein was housed some dark form of energy whose fuel required the flesh of men. He never dared enter the building, but he often watched curls of thundercloud-grey smoke roll from its chimney. The guards escorted slaves and captives into the building at odd times, young and old alike; none left.

The path continued straight, northerly along the edge of the crops. On either side, as he walked through the dead quiet, rose high cornstalks, too dense to see through. In the distance, the northeast sentry tower jutted above the crop line, a white silhouette cutting through the deep grey. A solitary light flickered near the top; an archer stood watch by an ever-lit torch.

He walked slower at the sight. A thought, of origin not his own, came into his mind: *a guard patrols the edge of the cornfield, just where your path runs east toward the tower.* No noise broke the silence save for the sound of his own footfalls. He trod as soft as he could; no fear forsook him at the warning, as fear ought to for a slave outside past curfew. A bold, immeasurable courage possessed his will, driving him forth, pushing him in a direction cloudy and perilous. His consciousness was no longer that of a normal man—he felt as if a beast of wilds unknown.

As a young man, he had played with his hoary sword, and by some measures had become a novice—but years had passed since last he held the cold steel: still, somehow, he felt as if his arms would know the motions should a strike be necessary. He glanced back in the direction of his hut, and saw the dull light of dying fire glow against the panes. Strange thoughts engorged his mind; his awareness sped from thought to thought, and, strangely, he felt a great calm sweep into his spirit. Time stopped for an eternity, and questions formed from a void: *what was the start of all this? When, in the eternal flow of time, did the cogs of fate start to turn? And at what point did they turn ill the fate of so many men?* Adacon turned

8

from the hut and looked northeast; the calm in his spirit boiled away, and the passion of Remtall set him ablaze.

He came to the edge of the corn. A sentry stood against a small tree, puffing on a slender black pipe; tufts of smoke filtered into the night air. The sentry did not look roused, or in an aware state at all for that matter; rarely did the sentries have anything to do at night except stand about and look at shooting stars. Adacon froze for a moment and unsheathed his blade. In his right hand he gripped the handle tightly and walked eastward.

Instantly, he ducked to the ground, lying flat against the cold earth. His nose pressed into the soil and he breathed deeply, replacing for a moment the smell of burnt flesh with that of tended soil. He rolled onto his back and looked up at the night sky, and in the direction of the sentry, let out a soft yelping noise.

As quickly as the sound had left his mouth, he rolled sideward into the last thicket of corn, concealing himself. Hard shoots grazed his flesh, releasing his blood along their stalks. The guard withdrew his pipe at the sound of the yelp and spun around quickly to face the direction of the noise. Through a gap in the undergrowth, Adacon saw a dumbfounded expression wrap round the guard's face as he looked for a source, baffled. The tower archer had been too far to hear the yelp. The man extinguished his pipe and looked up and down with great curiosity. Wearing an expression of unease, he trod slowly along the path southward, in the direction of the noise. He examined the ground around his feet as he walked; Adacon experienced a thought not his own: *he will see the broken earth, and where you lie hidden.* He readied his sword and clenched his teeth. The guard strode along with careful steps, coming within a single yard.

Looking closely at the crop line, the guard spotted the matted cornstalks; it was too late. Before the guard could draw his broadsword Adacon sprang up and hewed the man's torso at its center. Blood misted and the guard let loose a howling cry, unexpectedly loud. He quickly silenced the cry for help by slicing the sentry's throat with a quick thrust, causing him to fall dead to the earth with a thud. The strike had been fluid, precise—his body was not using its own faculties to battle, it seemed, but those of an alien bloodlust. His adrenaline, his passion, his body—they performed in accordance to what *had* to happen now, what *had* to be accurate and fatal.

He stood up, a wholly different being than last had stood upon the earth of Darkin in his shape, a murderer of men. He looked high enough to see broadly again over the top of the corn. The tower had heard the death cry; the noise had been too loud. He froze for an instant, paralyzed by a fleeting panic: something is wrong, he thought—I did not mean to be discovered. His adrenaline surged. A thought arose, and unsettled him: *they are coming.* Still too far away to be seen, he kept his eye on the tower, two archers manning it. One of the archers climbed down the tower ladder and the other stood in place. Adacon quickly ran out past the end of the corn trail and through a small clearing; the archers didn't spot him. Just beyond the clearing was an old barn, and to its west stood the restricted building, heaving rotten smoke from its chute. He darted to the far side of the decaying barn, safely out from sight of both guards.

As soon as he arrived on the side of the barn, a light struck out through the night air, shining down on where the first sentry had fallen. The light remained there, illuminating the surrounding area, as the archer now on the ground made his way toward the newly lit area. Adacon drew a quick glimpse of the area, edging to the end of the barn wall and peering around to watch for the guard's arrival. Blood had splattered onto his thin clothes, making them dirty and red; his face dripped with its warmth, and the taste of it possessed his tongue. Still, he felt calm and collected again, and he was not enraged. The possibility of freedom started to take on strength. It was almost tangible now, and only the guards stood between him and the unknown wilds beyond the plantation.

The archer on the ground stepped warily to the head of the trail that led south to the slave huts. Adacon watched the archer arrive and stoop to the ground to retrieve something—the dead sentry's pipe. The archer then turned southward and discovered the slain man's body; he gasped. Adacon wasted none of his opportunity for surprise, and sprang from his hiding.

The archer rushed toward the mangled body on the ground, shaken by the gruesome sight. Adacon ran at a full sprint for the archer's exposed back. With a clear motive, he raised his sword overhead and adjusted his momentum so as to strike down with great force upon the nape. A terrible horn sounded as his sword fell toward its target; the tower had seen the trap, and issued warning. The archer spun around fast enough to meet the falling edge with his neck. He slumped to the ground amidst a red fountain that steamed the cool air. One archer left, Adacon thought. He knew he would have to overpower the last archer from lower ground. He stole the bow and arrows from the fallen archer and found quick cover in nearby brush, dodging an arrow that whizzed by his head. The archer on the tower did not make a move—he stood atop the balcony and pointed the great light toward the foliage he had vanished into. Adacon waited quietly in the foliage for a sign of movement.

Minutes wore on, and his mind slowly trickled doubt about his situation. He wondered what would keep the archer up on the tower, as the lords bid their servants to fully control slaves at any cost, even that of their own lives. Then it hit him—with a shiver he realized that the archer was waiting for fellow sentries alerted by the horn. Three more would come at least. He decided not to wait for the incoming guards, and he dashed from his hiding place to a new one, closer to the tower. As he ran briefly into the open, another arrow slid by his frame, nearly tricking up his feet.

He crawled on all fours past huge thickets of ivy against a low stone wall. The wall ran southeast in a looping curve, out to the path leading directly to the tower, and the gate beyond. He remained unseen as he made his way east, face grappling with the earth in stealth. As the wall rose some, he turned his back against it and sat down, slowly removing an arrow from the slain archer's quiver. He knew his shot would depend on whether or not he could steady his hands enough to aim at the high target on the tower. The archer eyed the thick growths that hugged the north face of the wall, unable to see where the slave hid; the beam of light emanating from the tower revealed nothing. Adacon's face grew stern as the time for his deadly task came. He straightened the arrow against the string and centered its feathers in his sight. He decided to aim high and hope the arrow would arc; though he knew their make and purpose, he had never before used a bow and arrow. Still, he doubted he could hit the high target, despite a strange assurance overcoming him again. His attacks had been fatal and accurate thus far—maybe I can hit him, he thought.

He stood to fire, revealing his hiding spot. About to loose his arrow, he froze at the sudden clap of footsteps coming from behind. The footsteps were faint, twenty yards away at least, accompanied by muddled voices. He lost his focus for a moment to the distraction, but quickly returned his gaze to see the archer above fixing aim on him. Two arrows flew: the archer's spared its target; Adacon's did not. The form atop the tower grasped at his neck violently. The aim had been dead set. More red misted the night sky, illuminated by the torch harnessed to the tower balcony. The tower spotlight flickered out. The limp body toppled over the side of the tower rail and fell to the fertile earth, croaking until impact. Adacon began a mad dash at that moment, running directly to gain the tower. The trailing footsteps had grown louder, and he felt their eyes upon his back. The tower had seemed larger from a distance, and appeared smaller as he approached its ladder: it looked like a frail old piece of wood crafting, fashioned by wood slaves in the south. The old bars were sturdy though, and he quickly gained the high ground.

Three sentries came into plain view, rushing at the tower. He removed another arrow from his quiver and set it in place on the bowstring. He drew the string back and let the arrow fly, targeting the front most sentry. The arrow missed to the left, burying into the soft soil. He did not think—he instinctively reloaded the bow and fired again. The arrow hit, but not at its intended target; it glanced off the front guard's sword and flew into the archer that had been bringing up the rear. The arrow pierced through his lower left abdomen, leaving him helplessly wailing on the ground. Two guards rushed on—an archer and a swordsman; he reloaded his bow and fixed aim on the archer. Before he could release, the swordsman charged the ladder and haphazardly threw a knife skyward. He dodged the errant blade, but enough time had been saved for the archer to quickly take position behind the stone wall.

Adacon squatted behind the balcony's small rail to be out of sight. The swordsman grunted below, climbing the ladder with haste for the balcony. Adacon looked down through the floor hole where the ladder came up into the balcony. Peering down, he saw the top of a man's head rising upward fast. He felt no guilt as he fixed aim on the defenseless guard's skull and loosed another arrow. The force sent the guard tumbling back to the ground where, after a loud crack, blood pooled. One more, he tallied. The last archer sat hidden somewhere below, nowhere to be seen. With reckless abandon, Adacon flew down the tower ladder, hopped the slain guard at its landing, hit the earth, and ran toward the stone wall. He threw his bow to the ground and again unsheathed his sword. Gripping the hilt with both hands, he felt new energy course through his muscles—he stalked forth, and the fragrance of melted flesh bathed him once more.

He prowled the brush along the looping stone wall, searching the thicket where the archer had disappeared into. He froze to listen for noise—nothing. He grew impatient and started a mad search, untangling each piece of knotted brush. Suddenly, he heard the unmistakable sound of a twig snapping. It had come from behind.

He spun around to meet a cocked bow pointed at his face. The sentry launched an arrow at the slave's throat; Adacon reacted in time, reeling his sword upward in an instinctive reflex, severing the bow's sturdy frame. The arrow limply glanced from his neck, drawing a thin line of blood. The guard stumbled back in despair, and Adacon locked onto his eyes. They shared a brief moment of compassion before he swung his great blade around, this time horizontally at the guard's abdomen.

Snapping out of his momentary daze, the guard unsheathed his short sword and parried upward, causing a clangor of metal to break the quiet. Blue sparks of steel on steel fed Adacon's desire for freedom. The sentry struck back in the next second, thrusting powerfully in an upward slice at his torso—but he reacted as if possessed, countering without effort. The sentry wobbled off balance for a moment, stooping slightly to regain his footing—Adacon wasted no such chance, swiftly beheading the fazed guard. The guard hit ground with a thump.

A wail echoed from several yards away, and Adacon glanced to a still living guard, lying on the earth, grappling with an arrow stuck in his gut. He thought for a moment about sparing the helpless man, but memories of Remtall flooded in—there could be no mercy now. He thrust down once more, ending the cries, and a light filled his head…

The farm is free; at least for the moment. A fallen farm, he guessed, would take several days to replenish its guards; it was more than enough time to clean the evidence and make a swift and long departure. But he was not concerned with evidence; he felt that he had perpetrated no unlawful act. The words of his lost friend Remtall echoed in his head. This is the start, he thought. He sheathed his sword. The air had grown extremely foul, it seemed fouler than ever before, and he grew anxious to leave the smell behind. The landing of the tower ladder was painted scarlet, and Adacon had begun to leave his mark in the History of Darkin.

The gate to the outside world was fifteen yards away. He slowly walked the path. This is the start, he thought: there is no repenting this, not to the lords. He did not know where to travel once he made it beyond the farm gates, but he decided he ought to go east, in hope of finding free countries; he did not trust the slave lore, nor the tales of the elders, but he had no other hope. He knew it was more likely he would be picked up by sentries marching across the countryside, or by routing posts hidden throughout the land, only to be tortured and hanged. The guards of the lords had the right to sentence immediate death unto a slave. But fear was a feeling he now had no use for, it seemed—it was a newly estranged remnant of his old form. The sun leaked a hint of its first somber pink glow in the distance. Adacon wiped the blood from his brow and broke away from his past, through the farm's gates.

II: KREM THE VAPOUR

He had the clothes on his back, the boots on his feet, the sword at his hip, and the bow and arrows on his back, but Adacon did not have much else—certainly no food for making a long trip away from the farm. He knew he was not coming back, that he was leaving on a quest toward the hope that there were free countries in the east. It would be his new responsibility to find food and drink along the way, at whatever the cost.

He had not been hungry as he left the plantation, but hunger soon began to grow in him; he thought of the bread and water he received regularly on the farm, and how that was now a comfort of the past. The road leading away from the plantation was formed of dirt, and lined by green and gold shrubbery that outlined a dark red wood on either side of the path. He followed the path steadily into the morning, hearing the forest wake up for the coming day. From childhood he recalled strange memories of forest tales, stories whose origins were long forgotten. They were stories about curious things; tales of wolves and wizards, elves and trolls—the sort of lore that was meant to be believed for only the first quarter of your life. Stuff like *magic* and *spells*. He didn't believe in any of it, though he thought he would rather like meeting an elf. He had always heard elves to be loyal creatures of the forest, living at one with nature. The elves had no rule or slavery; they lived in harmony away from anyone else's concern, the fables told. Such was the kind of tall tale that had sometimes made him long to personify the stories, and embody a noble elf of the Red Forest.

Eventually the path led to a fork that split off heavily east in one direction, heading into what looked like a hot, sand filled horizon. The other direction jerked back and up north, deeper into the Red Forest. Relief came in not having to travel the wooded path any longer, as his quest called for him to move eastward. The entrance into the heart of the dangerous Red Forest is what the northern trail had been, he knew from tales, though the path itself was not labeled with any signs. The tales said that the Red Forest was full of evil things, and no sound-minded human should enter it alone. But the forest path was averted, and he made his way in the other direction toward a gloomy desert, slowly gaining glimmer as the sun came up. The weeds and grass around the path began to intertwine with patches of yellow sand, and a distinct smell arose; it was totally unlike that of the Plantation, not a pinch as vile. An aroma of warm bliss flowed in a delicate wind toward him, carrying the fresh smell of the dunes westward. The path leading out into the now cheerful desert seemed less than a few hundred yards, he realized.

Then, impulsively, he stopped walking for a moment, and glanced back one last time. Facing the direction of the life he was leaving behind, he felt his lingering stare hold all his memories in a single instant, one intense second of recollection, before melting away into passion. After several minutes, he looked away from the past, and set his eyes back upon the desert.

*   *   *

Adacon was a slave. Slaves did not get an education, especially any form of vital knowledge about the world or its geography. Slaves were given essential information needed to perform their duties. The information taught to a slave was always functional—it pertained either to how to use farm equipment or how to follow order. There were a select few whose dynasties were traced back to the most ancient times, slaves were told. These were the blood born rightful owners of Darkin. He was taught that the owners were gracious in that they allowed the poor to live on their land, and not only that, but offer them work on their farms. There could be no opposition because opposition meant death. No great powerful lords to control the great land of Darkin meant starvation and hunger for all, a good slave knew. It meant the absolute end to civilization. Still, he had always felt his mind was his most valuable asset, though it was restricted almost wholly. He had learned on his own to write, and had worked on his reading skills at night, absorbing books stolen from passing trade wagons.

He marched on, slowly starting to feel fatigued from the bloody scuffle he'd just survived. The sun rose slowly up and up, and soon the heat began to burn his skin. He wrapped his arms in a tight bundle, attempting to hinder the strong sun, but it didn't seem to help as the hot rays continued to scorch. He'd read about the desert before, yet never had it seemed in writing so cruel and hot. But it was hot, and before long he grew hungry and thirsty. The patches of green slowly fell out of sight behind him, as the path leading on through the desert twisted and trailed eastward.

He noticed his vision seemed blurry, but even still he thought he could see an unusual sand dune up ahead, spotted with discolorations. He wondered if the vision could be a mirage, but as he drew closer he realized the dune was completely real, as it did not change or vanish from his sight. It was not so large in size, and it seemed to have what looked like windows and a small door. He wondered who could inhabit such a remote house in the desert, and where they fell under the rule of the lords.

It was noon by the time he reached halfway to the small house. He dragged on, noticing as he got closer that the windows were actually small holes, plated with glass, carved from the hardened walls of the sand hill. The door was a faded green, and it had a small sign hanging on it, he could see. He paced on through the terrible heat, hard as ever up and down the dunes, as slowly his mind began to waver. He began to wonder what he'd just done. He had killed six men. The lords would torture and hang him if he couldn't find freedom in the east; if there was no freedom in the east.

Abstract thoughts rushed through his brain, many things of the strangest sort. He grew into a depressed state, deciding it was more than likely that the sand dune hut was a desert outpost for the lords. The structure hadn't appeared to be anything more than a small, hardened dune to him at first glance, and the door to it had been well hidden behind another nearby dune. Should there ever be any roaming guards passing by, they would not easily see the hut. But he had spotted it, and so he adjusted his path across the hot sand towards its entrance. As the door came within his sight, he could clearly comprehend the lettering on the sign:

> *'Molto's Keeping.*
> *Do Not Enter,*
> *Lest You Fancy*
> *Spirited Winds*
> *To Sear Your Soul.'*

He stood completely puzzled, yet completely enthralled. Though as a child he never talked of it, he always had a keen intrigue in the legends of *Vapoury* and its surrounding lore. Vapoury was the idea of using magic righteously, for the good of others, though magic itself was forbidden to be discussed by slaves, and was only spoken of in hushed tongues. He used to hear tales of the *Vapours;* the mythical wizards who used Vapoury, and could harness the natural elements for purposes of good. In one such tale there was a spell called the Spirited Winds, the same as was written on the sign. Though in all probability it was a coincidence, a stream of excitement poured through him, as he thought momentarily that perhaps Vapours were real, and their stories true.

Then a wave of fear poured through him. He knew, as slave legend told, that most of the magic users rumored to remain about the land in modern times were cruel and evil, only using their forces to construct a landscape of evil upon Darkin. The fear almost overtook him, but soon he supressed his worry, and curiosity devoured the fright in him. Still, he unsheathed his sword to be cautious, and made a slow pace toward the mysterious dune. He reached the tiny green door, froze for a moment, and then made an anxious knock. He hid his drawn sword to his side, deciding that an evil wizard might not kill him immediately should he appear unarmed.

The majority of slaves he'd known on the farm did not believe in Vapoury. None had seen it. The lords condemned the use of the word, and they named it a treacherous and chaotic fable. The rulers of Darkin believed with mysterious fear that the legend of magic was a bringer of ruin. The very act of reading about magic, or even openly speaking of it, almost always resulted in execution.

Adacon had always dreamt that there existed another world besides his own, one possible only in his dreams, where magic was a beautiful thing; he dreamt of humans and elves frolicking together on golden hills, using it only for Vapoury. This tinge of wonder in him had caused him to knock—any sane escaped slave would have made for the east until more civilization appeared, and worked from there on. But the moment had passed, and the door did not crack.

He briefly thought that perhaps the hut was an abandoned jail for some poor slave who had stepped too hard on his master's foot. The windows were in pristine condition; there appeared to be no cracks, or for that sake any chips in the green paint coating the door. A bird chirped in the distance, and the sound of the sand ridden wind grew louder as he stood still waiting. The sun was extremely bright and there was no shade for him, making sweat slowly bead on his forehead as the intensity of the day grew. His hand holding the broadsword slowly released its tension, almost letting the handle slip, as he sighed in disappointment. He knocked once more, yet still no response came. He tried the door's knob. It was locked. With a sigh he threw away his last hopes of anyone being inside, and turned around to face the pathless desert abyss, about to retrace his steps. No one was home.

"Yeh fallen tatter," came a raspy voice, seemingly from thin air. Adacon had turned his back as the words were uttered, and he quickly turned around to face their source. No one was there, but a small hidden hole had opened on the door's frame. "What chose you to disturb me? Has the great hawk of the sky met the humble serpent of the sea?" the withered voice continued. "Ah, I see you are a slave, escaped I presume. Forgive my queer tongue, and let me open the door." Adacon remained speechless as the tiny door swung open. Standing in the light now able to poke through the door was a small and silly looking old man, well robed in dark purple cloth.

He wore a purple cap, a strange looking assembly, lined with emeralds that appeared completely foreign to Adacon. He held aloft his left side with a marble staff, which looked rather valuable; its top was gemmed with amethysts and rubies. His face was well wrinkled, a yellowish tan desert color, filled with crazy hair that assumed the form of a beard encompassing a mustache. His eyes were deep green, and quite large, though his pupils were barely visible inside his irises. Adacon could plainly see that the odd looking man was weaker than himself, but he decided not to spare any caution for the appearance. He took his sword out from behind his back and pointed it at the small man in a menacing motion.

"Are you an ally of the lords?" Adacon asked viciously, gripping the handle tightly and preparing to strike down. To be safe now, he thought, he could only trust himself; a stranger's trust would have to be hard earned. He kept an intimidating glare on the old brightly clothed man, but the old man simply stared back with an eager smile.

"Fellow of the light, brethren of Darkin, calm your anger. I am not at all with a *label*, you see. I do not follow such organized rules for structuring life, but I embrace life all the same. Now let us have some tea, yes, that would be nice. Save the sun for another day, don't you agree? Today is a particularly harsh one. I think perhaps I shall have to set about making an awning for my front step. Perhaps the Lord Grelion should not get any sleep yet," the little man babbled.

The old man had a delightful sparkle in his eye; Adacon could not tell if it was virtuous or pure evil. Either way, the welcome greeting was a relief to him, and rest from the heat along with food and drink seemed too desirable to question.

"Thank you, kind sir," Adacon returned. "I am a weary traveler seeking refuge, and if possible, something to eat. I would be greatly in your debt if…" he was cut off:

"Tisk you—dabbling in your moral necessities. I am of your kind too, you know. I shall prepare for us some feast, as I suppose I can fix. But alas, it is time for you to escape this harsh golden eye, and breach into a cooler ambiance, down inside my den. Come, follow me, and leave your haste behind." The old man grinned deeply and turned, scuffling quickly back inside his hut. It was small making for Adacon, but he managed to squeeze through the door. He sheathed his sword again, realizing oddly enough that the hermit man gave no sign of fear at the sight of the blade.

The walls inside were quite beautiful, he soon discovered. The hall they walked was lined with endless shelves of books, then clear cabinets displaying wondrous rocks of all colors. Some seemed to glow and waver with a mysterious glimmer as he gazed upon them, but he kept his eyes mainly on the old man's back as they ventured down, descending the sandy corridor deeper into the mysterious house. Finally they came to a big open room with four larger corridors leading off in different directions. He noticed the walls were engraved with odd symbols, some of which were things he had seen before in forbidden books. His spine shivered. The old man turned to him and nodded, and without a word he walked with a strenuous pace toward the room's center. Once there, the tiny hermit paused to smell the air. He sighed, and gave another glance to Adacon.

"The sort of home that would make for comfortable living, eh boy?" he asked.

"I suppose, I am much cooler in here, and there's a pleasant aroma in the air. Do tell me we're going to the stove?" Adacon asked, feeling his stomach growl, reminding him of his hunger.

"Surely, I should hope, lest the trolls of Carnine have looted my good store," laughed the old man, letting out an enormous high pitched howl, seemingly too loud for someone with such a small frame. Suddenly, he began to run ahead of Adacon. They paced toward the left wall corridor, and he was surprised at the energy he felt rolling off the old man. They came to a hole in the ground at the end of the sandy hallway, and without a word the little man disappeared down a ladder coming out of the top. Adacon stood dumbfounded. He almost thought he could hear water dripping from below, but decided it was his imagination. Without shouting down to ask if it was safe to come, he followed the man. The ladder seemed to go down and down forever, and he began to grow faint after repeating the same hand movements over and over. Finally he came to the ground at the bottom and realized he was no longer standing on hard sand, but smooth grey rock. He looked directly up:

The ceiling of the great cave was sparkling like diamonds, and there were jagged rocks jutting their edges down toward the ground. High above was a tiny spot of light where the ladder had led down from. The height seemed quite extreme and he leveled out his glance, taking in a deep cavernous chamber. The sparkling room was enormous, one hundred yards wide at least, he thought in wonderment. The place looked like a palace carved from the inside of a giant rock. The most beautiful sight in the cave was a clear blue pond that sat comfortably in the center of the room. The water shimmered with reflections of the surrounding crystals and rocks that draped the walls and ceiling. He had never seen anything so beautiful in his life. He had a sudden notion, almost gone the next second, to kill the old man and spend eternity alone and at peace within the cave. But that thought snapped away, and reality returned with the sound of the old man's voice.

"So what do you think of my pool? I think it should be called lovely by some, though I reckon not even this could be seen as beauty to Grelion and his kin," muttered the old man, ending on an angrier tone.

"This place is beautiful, I have never seen anything like it," Adacon responded, still in awe. "This is your home?"

"This old place has been my home now for many of your lives lad, and with the sort of evil folk running around in this age, I am glad it is so well hidden. Anyway…" he spoke gently. "I've not had one visitor in the past century, I suppose, though mind you I do travel out a lot myself. It's a pleasant surprise for me to share this wonder with another—another like you."

"Like me?" Adacon recoiled, awed by the little man's reference to his extreme age.

"Sure you, lad" he retorted.

"Why me?"

"Because you are not one of *them*, and us who live apart from chaos and evil are as one," the man replied. "Do you not rebel against your oppression now, where it drives to sting?"

"I do, Though I don't know much anything about the world… I was raised a slave on a farm, just a few miles west of here. I know so little, except that I am a murderer now, and without a reason to live, except maybe to find freedom."

"Ah *Krem*, he's a good dreamer…" the old man muttered under his breath. "You cannot learn to be free unless you can learn to *love*, and you cannot begin to love, young lad, until you have learned to love yourself," said the old man, mystifying Adacon with the word *Krem*.

"Krem? I do not quite follow you..." responded Adacon.

"Oh, yes, of course—I am Krem, and it is the name I have known to be mine for as long as I can recall," Krem responded, chuckling to himself.

"And what is your stance on the oppression? Do you not feel the pain it has caused us all? I'm no longer a slave to the lords, and I don't care if they seek to kill me or not... I only hope to find some free place to go, and live if I can in peace."

"Ah, you have gone into worries—too many, I think, for now. What is your name, young lad?" asked Krem.

"My name is Adacon."

"Good Adacon, listen to me yet. A war has been spawned in you, I think. Never have I seen a slave so free from fear. And that quality in you I cherish. But this talk of oppression, what brings that?" spoke Krem.

"What? You don't know of the bondage, so close to your home? The controlling lords that use us as tools, and entitle us to no freedom? That is the oppression I have known for all my life," Adacon said with fury.

"If you have been treated poorly in the past, dear Adacon, I am deeply sorry for that. But it is now that a war seems to have risen in you, and we must focus upon the present. The *lords*, did you say? Hah, I marvel at that name you give him. Almost seems you think there to be more than one."

"I've always heard that there are a great many lords—the minority who rule the rest of the world."

"Partly you are correct young lad, as our country is controlled by a small group of people. But alas, there are no *lords*, as you propose. There is *a* Lord, whose name goes widely unknown in these times. It is Grelion. All the others whom you think to be the lords—they all work for Grelion."

"I can't believe one man could be responsible for all of this, and that one man could have that much power? I cannot fathom it. I was always told there were many lords, hundreds…"

"Hmmm… The lore in this age has run bleached, as I can tell from your beliefs. Grelion is the king of this country, along with everything save that which lies east of the great Kalm Ocean. Of course, under his absolute leadership are many lesser servants, but alas, he is the only true Lord."

"Where does he call his home? I will kill him, I swear, I shall run right into his home and cut his throat! To think, that there is but one person to blame for all the slavery and death—we must have his head."

"Ah, but you have so much to learn still, boy. Grelion is nowhere near this country. Like a true coward, he hides away from the land he rules over, and his exact location I'm not sure you could discover even if you had all the flying spies of Darkin. But his stench grows closer every day—I can sense his dementia ascending over our skies every night, his greed devouring our happiness. But enough talk of the sorrowful things we cannot yet change; we ought to have a proper meal first. Afterwards, we can discuss the fate of the world," Krem said, quieting as he stood from his chair near the cave wall. He walked away to the far right corner of the cave, toward a room that was cut from the rock—hopefully the dining area, Adacon thought. "Come along," the old hermit called back.

"I'm sorry, but I seem to be of a clouded mind right now, you are the first friendly presence I have known in a long time," Adacon said, trotting up to reach Krem.

"And not the last, let's pray. Now have a seat, and a bit of patience, young lad, it is time to be remedied of your hunger."

*   *   *

The dining hall was filled with splendid aromas of all sorts. Adacon sat himself at a table that was carved from the rock floor awaiting food, all the while being seduced by the growing smells. Finally, out walked the colorful little man Krem, effortlessly carrying two plates, each overflowing with food. There was bread and fresh cooked meat, along with fresh vegetables and fruit. Adacon was in heaven. This is no stale slave food, he thought jovially. He relished in the thought for another moment, and then realized that the food was now laid out before him on the table. Violently, he began to eat as fast as possible.

"Ow!" Adacon wailed. With a painful thud suddenly impacting his back, he stopped eating and looked up in agony. Krem had throttled him with his marble staff, and was now calmly watching the slave.

"Do you not release selfishness and greed before you eat? Ah, well, you should, rather than live this journey in greed, eh? Be settled for me to make a moment of some gratefulness, dear boy," Krem said passively. He began to speak again in a moment, this time in a gentler tone. "All of Darkin assembles before the great force of Gaigas, that the righteous fruits of this land may usher in a new serenity, renewing the circle of life whilst ridding the demons that haunt good men. I ask that you, Gaigas, Great Spirit of existence, unite our life with yours, as we thank you for these graces." There was a moment of silence after Krem's homage, and Adacon sat unmoving, unsure of what to do.

"Eat man," shouted Krem. So Adacon returned to his feeding frenzy, and he ate and ate until he felt his burst.

"Ah, this has been quite some meal, Krem, if I do say so," said Adacon in a humorous tone; he had finished off close to a full bottle of Krem's precious wine. Krem did not seem affected by his wine, and he thought for a second that maybe he and Krem were having different drinks.

"So what of this bastard—Grelion, you said was his name? We must find him immediately!" Adacon blurted out, returning his quest to mind, and spewing out the first thoughts that pertained to it.

"Do not be foolish boy. Should you attempt even another two leagues beyond my door, I do not give you half a chance at survival," Krem uttered, although it didn't affect Adacon's confidence.

"We must start east. If we can't find Grelion, we shall go on eastward until we find free natives. Then we will unite with them to build an army," Adacon said, as his mind swirled in patterns with no control. Krem interrupted him.

"*We*, hmmm? Who is this party you think to be assembled, that you speak of so surely in tone. You speak as if you are not the only one willing to die for your freedom," Krem said.

"I have myself, and that is all I shall need for the moment. I know in my heart there are others like me, there has to be—how could this way of life have been tolerated for so long? All those who share this passion for freedom will follow me. For I've never felt love, such as you speak of, and I shall free myself to find it, at all costs." Adacon glowered, and then he sighed, glancing to Krem's large green eyes.

"I'll tell you what I think, lad. You have the passion, and the virtue, you only need the path. I think it is time to bring about a relapse into the way of the ancients."

"The way of the ancients?"

"Heh, so young and passionate, and yet you do not realize how dangerous you are, or the constant danger you are in."

"I feel danger from nothing now."

"That is not true," Krem coldly replied.

"Upon a thousand leagues of this desert I swear to you, I will give my life for this cause," Adacon pleaded, feeling as though the old man could help him greatly on his journey, if only he'd believe his sincerity.

"Then your mind is made up. The quest should start in the summoning of a small band of fighters. You escaped from your plantation leaving behind no guards, correct?" questioned Krem.

"I killed them all, yes."

"It appears the goal of your quest is laid out plain enough in your mind, but the starting point remains shrouded in uncertainty," Krem said, and he drew in a deep breath before continuing. "I think the first move you might make, if you're inclined to take an old man's advice, should be made after a brief rest. Go, sleep upon my soft bed there. When you awake, return to your plantation and gather the slaves you left for the wilderness. Tell them of your war, and let your own eyes see who will stand with you." Krem pointed in the direction of a pillow-filled mat near the cave wall. Adacon didn't protest the chance for sleep, and he quietly lay down.

It seemed that nearly no time had passed at all when Krem's voice woke him from deep slumber.

"It is time now, lad. I have let you sleep too long. The sun is failing, you must go."

"Alright—I'll go," Adacon replied, startled to realize the old man hadn't been just some strange dream after all.

"I've no idea how far the next tower is from my farm, so there's no way to know if the farm has been found already by the lords. I mean Grelion. His men may already guard there again."

"Not yet, I don't think," Krem said.

"Do you know if more towers are near?"

"There is always a sentry tower nearby in this age, and that is why you must make all haste. Once you've recovered those slaves who will take to your cause, return here to my home amidst the dunes. We shall assess your next move then," Krem ordered. Without any more words, the old man led Adacon out of the pond room and back up the ladder into the main living hall on the first floor. He walked, still in awe over the magnificence of Krem's home, a marvelous cave palace encompassed in a sand dune. Krem gave a gruff farewell once they reached the green door, and he swiftly departed, thanking the old man once again for the food and rest.

III: THERE AND BACK AGAIN

The sun was slowly setting in the western sky. Adacon felt that at any moment he would awaken from a dream. His whole world had been flipped upside down, but when he contrasted the negatives against what his former life had been, he felt some happiness.

Shadows grew long and thin as he trod down the path, walking alongside shrubs that became small bushes and trees. The Red Forest formed along the shoulders of the dirt road, and soon the nocturnal animals hidden there began to make festive chatter and haunting calls into the dusk. He eyed the woods warily, expecting at any moment for a giant creature to come sprawling out onto his path. Slave lore told of wood golems, massive hulks known to be very territorial. More than a few runaway slaves were thought to have died by way of golem hammer, axe, or fist.

Darkness finally swallowed the sun, and there were few stars. The night looked mean, and he took his sword into his hand and decided to keep it there until he arrived at the farm. The woods were becoming denser as in the distance he could make out the dim light of the guard tower. He could hear no human sounds coming from the path ahead, and he wondered if the other slaves had already run off, perhaps into the wilderness of the Red Forest. A poor idea, he thought, as that would get them mercilessly killed by wild wolves or bears. But the farm gate drew near, and he prepared to enter his former home once again.

The entrance greeted him with dried puddles of blood on the dirt. The silence was almost eerie, and he did not move any farther into the farm. He looked around the corn field in broad angles, searching for any changes he could recognize in the scenery.

There were none; nothing had been changed, it seemed. And better yet, the lords, or Grelion, had not discovered the farm's downfall yet. He rejoiced, as a small piece of a large puzzle seemed to fall into place in his mind. Lord Grelion wouldn't know of the farm's downfall, he hoped optimistically, until the *morale* monitor rode in on horseback from what was called the Dark City. That wouldn't be for roughly a week, he calculated quickly in his head.

"Hello! Fellow slaves, can you hear me?" he called. There was no response for a long time, and then a whistling noise shot out into the night air, startling him. "Who's there? Who is it?" he yelled, tightly gripping his sword with both hands.

"It's not wise for you to shout so loudly—certainly not the *fellow slave* bit, at any rate," came a deep voice from a small distance away. Adacon looked in the direction the voice had come and saw the source emerging from a trail that led into the crops. It was a tough looking slave he recognized, an older man he knew to have worked on the other end of the farm. The man was greater in height and girth than Adacon, dwarfing Adacon's frame by comparison. He had long black hair that was tied back with string, a beard and mustache, and two black eyes set under thick black eyebrows. His cheek was slightly scarred beneath the left eye, and his features were sharply defined. They had never spoken before, Adacon realized.

"Hello brother!" Adacon said in an emotional yelp, realizing he may have found his first ally.

"Brother what? Have all your thoughts been brewed, as well as your concerns for safety? You should not talk so loudly sire, not with all the dead bodies about," the man responded.

"I have come to gather those who are willing to fight together with me for freedom; those who would rather die tomorrow than wake up a slave for the rest of their lives. It is that—a passion to break the oppression—that burns inside me. And I have met one so far already, outside this farm, who is on my side," Adacon replied in a quieter voice.

"No doubt then; *you* are responsible for the spilt blood I see here. Remarkable feat I daresay. I am impressed," the slave said. "And if what you say is true, then all that I dream of has come true, and the beginning of the end is at hand for the foul lords of Darkin. But I am more fit than most men, and I should account for the first *ten* of your army, I suppose. I cannot believe this day is come..." The man seemed extraordinarily enthusiastic about meeting Adacon now, and he wept happily.

"You want it as much as I, then. And you're willing to die?" asked Adacon.

"I have always been willing to die, if it meant a real chance to destroy the lords. And yes, if you are to lead this attempt I shall follow you, even if to death," the man spoke.

"I am Adacon. What is your name?"

"I am Erguile, to those that knew me. And you, Adacon, are the only one who knows me still. And so I pledge my life to destroy the lords, though I've no longer any weapons, nor any treasures to barter with. I have much in the way of a will to fight though, rest assured, and more skill with a sword than any man," Erguile boasted. Adacon reveled in the respect Erguile was bestowing on him. Respect was something never to be shown if you were born a slave, and the fact that Erguile was his elder made it more dignifying.

"And that will be all you'll need. I'll find weapons for you, and all who join me. Before I return to more pressing thoughts, I must ask where the rest are?" Adacon asked.

"They fled when the new batch of sentries arrived on the farm, randomly striking down slaves," Erguile said.

"New batch? You mean there has been word of the massacre here already?" Adacon gasped.

"You had no idea all the while? Hah, thought you'd gotten off plain free. No, I don't know how they did find out, but I believe it was in the earliest hours of the morn—they were running up and down the farm, just let the bodies of their own men lay and forked down slaves left and right. Then, after seeing the rest scurry away into the woods, they followed after to hunt them down. The whole lot of them except me gone into the Red Forest, save for those slain before they had a chance to run," Erguile said, lowering his voice and speaking closer to Adacon's face. "I suppose that is our favor, though, as the lords' men will never return from that horrid place alive."

"You too believe in the lore of the forest?" asked Adacon, sidetracked at its mentioning.

"I do not believe that any human ever to live could create such tales as it has without drawing from some truth."

"But what of the tales of elves? Have you read about their utopian cities, hidden deep in the forests, untouchable by man? And what of magic and the lore of mana? Have you ever felt those tales as well to have some truth?" questioned Adacon.

"I believe faery tales are just that—faery tales. I think you might like to fancy you'll meet an elf someday, but I'm betting you won't, and that sooner we'll both be hanged for treason."

"Have you ever heard of the *Spirited Winds*?" asked Adacon in a last attempt to pique Erguile's interest.

"No, I haven't," responded Erguile, "and magic is a myth if you ask me, along with the rest of it. Only thing I can count on as being real is the danger in those woods." There was a moment of silence, and Adacon appeared saddened by Erguile's skeptical response.

"I'll collect arrows from the slain guards. We have enough bows and quivers lying about for their purpose. We'll take their broadswords, too," Adacon said, changing the subject. "In my haste I never replaced this shoddy blade," he went on, waving his old sword in the air. He looked with sadness at his steel friend, recalling their time together. Erguile wandered off, looking around the guard tower for anything useful, as Adacon knelt to the earth, and placed his old blade, dulled to an almost round edge, on the soil.

"May another find you; one as young and brash as I was—I can't use you anymore—thanks..." Adacon whispered, staring at the blade with a head full of memories; he'd only been a boy when he first stole the sword and started practicing with it—not fully aware as to why he was doing so. It all made sense now, Adacon realized, and a single tear rolled down his cheek, as Erguile called out from tower ladder.

"What is it? Find something?"

"No, it's nothing," Adacon replied, and he brushed his cheek and stood to join his new friend.

There was no trace of any more sentries; it seemed they had gone as quickly as they had come. All of them had disappeared into the Red Forest to hunt the fleeing slaves. They hadn't taken any time to heed to their fallen brethren's gear, leaving everything behind. And so the two slaves went about taking the weapons left around the farm that they deemed suitable for their journey. By the guard post they found leather satchels in which they stored as much food as they could find—mostly corn and hardened bread. There were flasks of water on the slain guards as well, which Adacon and Erguile fastened to their newly stolen leather belts.

They decided not to check the restricted building for goods, as the smell was worse than ever, and they feared for what they might see. Adacon removed breastplates from two guards and wore one himself, then gave the other to Erguile. The quiver on Adacon's back was stocked to the brim with arrows. Erguile chose to carry two broadswords instead of a bow and quiver. Adacon had tried to convince him to take one, but Erguile argued his ineffectiveness with the weapon. At last the two marched to the gate, and toward the wilderness beyond.

*   *   *

"Can you fight?" asked Erguile in a smug tone.

"As a boy I practiced many long and hard hours with the sword I left back there."

"Good. And I reckon that was a poor question anyway, seeing as you killed all the guards… But me, I can really fight—was born with it in my blood. I may pay homage to you, Adacon, but I shall always be the greater swordsman," Erguile boasted.

"Fight as valiantly as you can, but at least you'll have others now, if only me, fighting alongside you—for your life, and its freedom," he replied, feeling satisfied to be in the company of one so confident as Erguile.

"You surprise me boy. All the times I had seen you go to and fro on the farm, looking like a weakling. And all the times I

38

had wondered when a rebellion would start. I marvel that fate decided it is you who should start it. And know that I don't agree with those who say *fate* is the great ruling God of our world—I believe we forge our own path in life," Erguile said. They walked through the gate and onto the tree-lined path. Adacon decided to prepare Erguile for what was about to come; meeting Krem.

Adacon explained about the dune house and its odd inhabitant who seemed at times crazier than wise, but more often just the opposite. He told Erguile just how shockingly old the little man claimed to be; how he said to have lived many of Adacon's lives. He did not mention Krem's door sign, if only to avoid hearing skepticism about what Molto could be, and what the Spirited Winds really were. Vapoury and magic, Erguile had already shown, were fictional in his mind. More talk of it now was useless.

They walked on and Erguile talked a bit about his own life. He, like Adacon, remembered little about his earliest years. His father had died when he was young, and he had been moved away from his mother at that time to a slave training program. They trained him similar to the way they had trained Adacon, they found by comparing stories. Also like Adacon, Erguile was without a family; at the least he was sure his father was dead and his mother a slave somewhere, or dead too. He had no brothers or sisters. It was when his father was killed, Adacon learned, that Erguile had begun to hate the oppressors. Adacon also explained the shaky idea spoken of by Krem: that there was a single Lord to the free world, a sole leader of the slavery. As Adacon expected, Erguile had never heard of Grelion. Still, Erguile fancied meeting the mysterious Krem already, for after Adacon's description Erguile had a strong impression of curiosity.

They grew acquainted as they trudged on toward the desert. Adacon was certain that Erguile's resolve for freedom was strong, and he dared not wonder if it could be stronger than his own. Their course continued, and soon the two found themselves leaving the Red Forest behind and approaching a cool and dark desert. The moons were almost directly above them in the sky, set between meandering clouds that concealed most of the night's stars. Adacon realized the lack of light would make it hard for them to find Krem's stronghold again. All around them were endless rows of dark dunes, all looking nearly the same. Adacon continued his conversation with Erguile, making sure no distress fell into his tone, as their path led them deeper into the abyss of the maze-like desert.

"So, how much farther do you suppose we have to go before we find this hermit?" asked Erguile with a trace of agitation in his voice. Adacon sighed, and for a moment stopped in his tracks.

"When I arrived earlier it had been midday, and the sun was still strong in the sky. I'm sure we've come the distance—if not more so—to reach the damned place; I just don't see the dune with the door in it, it's too dark," Adacon said, trailing off into silent thought. Erguile stood patiently awaiting his next words. "I think we might get ourselves killed before we find the place, if we keep walking deeper into the desert. Perhaps we should find a flat bit of sand and rest some, at least until the sun is upon us again..."

"You wish to sleep out here? Stay in this foreign desert all night without worry? You truly are mad, Adacon," Erguile retorted, but he reluctantly considered. "I guess you're right though. I can barely make out the dunes fifty paces from here," he said in uneasy agreement.

"Alright then, we'll set camp there," Adacon said, pointing into the darkness toward a flat plateau of sand. They walked in the direction Adacon had designated, and before long they found themselves sitting down on the cold sand. There was a deafening silence about the desert night, and for a good stretch the two weary travelers sat wide-eyed, staring up at a glowing moon. They didn't feel tired enough for sleep, and the intimidating prospect of spending a night in the desert had not completely withdrawn its fear. Erguile broke the quiet.

"Do you suppose Adacon..." He trailed off. "Do you suppose we could ever come to meet one of the lords—or this Grelion, if he truly exists?"

"I hope so—that we may wring his neck. I think we'll at least encounter one of his patrols before long. The little man, Krem... he seemed very wise. He told me he travels throughout the country often. I'm hoping he'll come with us, perhaps be our guide about the land. It would be best if we could increase our numbers before any real fighting—not that I don't think we're a strong army of two. My fears would have me believe that Grelion's sentries march throughout the whole country."

"I think you should take first watch Adacon; I fear I'd fall asleep if I watched first. Let me get a good hour or two, then wake me up and I'll cover us until dawn," Erguile said as he removed his swords from his belt and placed them nearby. He yawned deeply as he attempted to find comfort on the desert floor.

"You'll need your rest more than you know, I think. I don't know what tomorrow brings, but if what happened today is a sign of things to come, we'll both need our strength. Sleep well, Erguile the Brave, and for awhile yet I'll ward off the demons of the sand for you," Adacon joked, providing a needed respite of humor.

Erguile sprawled on the ground, groaning several times before finding a half-comfortable sleeping position. The sand was hard and cold, and made for a harsh bed, but fatigue had its way and Erguile fell fast asleep. Adacon sat rigid like a hawk watching

the surrounding dunes and the tranquil night sky, finally left alone
with his thoughts.

*   *   *

Many things jumbled around in the throes of his imagination, and
his thoughts changed as quickly as they came. He felt happy—and
in disbelief – that he'd managed to escape the farm, only to return
and find an ally in Erguile. It was Krem that most frequently
popped into Adacon's mind, and the odd little man started to seem
unreal to him. Could Krem have been some imaginary figure his
mind had conjured up from the heat of the sun? Perhaps the little
man and his palace under the desert had been a mere dream…

Adacon returned his thoughts for a moment to the farm.
He wondered if all the slaves had been captured and murdered,
and if there were new sentries upon the towers yet. Most likely it
was as Erguile guessed; the whole lot of them was swallowed up by
the beasts of the Red Forest.

Looking at the ground around their camping spot, Adacon
realized that although there weren't footprints on the hard sand
they camped on, they had to have left tracks coming from the
farm; surely there would be some at the beginning of the desert
where the sand was softer. The thought of guards pursuing their
trail into the desert made Adacon shudder. It crossed his mind that
in tomorrow's sunlight they might be able to track his original
footprints to find the way back to Krem's hideaway. Was the little
dungeon so secluded that it was by rare chance he'd even managed
to find it once among the monotonous dunes? Adacon started
questioning himself. He believed for a moment that guards would
surely find their tracks, and it would only be a matter of time

before they were hunted and killed. Then, from the black silence, Adacon heard a strange noise.

He glanced around warily, checking for any sign of movement or silhouette, but saw nothing. Keeping a watch was quite useless, he decided, as he strained to see the dune directly in front of him. Everything was black; even the moons had gone into hiding behind streaking clouds of charcoal grey. Adacon managed to stay alert, listening vigilantly for another hour, waiting for the noise to return. He tried to keep his mind focused on his task, but slowly he succumbed to his need for sleep. He decided to remove his sword and quiver to be a bit more comfortable.

Adacon slowly closed his eyes, feeling a rush of warmth come with the utter dark. He opened them; then closed them; then barely reopened them halfway. He slumped down until he lay flat, adjusting his arms to find any comfort possible. The thoughts in his head slowed to a trickle, and soon his mind became as silent as the dying desert wind. As he edged into unconsciousness a sharp cry tugged him wide awake.

It sounded like a horrible shriek—nothing he could fathom a source for. Though he'd never heard one, nor knew if they truly existed, Adacon thought the screech had sounded like a demon. Quickly he sat up and regained his bearing, grabbing his sword from the sand. The noise hadn't been imagined, he knew, and he wondered if it was from the same creature as before. He hadn't been alert enough to determine what direction the noise had come from; he knew by its intensity it had to be close. He stood up and gripped his sword tight, frantically scanning for anything visible in the blackness. No sound came, and he could see nothing amid the black dunes. Finally, after standing rigid for another half-hour, he reluctantly decided that the noise had been a harmless animal. It would be a much more fearful thing—he tried to convince himself—if the noise had seemed human. Without waking Erguile from his slumber, Adacon found himself lying down again and falling fast asleep with his sword on his chest, still gripped firmly by his right hand. A dreamless slumber overtook him.

*   *   *

Adacon awoke first and sat up to find he was sweating. The desert had grown miserably hot already. The sun had risen high overhead; it appeared they had slept long into the morning. He arose to stretch his limber form and rouse his senses for the day. The desert stretched all around him. He yawned deep and turned to wake Erguile, nudging him softly.

"Ack, I had the most horrible dream," Erguile said, startled as if from another dimension. "It felt real... I daresay I may have been in some other world. You and I had found Krem's house finally. We had begun to make conversation with the little thing when it soon became clear that he was a great evil wizard. He attacked us with jets of flames and fireballs. It was terrible... I remember my sword being melted from within my grasp. I sorrow to say he managed to catch you ablaze, and I would have been next I think, had you not woken me." Erguile clumsily rubbed his head and rolled over to sit upright. Adacon didn't respond to the fearful dream.

"It's hot today. I wouldn't have guessed in my little knowledge of desert countries that they were *this* hot. I knew they were said to..." Erguile stopped talking mid-sentence. Adacon had been facing the eastern sky—his back to Erguile as he listened—until the abrupt pause. Adacon turned around to see what the matter was; Erguile was staring at the ground beside them, and Adacon realized what was wrong. Erguile had gone to bed with two swords, the ones he had snatched from the farm; he had set them by his side, one next to the other—now there was one. Adacon quickly checked to make sure all his own gear was intact, having forgotten about the weapons until present. All of Adacon's supplies were still there, exactly where they had been laid out the night before. They stared in puzzlement.

"How in Darkin... last night you never woke me for watch; did you fall asleep?" asked Erguile.

"I'm sorry I did, but there didn't appear to be any danger. I kept a watch for most of the night, and I didn't want to wake you, thinking you'd need the rest."

"This makes no sense at all then. How could my sword be gone? I did go to sleep last night with two, didn't I?" asked Erguile, growing increasingly baffled.

"I'm most certain you did, I remember you carrying them the whole walk. But you're right... this is very strange. What on Darkin do you suppose would come upon us in the night and take for itself a single sword, leaving no other trace behind..." Adacon said, racking his brain. He decided not to mention the noises until Erguile calmed some. It dawned on Adacon that if anything had come in the night there would be some form of tracks in the soft sand surrounding their camp. They surveyed the area thoroughly but found no tracks but their own; they decided to give up the hunt and pick up their belongings. Erguile fastened his breastplate to his chest, which he had taken off for sleep—Adacon grimaced at the thought of wearing armor in the desert heat, and left his behind. They sat in silence eating a breakfast of bread and water before setting out.

"This truly confuses me, if not frightens me. I don't want to spend another night in this forsaken desert, no...I think we should be quick on our way to this Krem's dune—be he an evil wizard or not," Erguile said. He stood and drew forth his sword.

"Whatever stole your sword, do you think it could really have concealed its tracks in the sand here, to no error?" Adacon asked.

"I reckon it may have left some trace, lest it was a winged creature, or one with the powers to walk in the clouds," Erguile half joked. They set about another attempt, searching farther from the camp than they had first checked, looking again for any marks upon the sand.

"There!" Adacon cried. He pointed toward the tracks they themselves had left, still clearly visible as a scattered and broken line of ruffled sand winding into the desert. But it was not those tracks he had pointed at—there was another trail breaking away from theirs. The tracks led off in a different direction, disappearing behind a low dune.

"Perhaps we'll find our culprit yet!" Erguile said, feigning enthusiasm for a hunt in the scorching heat.

"Well, at least let's have a better look," Adacon said, and they walked over to the foreign tracks. The sand was soft enough to prevent any precise imprint, nothing detailed enough that the markings could be discerned as human or otherwise. They were, however, roughly the size of the marks a human might leave. The trail could definitely be followed, they both knew, but the path seemed to go on interminably into the northwestern horizon. Adacon was almost certain they had passed Krem's abode some way back, and he contemplated the futility of making an attempt at tracking the unknown thief.

"I doubt the sword would ever be worth our trouble. I don't know what lies farther north, save maybe danger. I think we would do best to retrace my original tracks."

"I suppose you're right. Let's do that then, though I don't think this incident will easily pass out of my mind," Erguile replied.

"Nor mine," Adacon returned. "I hope we find shelter from this damned sun soon though, and that Krem will have some answers for us."

"Let's hope we can find something at all in this godforsaken place…" Erguile said. Adacon and he started toward their trail leading back west. They followed it without trouble for a short while, and sure enough Adacon saw a new trail diverge in the distance.

"There, up ahead on the right. Do you see it?" Adacon said cheerfully. Erguile scanned the dunes.

"Yes, are you sure it is your path from before?"

"Most sure—I turned right some to reach the place, I remember. I'd suspected that we'd passed it last night, but there was no way to tell in the dark."

Sweating heavily, they reached the path Adacon had created the previous afternoon. They followed the old trail toward a dune that Erguile soon realized was more than just a pile of hot sand; a tiny green door came into view on its side, and he grew anxious as Adacon's tale was confirmed with his own eyes. The green door grew larger as they approached the hidden fortress, and Erguile could begin to make out little windows on the dune now, and before long the sign on the door was also visible.

"Krem'll be expecting us," Adacon said jovially. "He's an energetic old man, by all respects. I rather expect him to have food ready for our arrival." As they neared the door, Adacon began to describe the cool air, the glittering pond, and the filled dining room deep beneath the sand. Finally, they arrived at the door—Erguile read for himself the words on it:

'Molto's Keeping.
Do Not Enter,
Lest You Fancy
Spirited Winds
To Sear Your Soul.'

"Shall I knock?" asked Erguile.

"Yes."

"Alright." Erguile knocked hard on the door three times as he glanced into the covered windows anxiously.

"Last time it took him a good bit of time to open up, so be patient. Inside it's quite huge; he'll have to travel some to get to the front door if he's down below." It was only an instant, however, and suddenly a voice came from a secret hole in the green door.

"Still alive I see. And just as I expected. I take this to be a new addition to your company, laddy? I am glad to see it, though I had hoped you'd get more than one from the errand. A moment lads…" Krem said, speaking through the hole, and suddenly the hole closed up and the door swung open. Erguile was taken aback at the appearance of the small, purple-robed man; Krem seemed to perfectly resemble the evil wizard of his dream.

"Come in!"

"You are Krem, the lonesome hermit of the sand dungeon, I presume?" asked Erguile warily as they stepped inside the cool interior.

"Ah, 'tis I you script, lad. It is not a description that I would choose, mind. I think I shall befriend you anyway. I suppose slaves are a nice breed, though damned ignorant most of them are," Krem chuckled as he led them into his home, laughing.

"Damned ignorant? What does that mean, I wonder, coming from a small man who has secluded himself from the world inside a sand dune?" retorted Erguile. Already Adacon feared the tension growing between Krem and Erguile.

"Hush yourself and I shall let you have food. Does that strike your fancy, young lad?" asked Krem. Erguile did not protest at the offering of food, and Adacon felt relieved to see the tension die.

"And what shall I call you?" asked Krem as he led them farther into the cavernous hallway.

"My name is Erguile. I am a slave of the same farm as Adacon here. Alas, I am the last of our fellow slaves. The plantation was retaken at dawn yesterday. The others are dead now, along with the foolish guards that chased after them. No doubt—the Red Forest has had its fill by now."

"The Red Forest, a beautifully cruel place it is—in fact, it was not long ago I was traveling there and found the most peculiar creature; a marvelous beast that called itself Slowin. But I shall tell you more of the Deep Red when we are fixed with proper comforts, and you two are no longer ailed by hunger. Come! We must make haste, for Grelion never sleeps—no he doesn't—never sleeps…" Krem said as he led them through the cool cavern. Erguile fell in love with its beauty just as Adacon had. Krem brought them to the great room with four branching halls, and they briskly walked down the path that led to the ladder. Krem and Adacon quickly descended, followed by a reluctant Erguile, who made the mistake of peering down first. In a moment they were all standing on the floor by the great crystal-reflecting pond.

Adacon walked to the corner and seated himself in the spot where he had eaten before as Krem went to fetch food. Erguile had not thought about food since he had arrived below, instead training his eyes upon the beautiful shimmer of the pond.

"It's the most magnificent thing I've ever seen! I don't understand how such a place could have existed all these years without me having known. I am sorry, but I think I will stay here a good year before I set off with you, Adacon. I'm sure you wouldn't mind, would you?" Erguile said as he stood off to the right of the ladder, near the edge of the pond, staring at the water's wondrous illumination. The cave was eerily lit with no obvious source, and the ceiling shimmered with reflective sparkles, bouncing off the jagged rock roof. The pool was vast and clear, reflecting the glimmering ceiling, and no certain bottom could be seen within it, only a dark depth that descended beyond what eyesight was capable of seeing.

"I suppose if the pond has you so entranced that you won't be of any use in battle, I can let you stay here. But I doubt Krem will let you stay all alone in his precious palace," chuckled Adacon.

"Fine—then it shall be that once our quest is over, I'll first return here and spend a decade or two, marveling at this place, and swim evermore in peace—save when I grow hungry and hit up his food stores!" Erguile rejoiced. Adacon was happy to see Erguile in such high spirits.

The pond *is* that beautiful, Adacon thought, and Erguile's fantasy wasn't so different from the way he himself had felt upon first seeing the place. Adacon thought of things to come; he wondered: if such a marvel lay so close to their farm, what beauty could the rest of the unknown world have in store for them?—and what evil? But his thoughts only swayed for a moment, as before long a sweet aroma of spiced meat filled the room. Adacon glanced off to a corridor that led into a room filled with cupboards and saw Krem coming with a tray full of platters. Erguile smelled succulent food too, and he seemed to forget the pond already as he rushed to a seat next to Adacon at the oaken table.

"After this feast, I think I shall go for a swim," Erguile said. "How about you Adacon?"

"You will first have a good talk with me, Erguile, before I am to set you loose in my pool," Krem uttered as he laid the tray of piping hot meat on the table.

"This looks delicious Krem," Adacon said politely.

"Indeed it does! And I won't be able to contain myself much longer if you don't hurry your old bones Krem," shouted Erguile in a frenzy. Adacon feared for his new friend after the cutting remark, but Krem remained as calm as ever.

Krem began spreading plates around the table. There were several large chunks of meat—dark and light—covered in different blends of spices. Krem laid out more plates filled with plenty of potatoes, corn, rice and bread. There was wine again, along with several vials of rainbow-colored juices. At last all the food was properly arranged and Krem sat down opposite them. Erguile could barely contain himself and his hands began to fidget. Krem took a good while getting comfortable in his oak chair, then looked toward his guests.

There was silence, but suddenly Erguile began to grapple with the assorted meats and place as many as he could onto his empty plate in a barbaric manner. He began to eat, nearly forgetting to chew, shoving everything down his throat and almost causing himself to choke. Immediately, Krem lifted his staff at Erguile's head and brought it down with great force.

"Ow! The hell was that for old man? That hurt," cried Erguile, rubbing his head and dropping meat from his hands. Adacon knew Erguile's mistake, and sat in silence quashing his hunger for the moment in anticipation of Krem's words.

"Do you not give thanks to anything for the graces you receive? I suppose I shouldn't have expected different from you, coming from the same place as him. Ah well; that's the way of things, I guess. Now quit moaning lad, and fix a proper mind for giving thanks," Krem commanded, and then assumed a meditative gaze, closed his eyes, and spoke again.

"All of Darkin assembles before the great god Gaigas, so that the fruits of this land may usher in a new serenity, renewing the circle of life and ridding the demons. I ask that you, Gaigas, the soul of this world, unite yourself with us, as we thank you for these graces." Adacon recognized the words to be similar to the prayer he had heard before. "Now you may eat, Erguile…" motioned Krem. And all three of them began to remedy their hunger. In a good bit of time they nearly decimated the entire table's worth of food.

"I've had quite my fill," smiled a now bloated Adacon.

"As have I," spoke Erguile. "I suppose this meal alone requires me to drop any grudge against you, old man, even for beating me on the head."

"That it does indeed," said Krem. "We shall hold council now, and talk of the great journey to come. I expect you'd all enjoy a fresh pipe?" asked Krem.

"Most certainly! I can't remember the last time I had a fresh pipe," Erguile enthusiastically responded.

"Alright then, let's find our way to my fire den. It's up the ladder and a short walk from there," Krem said, and he was the first to stand up from his chair, disregarding the dirty table and plates. He began trotting towards the ladder. "Come on you wretched tatters!" he called back at the still sitting slaves as he began climbing up.

"I suppose we have to go," said Adacon, looking to Erguile. "I'll admit I would have rather stayed here and talked; my belly is full to its brim."

"Mine as well, but talk of war will get me moving," Erguile said emphatically, and he rose.

"I suppose. . ." Adacon said, and with some effort he removed himself from his chair, and the two climbed the ladder to the chamber above.

Upon arriving again in the room with the four separate halls they realized that Krem was nowhere to be seen.

"How do you like this? He goes off and leaves us alone in his palace," said Erguile.

"I guess we'll have to find his fire den ourselves. Come on." Adacon started off toward one of the corridors, the one farthest from his position.

"Krem!" shouted Erguile suddenly. "You tricky bastard, where have you gone?"

"That will be a good way to anger him, and get your head thrashed again," reproached Adacon, stopping at the sound of Erguile's shout.

"Serves the little bastard right, to let us alone and not wait up," said Erguile. Then, from far down the third corridor came a hooting sound, loud and seemingly from some kind of musical instrument. "That would be him now," Adacon and Erguile hurried down the corridor from which the sound had come.

They hurried down the long hall, taking in the odd decorations that were just as wondrous as the rest of the palace.

The walls were lined with mysterious trinkets, gadgets, and other artifacts fastened to shiny mounts, all of which neither Adacon nor Erguile could recognize. Some were the color of bone, and looked to be strange animal skeletons. Others were shiny and metallic, and whirred at their passing. At last they came to a small room with generous sofas and a large glowing hearth at its center. Little Krem sat in his purple robe, puffing on something that smelled extremely sweet. Erguile plopped down on the sofa across from Krem, followed quickly by Adacon.

"You had better serve me a fixing of that, old man," said Erguile.

"You've got some tongue, lad, but the rudeness I'll take as a trait for the better, as it shall come in handy when we deal with Feral Trolls. Here, I have not forgotten you both," Krem said, and then handed them their own pipes stocked with sweet smelling shreds of dried fruits and leaves.

"Thanks old man," cried Erguile, igniting the mix and starting to puff.

"You can keep those pipes—and these," Krem said, and he threw from his side two satchels, each made of leather. "I've put some dried meat and flasks of water in them already."

"Thanks Krem, it's much appreciated. These will be a great help," Adacon thanked him.

"Indeed," Krem agreed, puffing contentedly on his pipe as the nearby fire kept them from the growing cold. "Now, before I begin to talk, I am sure you both have questions you want to ask." Erguile almost jumped in his seat, and immediately asked the first question.

"I have more than a few nagging my mind, but this before all the others: is it true, as Adacon told me, that a Lord *Grelion* is the all powerful and *only* lord of this land?"

"Indeed he is, Erguile. And it's a sad truth, for that man has grown evil in all ways imaginable," Krem sullenly replied.

"I've a question that I wanted to ask you since yesterday, Krem—it rather pertains to you, actually. Who, or what, is Molto? I've twice looked upon that name on your door in confusion—and the Spirited Winds that the sign speaks of," Adacon asked, puffing pensively on his pipe. Erguile was distracted, deep in thought, quietly coming to terms with the truth about Grelion.

"Ah, an observant one you are, friend. Molto—that name is legendary from ocean to ocean, by those who remember the Elder Ages anyhow. It is said that he was the last of the great Vapours. It is my understanding that he lived in this very home before I came here, and perhaps even many years before that. The Spirited Winds, as you saw on my door, happens to be the name of a *spell*, one that when Vapoury was commonplace struck fear into the hearts of evil men, trolls and elves alike. In a great battle of the Elder Age, Molto waylaid a terrible evil as it descended from the North, single handedly stopping its advance. It was his powerful spell, the Spirited Winds, that defeated the evil Crawl Plaque, as they were called. His Vapoury alone restored an age of peace in Darkin," told Krem.

"Did you say elves? Elves of the forest? You mean to say they're not fable?" Adacon eagerly replied.

"Hah, elves are perhaps edging on the border of fable in this age, but I can assure you they have lived on Darkin for at least as long as humans have—I suspect much longer. It is said that in the first age of the world they inherited the good land from Gaigas herself."

"Gaigas—you keep saying that. Was she a queen of some land from long ago?" asked Adacon.

"Oh no, and above all, you should know of Gaigas. She is the good spirit of Darkin itself, the harmony and love within. Perhaps you'd like to think of her as *God*; I don't know the faith of slaves. She brings all that is good together, and works with those who are virtuous to guide and strengthen them in their trials against all that is evil and wrong." Krem paused to puff on his pipe. "Gaigas resides in the nature of all things positive and good. Some, who know the ways of the ancients, can draw upon her energy. This life force, or energy, is known as Vapour. Vapour can be drawn upon and stored in the spirit, should one know how to become at peace with Gaigas. It is a great and mysterious energy, the force a common man would mistake for magic, if he saw it used by a Vapour."

"This talk; I reckon it blasphemous and untrue. I have lived on this land for all my life, and not once have I seen a magician weave a spell, nor have I looked upon an elf," grunted Erguile, not believing a drop from the old man's mouth. With that, in an instant, Krem raised his right hand into the air and motioned at Erguile. Erguile's pipe suddenly rose up out of his grasp and into thin air, floating for a few seconds in nothingness. Then it suddenly dropped, and Erguile was quick to catch it before it hit the ground. Erguile was speechless, and he sat back quietly.

"That, my friend, is the Vapoury of air. Vapour itself arrives to us in many different forms, to assume all the different naturally occurring elements such as there are on Darkin. You both are familiar with fire and water, ice and wind. These are all attributed to the natural flow of Vapour from Gaigas, but there are many others that I have not named; some I would not dare name."

"I'm in disbelief...I don't...I don't know what to make of all this; if anything, I guess, I know now I can take all of your words as truth," gasped Erguile.

"Indeed I shall only speak truth to the followers of good, Erguile, but I am not a source of infinite knowledge—though you've yet to find that out," Krem chuckled.

"Krem, often I've heard slave-rumor of a place called the Dark City, an evil city, said to exist far to the west. Have you heard of such a frightful place?" asked Adacon.

"The Dark City—hmm; let me dig into my memory some." Krem smoked from his pipe and sat for a moment in silence. Erguile now sat at full attention, eagerly waiting for the next word to roll off Krem's tongue. It was clear he now believed everything the man told them. "The Dark City! Ah, I should have recalled the name sooner. Odd slang the slaves now have for it. Its rightful name is Morimyr. Grelion does not reside in that demonic city, though it is controlled by his underlings, and they govern absolute within its walls. His underlings are evil by all accounts, and I have had the ill chance of encountering a few of them in my time."

"You've seen this city?" Erguile said, breaking his silence. His tone had grown respectful.

"Indeed—I have been in it. But that was long ago, and I dare think much has changed since my last departure. How is it you came to know of Morimyr, Adacon?" asked Krem.

"It is the name we give to the home of our *monitors*, the huge, evil men who come each month to suppress any ideas of resistance," Adacon said, quivering at the thought of them.

"Ah, I see. Grelion himself has been known to come through Morimyr from time to time, out in the west. It would be complete folly, however, to try and go there and wait for him," said Krem.

"All of this feels like a load too great, I must say. I feel almost faint. So magic is by all accounts real? To think, all these years it was true. And Krem; you yourself are a wizard? For I have just seen you raise that pipe there into thin air," spoke Erguile, trying to straighten out all the shocking truths that were being forced into his head.

"Indeed magic is real, though its true name is Vapoury when used for good. But it is more important that you remember it is Gaigas's workings, not my own. Know also that I am no wizard; such as it is wizards are dangerous and ill-minded. The name of Vapour is given to those who justly wield Gaigas. I am merely a portal from which her power may flow, because I have harnessed it so. I suppose you can call me a Vapour—but I shall always prefer Krem to wizard. Wizards are named as the most evil of magic users in this age—and even though Grelion himself, along with some of his minions, dabble in dark magic, he despises its practice otherwise. It is true, sadly enough; the majority of those still able to manipulate Gaigas in this age do so for selfish purposes of gain. I am of a dying breed."

"Will you teach us how to use magic then?" shouted Erguile excitedly.

"Hah—lad, I wouldn't dare bestow upon you the powers of Gaigas, lest I wanted to be turned into a weed or some other wretched fungus. Alas, no one can learn magic anyhow, unfortunately, as it may have been possible in the days of old. You see, Gaigas is dying in this horrible age of darkness; only those whose Vapoury has existed since the time of the ancients can use it in this age."

"So you really are of ancient times?" asked Adacon, realizing that the small man in front of him had been alive longer than anyone could rightly guess by appearance.

"Yes, I was born long ago. And my age still collects into greater numbers yet—how many more I cannot clearly foresee. I do think, however, that my years are finally catching up with me. I feel in my remaining time that I should help at least in what ways I can; I may be of some use to cleanse the demons once more from this land." Krem sighed deeply, seeming to burden himself momentarily with the thought of his mortality.

"Perhaps you can tell us more about yourself, Krem—of your past?" asked Erguile.

"Now is not the time, and I don't think we'd have enough time if it was appropriate anyway. I shall use my past and its lessons in our task, however, whenever they can be used to aid our journey; I assure you of that, at least."

"So the quest I am undertaking with Erguile—we can count you as our third?" asked Adacon, fearing for a moment that Krem would let them loose toward the east unaided.

"I guess it comes to that, doesn't it lads? I can't sit around and let you have all the fun, now can I? Darkin, you see, has not always been this evil place that it is now. It was once wonderful and marvelous by most accounts; I plan to look upon that world once more before I die."

"Excellent! I am heartened already at this news. I have one last question to burden your mind with... What lies east? Be it we're going that way for our quest. . . I have always heard that there are natives, living under no man's law save their own; I thought if it was true we could bring them to our cause," asked Adacon.

"I have a great wisdom of this world, I can say without feeling boastful, and I have traveled all the way across the great Kalm Ocean. There are natives to the east, as your lore has told you. These natives, however, are not *all* friendly, and there are other, worse things, in the east—some I daresay more evil than Grelion himself, in their own way, be that possible even; for the east countries are home to the majority of the evil wizards left in

Darkin, and there are dark castles where dark wizards sit upon dark thrones, governing their own countries. The East, same as the rest of the world, also houses demons of many different forms. There are trolls and golems, goblins, and demonic wolves and dwarves. There are many wretched things in all the land that do not like humans."

"Why is it that the other creatures hate us so?" asked Erguile.

"Remember: it has not always been this way, and at one time every creature lived in harmony with Gaigas. We are all formed of the same root, the same love. This age of darkness can be blamed on several; but it is mostly Grelion's fault, his lust for power. He is human himself, and despises all creatures who are not—he has defiled the valor of men. Grelion is responsible for the burning of the non-humans in this country, and for the intolerance of Vapoury, Gaigas, freedom, and any open knowledge of these things. However—we can take comfort in knowing he has not entirely destroyed these things, though he has dulled Gaigas's presence in almost all hearts," Krem spoke.

"How is it that you have lived safely for so long in this desert stronghold? Surely you must be the kind of man he hates most," asked Adacon.

"Yes—I am of the mold that Grelion hates; he hates anything loving. But recall I am a Vapour, and in that right I still have the power to ask Gaigas to conceal me from all things with evil eyes. That is why I was overjoyed at your arrival, Adacon, for it had been nigh a century since anyone could see my home's door and windows. Should you have had any evil in your spirit, even a mere drop, the whole place would have looked to you no different than any other sand dune." Adacon sat absorbing all Krem had said, as did Erguile. There was more silence as the three puffed on their pipes.

"Alas it is time for a change in plans: I oppose the idea you suggested, dear Adacon. A journey east is not suitable for our company of three, such as it is. I know much of this fair country, especially the area surrounding the Solun Desert, and I hear many things. It is no coincidence that a most powerful rumor came to me from a winged friend the night before your arrival, Adacon. It is to go north, that I propose—out of this desert to reach the Vashnod Plains. It is on those plains that there lie two stone towers, prisons of Grelion. Rarely is there more than a handful of guards at each, I have noticed of late; and under cover of night I would have us assail one of the towers. Gaining that prison would strengthen our force a great deal, if the rumors hold true; an old friend of mine is being held there. His rightful name is Flaer Ironhand, and Grelion still knows not who he has captured—for if he did the tower would be guarded one hundred times stronger. If we can have this prisoner alone join us, we will be many times more powerful than as three," Krem said.

"Sounds like a plan to me, eh Addy ol' lad?" joked Erguile, tipsy with wine.

"Alright. We'll do that then, Krem. I trust you have a mind well enough for getting this rebellion off its feet anyhow. How do you think we should go about this attack?" asked Adacon.

And with that question, Krem began to lay out his plan, and it sounded well thought out to Adacon and Erguile, as if he had been contemplating the strike for some time. After a good while they finished outlining the plan, and Adacon and Erguile grew tired.

"The night grows old on us; it is now time to get some needed rest before our departure tomorrow. Tomorrow afternoon I will fill your bags appropriately, with enough stores to last us a good few weeks. Come—let us turn now to our dreams for restoration. I'll show you to your beds," Krem ordered as he stood up and extinguished his pipe. He walked out of the room, beckoning them to follow. Adacon and Erguile extinguished their pipes and stood up to follow. Krem led them through several intertwining passages and they reached first a luxurious room for Erguile, who said good night to both of them and went to his bed. Krem continued on, leading Adacon a little way farther to his room. Adacon reached a room, just as fantastic as Erguile's had been, and said good night to Krem, thanking him again for dinner. Krem turned and started to walk out, leaving Adacon to his peace.

"Wait, Krem…" whispered Adacon just before Krem was lost from sight. For a moment Krem disappeared into the hall before suddenly returning to the doorway. Something forgotten had suddenly flared into Adacon's mind, and his voice was filled with fright.

"What is it lad?" Krem said, facing him.

"I didn't want to speak of this in front of Erguile, partly because he doesn't know the tale in full. As we camped last night, and I sat watch, I heard a creature howl twice—I searched at length each time, but in the black abyss of the desert I saw nothing. After a long while my fear was lost to weariness, and I didn't hear it again. I went to sleep. When we awoke, we found that one of our swords was missing—one of Erguile's. We traced odd tracks leading away into the desert, out into the direction we were not intending to travel. I don't know what it was, but it scared me deeply; do you have any idea what it may have been?" asked Adacon, hoping Krem would have the words to dissolve his gnawing fears. Krem's visage was overcome with a look of despair that lasted only a moment, and then it returned to calmness.

"No, lad. I cannot say I know what it was. Do not worry yourself tonight though, boy, for you are in Krem's keep at least one night longer. Now get to sleep." Krem left and closed Adacon's door behind him.

IV: THE VASHNOD

Krem awoke first the next morning, uncannily early, and he made the others breakfast. Adacon and Erguile arose to the smell of freshly brewed tea and pastries, and the three ate in silence for a while.

"I have decided to make another slight change to our plans," said Krem, breaking the silence. Adacon and Erguile were still groggy, but Krem was not; he had been up since sunrise.

"What do you intend to change?" asked Erguile. "Do you mean to say we're not going to battle?" Erguile seemed upset.

"Hah, lad, don't fret—you'll have your fair share of battle; that I'm sure of. No, the change does not alter our chances of battle. Late last night, an unforeseen difficulty entered my mind. . ." Krem said. Adacon winced. "All that I wish to alter is our time of departure—I have decided we shall leave before noon, much earlier than we first decided. My reasoning lads, is that we shall reach the stone tower by nightfall, rather than in the middle of the night. We shall sack the tower under night's cover still; I just do not wish to be upon the dunes after dark."

"And why is that, old man?" asked Erguile gruffly. "Haven't you magical powers at your disposal?"

"Yes I suppose one might say so, but what I fear does not heel to my Vapour," Krem uttered.

"Eh? And whom is it you're speaking of?" asked Erguile, growing quite baffled.

"Do not be troubled—it is nothing that concerns either of you: we are going north to cross the desert before night has fallen, and that is all I will speak of it," Krem said. Never before had Krem seemed so stern in his wording, so sure in his resolve; Adacon still had not spoken yet, but he did not need to, for he felt he knew what Krem's concern was—Krem must have changed his mind after hearing about the sword thief, and so he decided he would not query the topic, at least not yet.

They finished their breakfast and thanked Krem accordingly; even Erguile showed genuine courtesy. Krem and Erguile seemed to be forming quite the humorous relationship, Adacon observed. It was both like and dislike together in one, but thankfully it appeared that neither of them took matters to heart.

To the slaves' surprise, Krem had already packed their sacks, having made time to do so early in the morn. Each one was filled to the brim, containing much food and water, along with some extra rations that might come in handy along the journey. There was also plenty of pipe-fill inside the sacks, Erguile soon found, as he prodded through his. Krem was attired in his usual garb—a dark purple robe and the emerald-encrusted hat—and he clutched his oaken staff in hand. Erguile fastened his armor in place and sheathed his sword. Adacon slung his quiver over his shoulder once again, and tucked his bow in place at his side. Time passed quickly as they made their last preparations, and then Krem held a prayer to Gaigas, asking for a safe journey. Soon it was midmorning and the party was set to move out—Adacon, Erguile, and the little Vapour Krem made their way out into the desert.

The sun was hot, already beginning to scorch Adacon's arms as they made their way northward in a direct line. Krem used a softly glowing blue sphere-shaped device he called a *Relic* to align their course toward the northern sky; when Erguile asked how the thing worked, Krem had only laughed and said: "It is my magical powers, lad." The three marched on under the rising sun, and soon Molto's Keep was far from sight.

"And what of the bright purple robe you wear? Odd as it is fashioned, more pressing on my mind is the notice it gives to those that might seek us," questioned Erguile, fearing the Vapour's stark appearance against the yellow dunes.

"Don't pay it any mind; you've forgotten my Vapoury, lad. Know we are concealed by my power," Krem answered.

"I will take your word then. So, you've a good knowledge of this world's map, is that right Krem?" asked Erguile as they pressed on, himself beginning to grow beads of sweat on his forehead from the overbearing sun.

"I expect I know most of what's out there, though I cannot account for all changes of recent, most of which I reckon are a product of Grelion's rule," said Krem.

"Well what might you call this desert we walk, if you were to call it something other than hell," Erguile returned.

"This forbidding place is known to all who have crossed it as the Solun Desert—the Solun, plainly put."

"Solun eh? And what of our farm? Adacon and I have known it by nothing other than the farm; I'm sure it must have another name."

"Indeed you have known it by no other name because it has no other name. All of the slave farms, numerous and scattered as they may be, are given numbers—nothing more. I believe the one you and Adacon escaped from is Felwith farm, number seventy-seven."

"Felwith? I've never heard that before, what does it mean?" joined Adacon.

"Felwith is the name given to those who most directly serve Grelion himself—they are his greatest minions. Morimyr is their home, though they extend themselves much farther than its cold steps."

"And what name do we give this tower we are now headed for?" asked Adacon.

"It is the tower of Ceptical, dear Adacon, and it is there that I hope we shall recover the greatest swordsman in all the land," Krem spoke.

"Hah! It is *I* you speak of, old man. I've been fighting with swords since I was a child. All through my slavery did I and some others form our own secret sparring titles. Hah, and it was always I who held the highest most rank," Erguile said arrogantly. "But not an easy thing, what we did. A good number of the men who came to fight with us were caught with their weapons, the dumb fools. Friends they may have been, but pity them I do not. It was their mistake to be not overly concerned with their going about here and there in proper stealth."

"I never had any idea such clans existed on the farm," exclaimed Adacon. "Surely I would have joined had any of you spoke of it."

"Yes, it was a very cautious thing, and I always spoke with the slaves whom I thought would fancy such a thing—you, young Adacon, never caught my eye as one to fight."

"I did practice as much as possible in my hut, with the space that allowed. I became quite good I think, over time. It was only after I slashed my walls a good dozen times that I stopped.

Still, I retained the fighting arts in my mind, as I had learned from the different books I acquired."

"I'm more surprised that you can read, Adacon, for I was the only other on the farm able to do so. How was it you learned?"

"I'm not sure—odd as it may sound—I suppose I was taught somehow, by someone, in my earliest years. As far back as I can remember I could already read fairly well, though I learned more over time as I found ways of getting books on the farm."

"Ah! You too learned to steal from the wagons! I thought I was the only one who knew it possible. Their dumbfounded faces must have looked funny upon seeing the empty wagons." Erguile laughed.

"Well I never spoiled an entire wagon, but I surely confiscated my share to read."

"Ah, I see. Well I guess you missed out on the fine tobacco that sometimes rolled through."

"Both of you seem rather learned for slaves, more so than I thought a slave ever could be," said Krem with a touch of bitter-sweet in his voice.

"Hah, and smart enough you are for a dwarf of a man, without the girth mind you, and at the ripe old age of who knows how many centuries past!" Erguile joked and they all laughed.

The three roamed deeper over the dunes of the unchanging desert, stopping only briefly here and there for a drink of water. The sun began to fall in the western sky, and the scorching heat began to subside at last. Adacon wondered about the thief as they walked in silence, and his mind played the night over and over again in his memory. The unforeseen circumstance Krem had spoken of, it had to be his own mentioning of the creature—what else could have made Krem change their plans? After all, Krem said that the news came to him late at night, and that was enough for Adacon, though Erguile must have thought old Krem referred to an insight of magic. Either way, Adacon felt a slight fear, mainly because he knew not what he was afraid of. But if Krem had reason to keep off the dunes after nightfall, Adacon believed that it had to be something terribly evil. There would be a time to question Krem; it was not now, and it would have to be in private.

"Do you suppose we'll actually reach the place anytime soon? I am growing tired, this wretched sand makes for hard footwork," grunted Erguile, fatigue in his voice.

"The Solun can be very cruel when it wants to be. I fear we may not make it all the way to the tower tonight, but we must reach the Vashnod Plains at least," Krem said.

"Have your estimates been misguided, poor Vapour?" mocked Erguile.

"No, but it is both of you whom I've misjudged, for our speed is lessened on your account," responded Krem.

"Pah! My account? Surely I am stouter of leg than an old dwarf such as you…" Erguile said.

"He's aided by unseen things Erguile, you must remember that," Adacon spoke up.

"It is not your fault anyhow—the Solun breaks the strongest of men under its glare," Krem reassured him.

"But will we be safe in the Vashnod for the night?" asked Adacon. "You spoke warily of staying out past sundown in the desert, so what of the plains?"

"My dear Adacon, to believe you are safe anywhere upon Darkin in the age of Grelion is folly, but I don't think we'll find trouble on the plains this night. It is mostly nomads roaming there, a desolate place really, and not many of Grelion's men patrol it," said Krem.

"Nomads? What sort of nomads?" questioned Erguile.

"The sort that take matters into their own hands, but if we are to leave them be I don't think we'll have trouble," spoke Krem.

"Good enough. I look forward to getting another taste of the food you've brought for us, and a fresh pipe," said Erguile.

"Come, let us hasten lads. I expect you two to be able to at least keep up with an old Vapour!" goaded Krem, and with that he broke away in front of them, increasing his speed to a mild run. Adacon and Erguile were quick to compensate for the difference in speed, and they caught up.

"I wish for a steed in this hour, and for the rest of our journey," panted Erguile.

"Perhaps before long you will have one," Krem said softly, and then winked at Erguile. They continued at a grueling pace farther into the Solun.

The sun now seemed to be in its last stage of life in the sky, and the desert finally began to change its climate. The dunes were lower now, Adacon noticed, and the sand seemed to be whiter; the dunes soon turned hard and firm. They pushed on, and the desert ran flat—the yellow sand had turned white and level. Up in the distance far ahead, very faintly, could be seen mountains. The distinguishable peaks in the fading light were shrouded in mist, and at least two weeks march away, Adacon guessed. It was comforting anyway to see a change of scenery, and for that matter an entirely novel sight.

"They're beautiful!" exclaimed Adacon.

"Enormous!" gushed Erguile.

"I assure you they're much bigger, should you stand in their foothills. They are known as the Angelyn Mountains," said Krem.

Before them was a vast plain, stretching in all directions as far as the eye could see. The plain was a great whitish-green lawn of grass with shrubs cropping up throughout its expanse. Here and there were patches of broad-leafed trees, though they were few, and in the distance were several emerald mounds.

"We've reached the Vashnod, and it has been too long since I traveled north," Krem sighed endearingly.

"And what are in those mountains?" asked Erguile, who hadn't withdrawn his gaze from the Angelyn Range.

"Many great and curious creatures—and cruel rock trolls—and also the home of the Reichmar," said Krem gleefully as they marched onto the plains. The sky dimmed further.

"By all means old man, what are the Reichmar?" asked Erguile.

"The Angelyn are beautiful to behold—ancient and massive in all their splendid glory—and as such they are fit to house the Reichmar. Alas, the Reichmar are the secluded dwarves of the north, a noble and proud people, though in this dark age they are despised and hated by most all."

"Dwarves! Ah, I will go mad on this journey for certain," hooted Erguile.

"It's fascinating. Why are they hated by most all, Krem?" asked Adacon.

"That answer you can find for yourself Adacon, I'm sure. Ask yourself who is *most* with the power to enforce hate in this age?" asked Krem. Grelion, Adacon thought to himself.

"Then they are oppressed the same as us?" Adacon questioned further.

"Surely they are. More so than slaves maybe, at times—a dwarf is tortured and executed without reasoning, should he be found away from the mountains. Grelion does not even respect them enough to grant them slavery, and so they have enclosed themselves deep within the mountains. It is their only safety; and even the cold stone of the Angelyn Mountains weakens with each passing day, as Grelion conspires to expose their cavernous city to his minions."

"So they are well hidden? Do they interact at all with the outside world anymore? Have they gone to total retaliation against anyone passing through their mountains?" asked Adacon.

"Well hidden, certainly, but Grelion has discovered their secret entrances by now. I'm sure that mistrust among the dwarves has escalated since last I heard news from the north, and I doubt they would take friendly to anyone not born of dwarven blood, especially a human. They are forced in this dark time to keep constant watch over their borders, and, rightfully enough, kill anything unrecognizable as a dwarf on sight."

"Might we chance gaining their partnership?" asked Erguile. "Often, in the lore I've read about dwarves, I've heard them to be a strong and courageous race: bold—and with battle axes just as bold." Erguile unsheathed his sword jokingly and swung it in the fashion of a battle-axe. "I still can't believe dwarves and elves are real. I will need to see one before I commit to belief in them."

"I don't think it would be wise to step upon their range, not yet anyhow. Eventually we may need their strength, along with the strength of all not tainted by Grelion's vile sway," Krem responded.

"Good enough, though I would love to see for myself how marvelous their city is," Adacon said.

"I have been to the Reichmar city thrice in the past twelve decades, but not once in recent times. In the elder ages I frequented the city often; it was indescribably breathtaking, and the people were only the kindest sort," said Krem. Adacon felt awe once more at Krem's extreme age.

"And this city should be considered more beautiful than even your home, Krem? I don't know if I can fathom such a place. What is the city's name?" asked Erguile.

"Dwarfton, you could call it, as most humans do. It has a dwarven name also, which is Ascaronth."

"I would most like to visit Ascaronth, when the time comes that we are able to do so," said Adacon.

"And certainly enough we might, when that time arrives. But now you must turn your eyes to the far right of our path; for it is to that opaque shadow on the horizon you both have failed to see that we must now cut our trail toward." And with that Adacon and Erguile gasped in unison, as their heads turned to engage the silhouette of the Tower of Ceptical. It was a menacing spire to the slaves, standing as the tallest unnatural structure either of them had ever seen. The sky was darkening and the tower was blending into deep grey clouds. Both of them felt a great sensation of fear in their hearts upon seeing the prison.

Some miles to the right of the tower was the dim shape of an enormous granite faced wall that flattened out at the top like a grand table in the sky, high above the Vashnod floor. It was long and tapered off to the south, away from them with no end in sight.

"And what is that high ground?" asked Erguile.

"The Rislind Plateau, and the only way north save through the Angelyn Mountains," responded Krem.

Adacon shuddered again as he returned his gaze to the Ceptical Tower. He pointed at it and spoke.

"*That* is what we must sack?" Adacon said in a shaky tone.

"Indeed—and we shall by tomorrow, lad. But the tower is still a half day's march. Do not fret; we will be forced to make camp tonight on the plains," spoke Krem.

"These plains will do fine enough. There is never enough rest before battle. Where do you think we might find a fitting spot?" asked Erguile, eager to have more food and sleep before assailing the tower.

"Perhaps we could make camp near a patch of trees Krem? We would be more concealed than out in the open plain," proposed Adacon.

"And by the trees we shall camp then, but not before we march until the moons are ripe to fall," said Krem, and with that he checked the face of his Relic. He seemed to grunt something to himself and then they continued. Adacon and Erguile marched in awe of the mountains and the foreboding tower jutting in the eastern sky. The yellow dunes were fast behind them and out of sight.

They walked on without affair until the moons reached their limit in the black cradle of the sky, and Krem spoke the first words in a seemingly long forever:

"It is time we had some stew fit for our lagged muscles; what do you think, Erguile?" asked Krem, humor in his voice for Erguile's amusement.

"You have my mind, Krem. We'll set camp then, and look at that," Erguile said pointing off to a small hill covered with trees. "Is it not perfect for our purpose?"

"Wonderful!" shouted Adacon, and he ran ahead to look at the emerald hill that rose from the Vashnod floor. The other two caught up to him, and soon Krem made camp and had a fire going, above which sat a small pot, in which was boiling a delicious smelling stew of spiced meat and vegetables. Erguile sat nearby and puffed contentedly on his pipe. Adacon stood alone at the edge of the hill, staring off in all directions, mesmerized by the foreign landscape. In a moment Krem started to pour the stew into clay bowls.

"Come on lads, dinner is served," called Krem. Adacon came and they gathered around the fire. Each sat with a bowl in hand but did no more. No one spoke—no one dared. Finally Krem seemed pleased enough at their discipline, so he spoke.

"We shall give homage to Gaigas in our own minds from now on, for from our pondering of her can we learn much about this journey of life," Krem said, and the three fell to complete silence. An eerie tranquility overtook the atmosphere.

Adacon immediately fell to his own world of thought, forgetting to give homage to Gaigas. Just a few days before, he had been inside his own prison, a part of the unending oppression; now he was completely free. Life would be completely unlike anything he had experienced before, and it seemed that each new day was bringing more excitement than the last. His mind flourished with a thousand fascinations and fumbled with a thousand questions. It was almost too much, but all of it was beautiful.

Erguile seemed content enough after a few seconds to begin feasting, but he held back. It was only after Krem opened his eyes at last that they began to eat. The stew was extraordinarily good. The slaves gorged themselves and when it was gone they wished for more; but there was no more stew, and the night had grown colder.

"Now that we are properly full it is time to settle into our comforts for the evening. I will be our watch for this night; I do not feel a need for rest just yet," Krem said, and they went about making the site as comfortable as it could be. Soon Adacon slipped into fantastical dreams, and Erguile fell into a dreamless slumber, while Krem kept watch over the dark plains.

*   *   *

It was still the middle of the night, Adacon knew, as he opened his eyes and saw a star-filled sky above him; the clouds had cleared, allowing a view of glittering space dust. Why am I awake at this hour, he wondered, realizing he should be sleeping. The reason became apparent in a moment; noises drifted through the air behind his head. It was not very close, but near enough to hear. Adacon rolled to his side quickly, seeing Erguile still sleeping peacefully. Then Adacon froze—he recognized the noises to be voices—one of them was Krem's.

In a state of alarm, Adacon first acted as if he were still sleeping, but he carefully raised his head to peer in the direction of the talk. He was taken aback at what he saw. Standing next to Krem was a swirling aura of light, something that vaguely resembled the shape of a human. The aura was scarlet and gold, flickering slightly. The form seemed twice as tall as Krem, and it appeared to be having a conversation with him. Although Krem's voice could be clearly made out, when the form spoke it seemed only to hiss in a syncopated rhythm, and Adacon could not make out a word. Krem seemed to understand at any rate, and the two were chattering on.

Adacon tried edging closer to hear Krem better, nervous of being seen or heard. He wriggled quietly, leaving Erguile alone. Finally—either by wriggling closer or by being fully awake again—Krem's words could be understood.

"Be it may that your power has been accelerated Zesm, I would ask you to remember our last meeting," Krem said in a cold tone, one unlike any used with the slaves. A syncopated hissing came in response, and Adacon turned his head up and around once more to catch a glimpse of the form, only this time the form was gone, and in its place stood a tall, hunched human. The man was built of threaded muscle, wrapped in greyed bandages, with spotty leather armor hanging off here and there. On his head was a dirty type of turban, and on his side was sheathed a bloodied broadsword. Adacon rolled back to his mock sleeping position: the thief, he thought in shock. He continued to eavesdrop intently, and the hissing noises of the thief's voice had been replaced with a heavily accented voice in the common tongue.

"You may have defeated me once before Krem, but even then you failed to destroy me. Behold—now I am of a different vein than before, and you ought not anger me, and rather do as I command. Return south whence you came, and keep with you the minions of Grelion you have taken," said the mysterious voice.

"I will do no such thing," responded Krem.

"Krem, I did not wish for it to come to this," returned the voice.

"So it *is* Grelion you aid once again, and no doubt his power that has restored you. Let black magic pour through you, and even still you will find no ground to stand on against me, poor Zesm—Zesm the Rancor," goaded Krem. "Black magic will not win out against Vapoury in a duel; even you should know that."

"Alas, it is not Grelion that I aid, but *Vesleathren* himself," replied Zesm.

"Liar," Krem struck back angrily. "It cannot be; Vesleathren was killed at the end of the war."

"He is well and brooding, Krem. Know his power, and mind your route back to the desert," Zesm said. "Vesleathren still commands the Feral Brood!"

"Impossible, it's not true. He died long ago. Flaer Ironhand slew him ere Aulterion ended the Feral War," contested Krem.

"So goes the tainted lore of your brethren—Flaer gained nothing more than Vesleathren's blade in that war, and Vesleathren fled north long before Aulterion's blast," said Zesm. "Hear me now, Krem, feeble sand hermit—Vesleathren unmasks his purpose soon for all to see, and you ought to return to hiding. I'm afraid if you do not I shall return tomorrow night, and all three of your lives will be ended: this is my master's bidding." With Zesm's last word a violent rustle sounded and Krem let out a gasp. It seemed the stranger had disappeared, but Adacon dared not stir to check. Krem's footsteps could be heard returning toward the campsite. Adacon remained wide awake for some time, his mind racing, trying to make sense of anything he had heard. What he soon felt was an ominous shadow of darkness covering their quest; after an hour of worried thoughts, Adacon decided he had to bring it up with Krem in the morning. If anything, their lives were preserved for one more day, as Zesm had ordained.

*   *   *

Morning broke and Erguile awoke first. He started to take food for breakfast from his satchel, before kicking Adacon.

"Ugh, hello…"

"Time for something to eat, I expect," said Erguile. "Only where's the little man gone off too?"

"Wha..?" said Adacon rubbing his eyes. Groggily he peered around looking for Krem, but there was no sign of him.

"Up and ran off I suppose. Maybe we have to sack this tower as two now?" said Erguile, only half joking. "Would have liked to have him with us though, with that Vapoury he had. Still, I think we're up to the task—if it's as ill-guarded as he said." A jolt of fear ran through Adacon, though Erguile seemed confident enough not to be distraught by Krem's disappearance.

"He can't have just run off. He must be off to scout ahead. He'll be back soon," said Adacon.

"Maybe, but we can't stay here too long if he doesn't come back," Erguile asserted. They prepared for themselves a breakfast from the food stores Krem had given them, and Adacon told Erguile the details of what he had overheard in the middle of the night. The morning rolled on as they ate, and Adacon reworded everything that had been spoken. He described the deranged looking Zesm. He talked about the aura Zesm had formed from, the hissing noise he had been making, and then Adacon decided to finally tell Erguile about the noises he had heard the first night they camped together in the desert.

"Why didn't you tell me—better yet wake me up right then and there, hearing noises and such?" said Erguile angered.

"I felt I was doing you a favor, letting you sleep and gain your strength. Besides, like I said, I saw nothing that night, and I thought the noise might have been imagined at first," responded Adacon.

"Sure, but you heard it twice!"

"I'm sorry," Adacon said limply. "But this Zesm, when I saw him last night talking with Krem, I glimpsed a broadsword on him."

"What? Mine surely!" Erguile raged.

"But it was bloodied. Yours was clean."

"So he may have killed with it after he stole it."

"But then why not kill us as we slept?"

"Who knows his intentions, but on account of your story he sounds like a powerful enemy of ours—it *is* strange he didn't slay us though."

"Last night, this Zesm spoke of a master. Perhaps he was doing only as commanded."

"Perhaps, but either way I will slay him on sight if he dares to cross our path again."

"But even Krem seemed to fear him once he mentioned a name—I think it was Veh—Ves..." Adacon trailed off trying to remember the name.

"The old man feared him? That's hard to believe, for I could sense no fear in that old man."

"Whoever it was, Vessomething, it was after his mentioning that Krem spoke with fear in his voice. It seemed it was the master of Zesm's."

"I don't like this business about phantoms, and I think we need to set forth toward the tower. We've waited longer than we should have already. Let Zesm try to murder us before the next day comes, and we'll see which man is sent to his grave," Erguile said confidently. Adacon didn't like the idea of going on without Krem, especially considering the threats Zesm had made. Erguile was right though; hours had passed, and too long already they had been sitting idle, awaiting Krem's return. So they silently gathered their supplies and began their march northeast towards the Ceptical Tower, now shining in the full light of day.

They paced on over the plains, enjoying a cool wind that was sweeping in from the east. The day passed lazily, as they marched uninterrupted for several hours.

"Aren't you worried about his threat to kill us if we don't return to the desert?" asked Adacon nervously as they marched.

"Hah! Let him come, and meet my steel fang," responded Erguile, and he drew his sword and swung it through the air.

"You're quite fearless, and a comfort for it," smiled Adacon. "After all, if we return south I suppose our danger remains the same. Either way Grelion will want us dead, and north or south we know not the way. At least we may try for this swordsman in the tower."

"And maybe others more than him, as Krem foretold," said Erguile. "Won't be long before we have a proper band of fighters I think." With a slight boost in their morale the two sped across the plain at a hastened pace. The sun started to fall westward in the sky, and there remained a cool breeze as they trudged closer to the tower. It wasn't until the sun was almost halfway down in the sky that they decided to stop for a meal. The tower was very close, only several hundred yards away: it was at least ten times as tall as the towers on the farm, Adacon reckoned, and it was made of plain, unremarkable grey stones. A dark and massive wooden door could be made out at the base of the stone tower, and a shoddy gravel road ran away from it. The slaves chose a shady area behind a tree-laden hill for their resting place, partly so they wouldn't be spied upon from atop the tower's balcony, and partly so they could start making an early dinner.

Dusk began to creep upon them as they ate. Soon the meal was finished, seemingly as quick as it began, and Erguile was complaining that had Krem still been with them they would have been able to smoke their pipes; with no Krem magic to conceal the smoke trail in the sky, they were forced to go without.

"Alright, I suppose we had better do as Krem meant for us to, despite that he's a deserting coward," said Erguile. They went over their original design—to take the tower by way of a secret passage at its rear; after getting inside, they were to go up the staircase leading to its highest room, near the upper balcony: the cell of Flaer Ironhand. At the balcony, as Krem had told, they would find Bulkog—troll guard of Ceptical—carrying a circlet of keys, one of which would open Flaer's cell. Krem had spoken to them briefly of Bulkog's ferocity, and of his weakness for hallucinogenic pipe-weeds and liquors that came through by way of farm trade. If they were to have some luck, Bulkog the Vandal would be in a stupor and drunk.

"On after me, Addy," Erguile ordered. They crept, heading out into the open darkness, leaving their concealment beneath trees. They followed the gravel road that lay in the front of the tower—it loomed up in the night sky before them and its great balcony appeared as a crown from which a spire needled out toward the stars to a black point. To their great relief there didn't appear to be any guards above—no one was watching. The tower was tall, but it was not very wide, and when they had finally gotten close enough the two slaves swiftly darted across the road and around its circumference. There were still no lights coming off the tower, and Adacon felt reassured that they hadn't been seen.

"Doesn't this place look abandoned? No guard on the balcony, no scout, no torches?" questioned Adacon.

"Don't think too hard on it—you might spoil things," replied Erguile with a wry smile. They crouched hidden amidst shrubbery that ran wild with vines and weeds that hugged the tower's foundation. Wasting no time they began to scour the earth for the secret entrance Krem had described to them.

"Found it," Adacon yelped immediately and too loudly.

"Quiet—we still have an element of surprise working for us. Do you want to lose that along with the old man?" Erguile chided. Adacon began to uncover the earth around a rusty old iron padlock; it seemed to be on the face of an inlaid square door, two yards wide and level with the soil. It looked as though it led down into a cellar just outside the tower.

"And how are we supposed to get past this?" asked Adacon dumbfounded, staring at the lock.

"Don't remember there being mention of a lock…" said Erguile. They took turns fiddling with the padlock until they both gave up exhausted; the frustration had got so far as Erguile taking a swing at it with his sword, disregarding the noise it would make. Still, there was no sign of activity or noise in or around the tower.

"What can we do now but enter in from the front," Erguile acquiesced.

"That door may be locked as well, and we could be walking right in on them," replied Adacon.

"Well I don't see any other choices, but it doesn't seem to me there's anyone here to be walked in on."

"Maybe we should press on—leave this place and head toward the Rislind Plateau, then go on further east," suggested Adacon. "Maybe Krem was wrong about this tower. Maybe it *is* abandoned."

At that, a loud cracking noise sounded, and both Erguile and Adacon exclaimed in horror at what they turned to see: fallen to the ground from atop one of the trees they had been sheltering near was a mass of silver metal in the shape of an enormous man. It looked as though it had been perching atop a branch—around its body were long splinters of wood.

"What in the world," Adacon whispered. They both drew their swords.

"Keep it quiet now; maybe he's not dead," whispered Erguile.

"What should we do?"

"Follow me, and be ready to strike it," he uttered quietly as he stepped toward the tree less than twenty yards from where they stood. Cautiously, he made his way within ten yards of the hulking silver mass, Adacon tailing him. Adacon came up alongside Erguile as they finally came within striking range. They were now only several yards from the creature, and they stood in awe at the sight: the man was not truly a human at all, but some kind of a rock-like being; he was shaped much as a man would be, but larger than anyone either of the slaves had ever seen. The giant dressed in a leather chest-piece and greaves, and he wore faded boots the color of soil. His head had no hair, but was tightly bound in russet cloth above his eye line. On his belt there was a dagger big enough to be a man's sword, and he wore gloves on either hand with finger holes cut in them to let his silver fingers through. The mass of silver began to move.

"Ugh, fallen again in my sleep—weak trees here," spoke a deep voice.

"Name yourself—enemy or friend to slaves of Grelion?" shouted Erguile, forgetting his stealth and brandishing his sword.

"I'm sorry—didn't see you there," the silver giant said slowly.

"What kind of man are you?" Adacon rattled off in shock at what he was seeing.

"I am no man, Sir Adacon—I am Slowin, golem of the Red Forest, protector of the earth there," retorted the silver mass. The two slaves stood aghast.

"Slowin?" Adacon gasped. "A name Krem spoke of, and you said mine."

"Yes, Krem told me of your journey," said Slowin. "It is why I am here, and far from home."

"A friend of Krem's—I suppose we're in no danger from you then. Still, we have this tower to sack, and we are too loud," Erguile said, regaining his composure.

"It is that very task that I can assist you with," Slowin said, standing up to full height. He was colossal, nearly twice as tall as Adacon, and of magnificent girth.

"How is it you were able to hide here, so close to the tower?" asked Adacon.

"Krem's Vapoury of course," responded the silver golem.

"Where has he gone then?" Erguile asked.

"He had a grave errand—unexpected, it sounded when he told me," Slowin replied.

"It had to have been something with that Zesm," Adacon chimed.

"Quiet," Erguile warned. They had forgotten stealth, and were talking loudly, since the crack of the tree and Slowin's crash to the earth.

"Don't worry Erguile," Slowin reassured. "Bulkog is drunk and hallucinating in the tower, and the other guards have fled in haste two nights ago at hearing word of Zesm the Rancor's return."

"You have been in the tower already?" questioned Adacon.

"No, Krem told me last night, after summoning me from my rest."

"That bastard—doesn't let on all he knows does he," Erguile spat.

"I owed him a debt, and I am repaying it now, as an escort for you both," said Slowin.

"Are we in no danger now then?" asked Adacon.

"Of course there is danger; but rest assured, while you are under my watch, no harm will come to you," Slowin said, standing as a hulk with his arms crossed over his otherworldly construction of a body. His stone skin seemed to be made out of something metallic as per its sheen, and his enormous frame appeared to be organic; there was fluidity in its design not apparent in the crafted machines of men.

"And enough questioning, for haste is set upon our errand. Enter, and do as was your plan at the start," Slowin said, and he strode toward the tower. The slaves followed, and when there Slowin drew forth a mallet that had been hidden on his back under garments. After hoisting his mallet, he brought it down with great force upon the padlock. Out rang the clangorous echo of metal on metal, and the padlock lay broken apart.

"Aren't you going to come?" asked Adacon, as Erguile already began lowering himself through the door into the cellar below.

"Ahaha! I had forgotten the humor of humans—does it look like I might fit through?" Slowin laughed loudly, throwing caution to the wind. "Now go, make haste."

Adacon followed Erguile down into the cellar, and soon they were half crawling in a dank and dust filled cavern with no light. The cellar was wide but not tall enough for either of them to stand, and they could see nothing but a soft trail of starlight coming from the open door.

"And what now, how are we going to ever find the way in from here?" Adacon grunted.

"Krem didn't account for this part then, did he," Erguile groaned. At the last word of Erguile's a thud came from behind them. Spinning around, they saw a small orb of glowing white on the cellar floor, fallen in from the door above.

"Use it well, slaves. It is my light for times such as these," called down Slowin. Adacon picked up the shining orb—feeling like a heavy ball of marble—and realized that it sent a shaft of light toward whichever direction he thrust it.

"A magic trinket from a golem—our journey grows queerer by the hour," Erguile chortled.

"Thanks Slowin," Adacon called up, and he turned toward the dark parts of the cellar. Once lit, the layout of the den was simple: a floor of orange sand, wooden crates, and several sacks scattered about an otherwise empty chamber. Toward the end of the room against the opposite side was another door: a small wooden square that appeared to have another lock on it. The slaves hurried toward it, hands ready by their sword hilts.

"Another lock," Adacon said, frustrated.

"Pay it no mind, this one I ought to handle fine," Erguile said, and then he reversed his position so as to set his back against Adacon's. With a heave, he thrust both feet forward, cracking the wood. Again he assaulted it, using Adacon for leverage. With a loud splintering crack the door caved completely in, and new light poured forth. The small orb in Adacon's hand suddenly went dark; it became a lifeless mix of grey and black. Erguile went through first, followed by Adacon. In a moment they both were standing in a wide dungeon hall ten yards high. The walls were bare, and there was no sound except for the droning crackle of torches that intermittently lit the hall.

"Look, stairs," pointed Adacon, and they ran for a nearby staircase, their swords out and ready. They clambered up the tremendously steep staircase, Adacon leading the way. After many times around the circumference of the tower, each flight becoming increasingly vertical, they came to a foyer walled with inlaid jail cells and a path out onto the balcony. They entered into a small

87

room laden with crimson carpet, on which stood several tables. On the tables were spilled tankards and flasks, as well as several upright beakers containing a thick brown liquid. On the wall hung what looked to be a giant decorative hammer. The slaves noticed an odd aroma, sweet yet pungent all the same. It wafted to them from the balcony entrance.

"Bulkog," whispered Adacon.

"He must be on the balcony," Erguile whispered back. They gripped their broadswords and quietly paced toward the balcony. The air was cool and a slight breeze rolled in from outside, carrying the odorous pipe smoke. The slaves turned a corner to face the precipice, and there they beheld the source of the aroma:

Pipe in one hand, hoary blade in the other, stood Bulkog; he appeared, however, unlike anything Adacon or Erguile thought a troll should look like. Both of them had seen illustrations of trolls, and this looked nothing like one. Bulkog was bigger in size than Erguile, almost two-thirds as big as even Slowin the golem. His skin was yellowed and dilapidated, oozing brown syrup from its pores. His head was poorly constructed, as if he had been misshapen in childbirth or beaten savagely in the face. His hair was wrapped up in leather bindings, and the mess of it that could be seen was greased and grey. He wore thick silver armor on his legs and shoulders, but his chest was bare except for a rotted black shirt. At the sight of the slaves Bulkog coughed deeply and dropped his pipe. A trickle of brown paste slipped from his lips, suspended itself in midair, and finally sagged to the stone floor of the balcony. Reaching for a sword, Bulkog spoke:

"What's this—vile thieves of Zesm, come to steal from my hidden stores? Hold still and I will rend you both asunder—"

Adacon and Erguile began a full charge and Bulkog
stepped back to parry with his long steel.

The blows fell hard, but Bulkog deflected both without
effort; Adacon's sword glanced off the troll's shoulder armor, and
Erguile's strike was rejected by Bulkog's own blade.

"Feel the bite of *Ettlebane!*" roared Bulkog, and in their
recuperation from the parries, the deranged troll bolted past them
back into the red foyer. Adacon and Erguile, temporarily stunned,
rose again to action and gave chase. They confronted Bulkog in the
foyer as he was taking down from the wall the massive hammer of
war.

"Heel now to *Ettlebane* and *Mirebane*, blade and hammer of
the Feral Dynast—or do not, and seek a prolonged death!" raged
the drunken Bulkog, wobbling as he swung Ettlebane his sword in
one hand, and Mirebane the war hammer in the other.

"Seek this," replied Erguile cockily, and he swung violently
at Bulkog's head. Bulkog was drunk, but he retained his speed and
blocked Erguile's attack for a second time. At last Bulkog struck,
flailing forward with both weapons at Erguile in a north to south
swing. Erguile quickly rolled aside, diving headlong onto the floor,
blood blending into the carpet as his leg grazed the steel at his
ankle.

"Ahgh," Erguile moaned, slowly regaining his feet. Bulkog
stood over him ready to finish when Adacon came from behind;
his sword bit directly into Bulkog's shoulder, just between where
his armor met his neck.

"Ugh—runt," Bulkog violently screamed, "I'll kill you!"

Adacon tried desperately to remove his sword from
Bulkog's shoulder but it wouldn't budge; the cut had been a severe
depth and the blade was buried in muscle. Bulkog twisted around

to face him, and Adacon lost grip on his sword. He recoiled in fright, cowering with his arms over his face.

"Time to die, you rotten human; feel the death pang of Feral steel," Bulkog bellowed as blood oozed down his chest from the fresh wound. Raising his hammer high over Adacon's head, the mallet descended; Erguile had rolled near, and as the hammer fell, he stabbed down fiercely into Bulkog's feet, causing him to tumble. Adacon jumped aside as Erguile regained his footing and yanked from Bulkog's neck the broadsword. He tossed it over to Adacon and they were both armed once more. Bulkog was writhing about on the floor, howling in agony, his back to them. The slaves made ready for a unified death blow; they sent their swords down upon Bulkog's spine, but as the tips were about to sting him a bright red flash of fire burst upwards from the troll's chest. A great force followed the fire blast and the slaves were thrown back against the stone wall. Erguile looked over to see his friend unconscious; Bulkog rose and limped over, faint with blood loss yet ready enough to finish off the intruders.

"Now you have made me disobey my master and use *magic*. On such pathetic enemies as you two are—what a waste to lose his trust over this. But I will not be slain by humans on this or any other day, master's will or not," Bulkog rambled, half to himself, as he approached them. Gurgling blood poured from his mouth. Bulkog dropped his weapons and grabbed the dazed Erguile by the neck with his fists. He lifted him up and choked him, finally slamming him against the wall.

"Die now at last, human," Bulkog said, and he thrust his sword into Erguile's neck. Just as the blade tip pierced the first layer of skin, a great white light blinded Bulkog and burned his eyes so that he fell backwards and to the ground. Adacon stood over him then, pointing Slowin's orb of light directly at the troll's eyes.

Bulkog cried in pain, and the light of the orb seemed to intensify more than it had in the cellar; the orb seemed to draw in from an ambience of light to a fine pointed beam, and the energy caused smoke to drift up from Bulkog's eyes, seeping between his fingers that failed to shield them.

"Bastard," said Erguile, who had come to stand beside Adacon over Bulkog. Erguile picked up Mirebane, the Feral hammer of war, and brought it down without mercy on Bulkog's skull. The crunch echoed loud, and on Darkin Bulkog the Feral made once more a howl but never again; the haunting call cascaded out through the balcony and into the night sky, loud enough for Slowin, far below, to hear.

"In here," said Adacon. He led the way through the entrance to the jail. Inside was a circling wall of thin-barred cells, tiny and cramped, all hugging the fringe of the room. They were empty except for one; in it was a hunched man, balled on the floor underneath a mess of wild brown hair, clothed in stained rags. He appeared asleep or dead.

"That must be him—the keys," remembered Erguile, and he ran back to grab the keys from Bulkog's corpse. Adacon approached the cell door and peered down.

"Hello, Flaer? We've come to free you," Adacon said. He trembled, still filled with the adrenaline of facing Bulkog. From the crumpled man came no reply. Adacon repeated himself to no avail. Erguile returned with the keys and quickly opened the door. With a rusty creek it gave way and he shook the man.

"Come on, we've got to be off now," Erguile pleaded, shaking him. After another bout of shaking the man came around, opening his eyes and peering up. Slowly he got to his feet.

"Are you alright?" asked Adacon. There came no answer, but a moment later the man nodded his head.

"Can you speak?" asked Erguile, and the man shook his head side to side.

"*Cursed*, I'll bet," Adacon guessed. The man nodded to confirm. "Are you Flaer?" he asked, and the man nodded once more. His face was long and shaggy, appearing like an overgrown animal.

"Damn it—I can't free his hands," Erguile groaned. Adacon looked down to see Flaer's hands shackled in what appeared to be a smooth black contraption made of something with no interlocking pieces. The shackle, it appeared, was a black steel figure eight that somehow bonded Flaer's hands tightly at the wrists; there were no keyholes or features of any kind. The bracelet was in fact one smooth unit.

"Better get him down to Slowin," stammered Adacon, and Erguile agreed. Flaer followed without protest, and the three descended the tower. They exited the front doors instead of going through the cellar, and Slowin was already there awaiting them.

"Well done; are you hurt much?" Slowin asked, noticing the blood on Erguile's neck and leg.

"Minor cut, nothing worth paying mind," Erguile said. "But Bulkog was no common foe, drunkard or not."

"He's dead now though, I gather," returned Slowin, glancing to Flaer who kept his head down. "Flaer Swordhand—an honor to make your acquaintance," cheered Slowin, and he hugged Flaer heartily; Flaer grimaced.

"He cannot speak, nor can we free his hands," Adacon informed.

"That is the least of our trouble, as I expect Vesleathren to be greatly angered by this meeting we conduct here; we who are among the freed Flaer Swordhand and felled Bulkog," said Slowin. It appeared Adacon was ready to ask more questions but Slowin spoke again:

"We must travel immediately, in all haste, farther east and up onto the Rislind Plateau. Not until we reach the Saru Gnarl Cape will we be safe to rest. Come," And with Slowin's order the company of four departed swiftly into the night, marching east from the sacked tower of Ceptical along the slave trade route.

V: THE BRIGUN AUTILUS

The party traveled through the night in silence, stopping just before dawn to rest and eat. There was not much talk, and Flaer's silence brought an air of gloom upon the slaves. Slowin made little conversation, averting questions when they came up.

"We will rest here briefly, now that we have reached Rislind and are upon the Plateau," Slowin told them. A small fire was started, and in the early morning twilight the four sat around, eager for a chance to sleep.

"Can you not break Flaer's bonds, Slowin?" asked Adacon.

"No, they abound with evil magic, the magic of Vesleathren. I cannot break them," he responded.

"I have thrice heard that name. Who is Vesleathren?" returned Adacon, as Erguile stood near to Flaer and curiously raised his sword.

"I'll break it. Hold still, Swordhand," Erguile said, preparing to strike at the black cuffs binding Flaer.

"No—do not strike, else lose your blade's edge," Slowin gasped.

"Just think I have the power for it; there's no intention of harming him," Erguile solemnly moped, sitting back down.

"It is folly to play at Vesleathren's magic; believe me, I have tried it before," Slowin went on, restoring order. Flaer remained downtrodden, hanging his head in lethargy. "Vesleathren is the heir to the Feral Throne of Melweathren—Melweathren the Admiral of the Crawl Plaque during the first age of this planet, who was defeated in battle on this very plateau by a Rislindian, thousands of years ago."

"What is Crawl Plaque?" asked Erguile.

"That is the name given to the first army of the Feral Brood, a race brewed of corrupt magic; dark mana sustained their life and power," answered Slowin.

"That's what Bulkog spoke of, Feral Dynast something," said Adacon.

"It is much as I feared then, and Bulkog the troll had become of Feral genetics. Lucky you are to have survived his encounter."

"What of Grelion? Is he not our most treacherous foe?" asked Erguile.

"Long had it been thought that after the old war, which Molto the Vapour ended by casting Spirited Winds, did the Crawl Plaque expire out of existence. Few were those who knew that Melweathren had an heir, named Vesleathren. Vesleathren brooded, conspiring for long years, preparing a Feral army that would once again try to sack the entire country of Arkenshyr."

"Arkenshyr? Where in Darkin is that?" questioned Adacon.

"Hah! Poor slave, it is here in Arkenshyr that we are now, and one of the five countries of Darkin it is," Slowin replied. Adacon tried his best to keep up with everything he was being told, as did Erguile; they both looked dumbfounded and confused.

"And so he invaded, and another great war was fought; the five countries united, unifying in Arkenshyr to battle Vesleathren.

Then, for a second time in history was a war ended by a great Vapour. At last Vesleathren was thought dead, killed in the final blast, but the world was weakened so by this war that the scattered Feral ravaged the lands, reproducing endlessly. Leaderless they were, but they pillaged everything nonetheless. No unified power of good was left to oppose them," Slowin told.

"Was there no more left of the Five Country Army?" asked Adacon.

"No, not enough to contest the ill-spawned Feral Brood. The rape of the countryside continued for many years, until finally a brave soldier rose in ranks from the north country of Hemlin, and united enough free men, elves and dwarves to drive back the Feral Brood. And the Feral were slain on sight, until they were all but gone entirely from the face of Darkin. This leader came to great power over the world for his triumph; but in the time of peace that followed the Feral cleansing he grew restless with greed. His great favor with the cultures of the world won him entitlement to whatever he pleased, and soon his greed overtook his valor."

"What was this leader's name?" Adacon queried, fascinated by the tale.

"Grelion Rakewinter."

"Grelion!" Adacon cried.

"Can't have been him," Erguile said. Flaer shook his head and lay down for sleep.

"It's true. But now Vesleathren has returned, from the grave it seems. And he has already been offering his dark magic to those who will take it. Bulkog certainly accepted, and he had already become Feral when you came upon him in the tower."

"That explains the fire blast he used on us," Erguile realized.

"Vesleathren will aid those who assist him, granting them great power through his black magic; even Grelion will be deeply fearful at his return," Slowin foretold.

"Black magic? Is that not Vapoury?" asked Adacon.

"No. Black is the name given to magic that has a purpose selfish and destructive. That is why Vapours are known separately; they wield magic to righteous ends. Though they use the same source, they use it for good, and so it is Vapoury."

"Good wizards against evil ones?" Erguile surmised.

"Precisely. Valiant Vapours against black mages. Vapoury against Black Mana."

"But, as Krem said, all magic comes from Gaigas. Why then doesn't Gaigas restrict those wishing to do harm with her energy?" Adacon quipped.

"Because Gaigas has no control over how living creatures use her force; she is not a conscious entity, as Krem might have you believe."

"This is all very grand, but I am tired from battle. Grateful I am to be heading east and no longer confined to slavery, but alas, I need rest before we continue—and before my head is filled with more dark lore," grumbled Erguile.

"Indeed, even silver golems require rest, though I prefer treetops to beds of grass," said Slowin, and he left them for a nearby maple tree. After Slowin had climbed the tree to an astonishing height, he called down good night, though early dawn was breaching in. Adacon made a spot for himself and gave up trying to make sense of all that Slowin had told him; he truly was exhausted, and felt at least some comfort being in the company of Erguile and the golem. Flaer was useless however, until his bond was broken. Adacon shut himself down before thinking further, and fell fast asleep.

*   *   *

They hadn't slept long before a loud chatter of birds woke them all up. First up was Erguile; he stretched and looked about. They had come off the plains and were now upon the Rislind Plateau—the plateau was mostly flat with bright green grass that ran high and intermingled with flowers of white, purple, and gold. Trees were clustered here and there—maples, oaks and pines. The trade road had led them southeast, but it looked to soon turn back north by cutting left ahead, back down the plateau. Erguile saw a fork where the road cut north; a smaller dirt path in the grass remained on the plateau and climbed higher up, east and toward the far precipice. In the direction of the dirt path was a stream, just visible between a burgeoning line of trees. In the direction of the trade road was another tower, faint in the distance, very far off, appearing identical to Ceptical.

Before long the entire outfit was up and moving. Erguile had prepared a small meal for breakfast—mainly bread, water, and stew. After eating, Slowin told them to follow his lead, and they began a slow pace toward the fork ahead. The sun was cooler than before, and it seemed that autumn was approaching faster each day. Nobody spoke, but both slaves felt cheery in their new fellowship; it hadn't been long, after all, since they had been alone and locked out of the tower.

They followed the gravel road and came to the dirt path that curved up and away toward the southeast. The new tower, a twin to the one they had rescued Flaer from, now stood largely in the horizon to their left.

"The *Brigun Autilus* is there," Slowin said. Flaer nodded at the mentioning, and the four set off down the trade road, away from the dirt path, off the plateau and toward the tower.

"What's the Brigun Autilus?" asked Adacon.

"Flaer's sword. It was Krem's sincerest wisdom that we reunite Flaer Swordhand with sword," Slowin hooted, and Flaer winked. "And best to do so now before Feral Broodlings come to claim these towers." The four hurried on toward the tower until they were within several hundred yards. In front of the tower they could see a single guard pacing. Behind a squat of bushes and small trees, the four huddled.

"What's so special about a sword that they'd want to guard it?" asked Adacon.

"Can't be much better than mine," Erguile remarked, sun glinting off his blade as he drew it from his sheath.

"Ah, but how mistaken you are Erguile," Slowin chuckled. Flaer looked over, and Adacon caught what he took to be a smile.

"What do you mean by that, Slowin?"

"I mean that the power of the Brigun Autilus is so great that it will destroy those black bonds—" Slowin said, pointing at Flaer's cuffs.

"Impossible, how could his sword be that much more powerful than any other?" Erguile cried in disbelief.

"Think of what we've already seen, Erguile—how is it you are shocked to learn that a sword can possess great Vapoury within its steel?"

"Wish *I* could have had a shot at those cuffs, either way," Erguile moped.

"Stay here, both of you," Slowin said to the slaves, ignoring Flaer. "I will return shortly." And with that Slowin took off at a blinding speed; the crazed sprint looked quite unusual for a creature of his size. The silver golem gleamed, reflective sheen glaring in every direction as he motored toward the front door of the tower.

"What's he doing—in broad daylight? Sticking out like a sore thumb; he's going to get himself killed!" Erguile said, about to run after the golem. Flaer grabbed him on the shoulder to stop him from chasing after. Erguile looked to Flaer, and Flaer merely winked, nodding toward the tower.

Slowin approached the confused guard in front of the tower. The guard paused in shock before finally drawing his sword, but Slowin smashed right through him; in one motion he trampled the guard and smashed through the entrance, rending it open. The front door had appeared made of iron, but with a tremendous clank Slowin had broken right through with his charge. The guard was motionless on the ground, appearing dead.

"Why couldn't he have done that for us last night?" a bewildered Erguile said in awe.

"What power," Adacon gasped.

The three waited in relative silence, watching the balcony atop the tower for any sign of activity. Finally, two guards flew over the side of the balcony as if heaved by a cannon. With violent screams they crashed to a soft thud into the earth below. Slowin suddenly appeared on the balcony, waving something bright in his hand; it was a glowing sword. To the slaves' astonishment, at the next moment, Slowin heaved himself over the rail of the balcony and began to plummet straight down to the earth.

"No!" Adacon shouted, and all three of them ran toward the tower.

Slowin landed with an enormous clap that sounded like thunder. The ground quaked under the runners' feet as they approached him. Slowin appeared unfazed.

"My god, I would wager you are no ordinary golem," exclaimed Erguile. Slowin raised the throbbing sword above Flaer, and Flaer knew to turn his back; the bright sword glared as it contacted the black cuffs. The figure eight sparked and broke apart. Flaer grinned wide; he turned to Slowin and took the sword from him. Suddenly, the throb and glow left the sword and it appeared as ordinary steel. Flaer bowed in thanks to Slowin, and Erguile and Adacon went to examine the shattered pieces of the black bracelet on the ground.

"Amazing," Adacon whispered in awe as Flaer slipped the sword into his leather belt, sheathless. The sword was longer and thinner than a broadsword, and its ricasso was wrapped in faded leather. The handle was grey and leather-bound, and the side of the steel blade had a black engraving that formed runic symbols.

"Why couldn't you have done that last night, golem," said Erguile; he was half-amazed, and half-angered.

"Krem thought it would be best you experienced combat to gain experience," Slowin retorted. "Although had I myself known Bulkog to be Feral I would have intervened, I think." Flaer appeared in the best spirits Adacon had seen so far, and soon the four were marching back the way they had come, toward to the previous fork in the road.

"The sword shone brightly in your hands Slowin, then it faded when Flaer took it," Adacon mentioned.

"Yes, the Brigun Autilus can be focused only by its rightful owner. Had I held it much longer it would have scalded me to no hope of recovery." Slowin showed them his hand where it had gripped the sword. His gloves had been burned through at the spot where he had held the handle, and his silver skin had become black and charred.

"I thought I smelled burning ore," roared Erguile, and at that all four of them laughed, though Flaer inaudibly so.

Morale was high as the party followed Slowin. He led them back to the fork in the gravel road, and this time they took the eastern way onto the dirt path, leaving the slave trade route behind.

"What course is upon us now?" Erguile asked eventually.

"We travel tirelessly east now, through Rislind and on to the Saru Gnarl Cape," Slowin proclaimed.

They marched long hours without stop on the dirt path, all the while alongside a stream that had grown to become a river. In the distance beyond the meadow they walked through was a small mountain range. It was a dwarfed cousin to the Angelyn Range, but still the sight excited Adacon.

"Is the ocean grand?" he asked curiously.

"Indeed. It is ferocious as well. Once across the Kalm Ocean, however, we will find refuge and counsel, and then I will be relieved of my task, and set free to return home to the Red Forest."

"What of Flaer's failed speech? Is there no remedy?" asked Erguile as Flaer issued a sidelong glance.

"We shall find a cure as soon as we are able to; the mana of Vesleathren runs deep in that curse, and I alone can do nothing against it," Slowin answered.

"Surely you possess some magic Slowin; this orb saved our lives against Bulkog," Adacon said, pulling the orb from his pocket. The orb was without brightness in the light of the sun.

"I possess some unique power—though if I use magic not even Krem can say," Slowin replied, confusing the slaves.

"What's that mean?" Erguile asked.

"I am not like other golems. Truly I am not of their race, though it is more like them than any other being I appear. True golems are made of stone and tree, plant and rock. I am different as such, I am a metal golem."

"And there are no others?"

"No."

They carried on, resisting the urge to continue an unending line of questions. Finally they reached the mouth of the river, a vast lake that ran into a waterfall at the precipice of one of the first mountains in the small Rislind range. The mountain range was tree-covered and sprawled in a circular fashion; shades of deep green shone brilliantly in the midafternoon sky. A mist clumped about the mountaintops, thick and wide. The lake was surrounded by burgeoning forest of a great many earth-shades; a mix of blue pine intensified amidst cedar and maple, covering thickly the lake edge and the slope of the nearest mountain. The group went along the side of the river toward the birth of the tree line. They stopped suddenly before entering; Slowin addressed them:

"This is the way into Rislind Village, whose eastern gate will take us by road to the Saru Gnarl Cape," he told. "Be wary of the frightful things that make this forest their home."

"But you're here to protect us," Adacon said.

"I am, and so is Flaer—but even we do not see all the spies of Vesleathren. Dark things abound this age of our world. Let us make haste toward peaceful rest in the village."

They pressed in through the forest wall, leaving any remnants of the dirt path behind. Once within the forest shade there was no proper path, and Adacon questioned how they would find their way without getting lost—then he remembered Slowin was a forest golem.

"Rislind Village is hidden to passers, nomads and spies alike. No trade routes run this way, and Grelion knows not of its existence. There is a secret way into the valley within the mountains, known to but a few who are still friends to Krem. This pass is what we seek now."

Slowin led them up a path that seemingly had never before been trodden; hazardous thorns and jagged boulders sprouted amidst massive trunks of birches, maples and pines. Scattered about the forest floor were trickling streams running between the boulders. Eventually the party tired, and panting they sat to have a drink.

"Ah, how refreshing," piped Adacon, drinking his fill on all fours. They drank heartily until each was satisfied. Erguile broke out a stale loaf and passed it around.

"Slowin—you eat and drink the same as a human," remarked Erguile.

"It is true; I need the same sustenance as you," replied Slowin, "and I assure you that I need rest just the same too, though it may not seem so."

Adacon looked up at the steep incline of their intended path. It appeared to grow more technical, giving way to bare-faced rock that went nearly vertical amidst the trees and shrubs.

"This path grows treacherous," Adacon thought aloud.

"It is not much farther to the entrance," Slowin remarked, and then he turned to lead the trek upwards. Flaer seemed in happy spirits for the climb, though being unable to talk seemed to weigh on him now—often would a look overtake his face when conversation began, as if he wanted to add his thoughts; too long had he wasted away in the rusty confines of Ceptical, deprived of merry conversation.

They climbed farther up over bare-faced rocks, and even Slowin, whose size belied his agility, climbed with grace. As he reached a higher ledge he unearthed a small tree and sent it hanging over down toward the others. Holding fast, Slowin called them to climb up; one by one, each made his way up to Slowin's ledge. In front of them now was a vast wall of vines and dense thorn.

"This is the Plant Wall of Rislind, enchanted by none other than Krem himself," Slowin told them. "Use caution even after we have silenced it."

Suddenly the wall of vine tendrils began writhing in offense at their presence. A vine snapped out and then another, sharp thorns scraping the air in a deadly frenzy. Adacon and Erguile backed away. Flaer pulled out his sword, and he appeared ready to dismember the mass of livened vines and bramble when Erguile suddenly spoke up:

"Let me have at it first, Flaer."

Flaer smiled and paused. He sheathed his sword and issued a good luck gesture with his hand. Adacon looked frightfully at the plant, then at Erguile, then at Slowin who smiled also. Erguile stepped forward and hacked at a lashing vine. The vine was cut in two, but the plant retaliated; a thorn shot deep into Erguile's arm from its opposite side. Erguile groaned and backed away. He regained his composure and charged back at the plant.

"Do you have a death wish? Let Flaer do it!" Adacon warned.

"Never mind that," Erguile pressed, and back to strike at the plant he went; this time his hack missed entirely and his feet were caught in a thorny tangle. Swept to the ground, Erguile slashed about frantically, but a vine suddenly coiled around his sword and ripped it from him. Adacon looked side to side and saw

Flaer smiling even broader, and Slowin still looking on without reaction.

"Help him!" Adacon burst, and then he ran at the bramble, courageously slashing at tendrils that were coiling around Erguile. Soon Adacon was gripped in a tendril vise the same as Erguile, and it was only when blood began to trickle down the foliage that Flaer jumped into action; he severed the limbs of the plant with great speed. The plant lay dead and in pieces amidst a pool of jade ooze, and the slaves rubbed their grazed heads and arms.

"What a mess that was," coughed Erguile as Slowin helped them both to their feet. Behind the bramble, which still twitched violently on the ground, was a cave of earth and rock leading through the mountain, a tunnel down to the Rislind valley.

"Amazing," ushered Adacon, following behind Slowin and Flaer into the cave. The cave was cut squarely and led down and still farther down, descending to the eastern foothills of the range. After a long and eventless journey they exited finally at the bottom, stepping once again into forest.

"Won't the secret pass be revealed now?" Adacon asked.

"For perhaps an hour, yes, but Krem's enchantment causes the plant to regenerate swiftly to full girth, as strong as before it was cut down," answered Slowin.

Eventually the trees of the foothills thinned out and the earth became level yet again. In front of them appeared a field, treeless and wide, filled with opal flowers. Several horses roamed in the distance, heedless of the wide Rislind Mountains that afforded them safety by ensnaring their fair lawn in secrecy. In the center of the field were buildings; small thatched structures sprouted roofs the color of faded wheat and walls molded of ocher mortar. The party set across the field toward the village as the roaming horses stilled to gaze.

"Free horses—they are incredible—I've ever only seen them hauling trade carts, dispirited and filthy, never so beautiful," Adacon beamed.

"We will find free living humans and gnomes here, and a peaceful race of trolls as well," Slowin explained. "Make sure to be properly polite and respectful to all you meet. They are very protective of their seclusion here, and rightly so. It is only in knowing Krem that we may trespass here." Adacon restrained his joy at hearing about the different races, each coexisting peacefully in the village.

They reached the edge of the village just as the sun slipped behind the westernmost peaks. Adacon studied the sky around them; it seemed they were encapsulated within a circular band of emerald mountains—it was as if the range was especially formed so as to conceal Rislind Village from the world. The village stood squat in the middle of the valley floor, and only upon reaching its gate did Adacon notice a stream running silently in from the east. A small post stood by the gate Slowin had led them to. Standing there was a tiny man, smaller even than Krem, and Adacon likened the little gatekeeper to sketches he had seen of gnomes. The gnome stood about as high as Adacon's waist, and his hair was pushed underneath an odd triangular cap, colored brightly sea green. His entire tunic, for that matter, was sea green, except for a copper belt that held a brown sheath, in which sat a shiny dagger. The little man wore bole colored boots and gloves. The gnome's hair was weathered auburn, and he had a patchwork beard and mustache. His eyes were small and black, but deeply set.

"Slowin, the oddest golem in all of Darkin—what brings you and this strange assembly?" asked the little gnome in a surprisingly deep voice.

"Ah, good Remtall! Woeful are my tidings," Slowin replied. Time went by as Slowin explained to Remtall the whole story and their journey so far. Finally Remtall exclaimed:

"This cannot be Flaer—that Flaer who aided my passing into this village so long ago?" stammered Remtall, and the two embraced; Flaer lit up with glee.

"It is, though a hex is upon him now, and his tongue has been bound," Slowin uttered.

"I am stricken to hear it, that and all the ill tidings you bring," Remtall said. "Alas, we will find you ale, and beds to rest in for at least one night before you set out again farther east." Remtall at last turned his attention to the slaves, and for the first time heeded them.

"And you two I suppose play some role in this flight. Pleased to make your acquaintances, freed slaves of Grelion, and welcome to Rislind!" With that Remtall heartily shook their hands. "Come, the sun sets, and the inn thrives." Remtall began to lead them into the village when Adacon let out the thought that had been gnawing at his mind.

"Remtall—I knew a Remtall; he was my only friend on the Slave Farm I come from. He was no gnome, taller than myself almost," Adacon said. Remtall gasped.

"It cannot be!" Remtall exclaimed.

"Surely you did not know him?" Adacon replied. Remtall lowered his head in sullen thought and then raised his eyes again to meet Adacon's.

"Sad is my heart already at such dark news as Slowin brings; let us not speak further of this matter until we are within reach of tankard and ale—come quick!" Remtall spat desperately, and he raced ahead of them toward the biggest building in the village, presumably the tavern inn.

The party traced Remtall through the town, the slaves curiously glancing around the small village. The houses and buildings all looked similar; they ranged in size but each had ocher walls and a yellowed roof. Along the way several villagers walked about, one of which Adacon recognized for a troll, albeit a much friendlier looking troll compared to Bulkog. Many of the town folk gave cruel glances at the outsiders, and their only assurance was Remtall leading them on.

The troop came to the inn entrance, a giant oak door with a sign that boldly read, "Deedle's Tavern & Inn."

In went the group, one by one, and Remtall led them to a secluded table near the back of the place. The inn was fairly crowded for such a small town; Adacon glanced around warily, absorbing the strange faces. Such a concoction of mixed people Adacon had never before witnessed. Erguile too was wary, glaring around the wide room, until a tankard of ale was slammed down before him. A friendly barkeeper had hurried over to the table and set the pitcher down, along with five frothing tankards.

"Happy to oblige guests, and friends to Remtall," said the keeper. Remtall had wandered off momentarily, frantically looking for a chair big enough for Slowin; the giant golem had been pulled aside by some strangers who knew him, and alone at the table sat Flaer, Adacon, and Erguile. They each drank greedily and quickly poured seconds.

"This is a bizarre place, magnificent too, of course," throated Erguile as he tore through his second tankard.

"It is—I wish I could meet some of these folks, what I could learn," Adacon said. Flaer smiled and patted Adacon and Erguile on their shoulders.

"Good to have you with us man," retorted Erguile, gripping Flaer's shoulder in turn.

"Yea, Krem spoke very highly of you. We are every bit comforted at your presence," Adacon spoke in between gulps. "After all, the best swordsman in all of Darkin!"

"That bit is contrived, but tonight I shall honor your skill just the same—a toast!" Erguile said cockily, then raised his glass, and so then did the others. They drank healthily the first pitcher to completion by the time Slowin returned to the table at last, toting an enormous stool. He sat on the fringe of the table and looked for his ale. Quickly he drank it and looked to refill, finding the pitcher empty.

"A powerful company of drinkers, I dare say," Slowin laughed. Just then Remtall reappeared, new pitcher in hand.

"Sorry to keep you all waiting," he said, placing the new pitcher down and finding a seat next to Flaer, opposite Adacon and Erguile. "I had to call a guard to remain at my post. Even in peaceful refuge such as Rislind we must never become complacent when Grelion is alive and seeking spoils."

"And I sorrow to bring news worse, Remtall, as we are again in Vesleathren's wake," Slowin said.

"I can't bear to think of that—it is too wretched; and this news of yours Adacon? My heart dreads to know of your tale, but please. . ." Remtall pleaded, engaging his tankard again.

"Remtall was the name of my friend in the slave camp. He was my only friend before I deserted the farm and met Krem in the Desert. He was murdered, hanged for defiance by the Guard," Adacon told. At that Remtall wept openly, and he trembled. Slowin tried to comfort the tiny man.

"What is it?" Erguile questioned.

"Was this Remtall of fair golden hair, with eyes of aquamarine?" cried Remtall.

"Indeed he was—but how can you know that?" Adacon resounded.

"Remtall Olter'Fane was my son—and I am the father of your lost friend," burst Remtall, falling into tears and drinking deep of his ale.

"But how can it be so? You are a gnome; that boy was a tall and mature man," questioned Erguile. Remtall did not respond, but looked pitifully into Slowin's eyes.

"Forgive them, for they are slaves and know not of the world. Erguile, Remtall's late wife was human, and can the height of a human or a gnome be created by such a union," Slowin explained. Remtall continued to cry and drink, and the others drank in turn while hearing the tale of how his son was stolen with other children of Rislind seventeen years prior.

"It was Zesm the Rancor! That dirty rogue, allied to all who might pay him well with black magic. I shall have his head yet," an enraged Remtall blasted. Many in the tavern turned to look at the scene, but only briefly; Flaer turned toward the gawkers to reflect their poor manners with a fiery glare of anger. Momentarily his sword glowed, bright enough for every patron to see soft light rising above the table. Startled by the Brigun Autilus, the patrons went back to their own affairs, and the light disappeared.

"You cannot be certain it was Zesm, can you? He was in hiding for the longest time after Krem defeated him in battle," Slowin recalled.

"There were many children taken that night, and one witness alone; and Zesm's hunched figure is unmistakable," said Remtall.

"Who witnessed it?" asked Erguile.

"'It was me! And I ran after him and his carriage, through to the edge of the foothills; it was dark and I lost him there—aided he was by something magic and unseen," Remtall said. "How any horse-drawn carriage could make a way through the Rislind Pass I do not know, lest black magic worked in it."

"Zesm is now allied with Vesleathren, and his power is returned stronger than ever; he is hunched no more," Slowin mournfully admitted. "This I learned of late from Krem, just after he learned from Zesm himself, mere days ago in the Vashnod."

"But how is Zesm to be trusted? He is ever the liar," a drunken Remtall contested.

"Krem sensed Zesm's power; he said it to be fiftyfold the power of the old Zesm," Slowin said.

"I overheard him speaking; I heard him say he would return the next night to kill all of us, and it has been three nights now with no sign of trouble," Adacon added.

"The liar, as I'd expect," spat Remtall.

"It is no matter. I have faith in Krem's portent, and he assured me Zesm will fall, as will Vesleathren, ere a Feral Army can be made again," Slowin said.

The company sat momentarily in silence, and drank further into the evening. Slowin and Remtall made small talk for awhile, and the slaves chimed in with questions whenever they became confused, as often they did. Finally, Remtall returned to a serious consideration, and looked to Slowin.

"What truly is your errand in the East?" the gnome asked. They were well into their fifth pitcher now, and Flaer had closed his eyes to rest. Food had come to the table too, and with the fourth pitcher the group had feasted.

"We purpose to cross the Kalm, to the free city of Erol Drunne in Enoa," said Slowin.

"Enoa? How do you expect to find a ship out of Saru Gnarl? Grelion is the keeper of that city, and it is the primary port of all his slave trade from Enoa to Arkenshyr! And should…" Remtall stuttered with drink, "—should you even somehow find passage across the Kalm, you would find no captain willing to go the route."

"What's wrong with the route to Erol Drunne?" poked Adacon.

"Wrong with it? I'm sorry, I forget quickly in drink that you are a slave, but the Erol Drunne pass is certain death," Remtall shouted in stupor. The patrons in the bar knew better than to look at the commotion.

"Perhaps, but I am privy to information I cannot disclose here and now. And it is you, Captain Remtall, whom I seek to guide our vessel," Slowin blurted out.

"Me? I—I haven't sailed in *twenty years*!" shot back Remtall.

"Rightly so, but for most of your life you lived at sea, and in your time you were the best there was, as pirates go," Slowin responded, taking a quick sip of ale, unaffected by his alcohol.

"I cannot do it, it would be suicide," Remtall exclaimed.

"I don't think it would be, not with you guiding the helm," Slowin insisted.

"I have never attempted the route, not even in my most daring years as a youth."

"It matters not, for this is our hour of need, and yours alike. Rislind will not sit long hidden among the mountains—not while Vesleathren plots to assail the whole of our world," Slowin came back. Remtall sat sullen, head turned down. He was obviously considering it, albeit drunkenly so. Slowin revealed his trump card:

"It is the only way of avenging your son. It is only by reaching Erol Drunne that we may defeat Vesleathren, and Zesm in turn."

"Aagh—alright. I will attempt it, but gaining a worthy ship out of Saru Gnarl I will not engage in, for I think that errand to be more foolish than making the sea-trip to Erol Drunne," Remtall exclaimed.

"Alas, securing the ship is my task, with the aid of Flaer, I hope," Slowin said. Flaer briefly looked up, not apparently asleep after all; he nodded in agreeance.

"And us too," Erguile rallied.

"Yea!" Adacon chimed between burps.

"But of course," Slowin responded, and he began to tell of the plan he had in mind for stealing a ship worthy to cross the ocean. He talked long into the early morning until it became ineffective to talk further, as the ale had taken its final toll on them for the night. It had been thoroughly outlined that Slowin, Flaer, Adacon and Erguile would travel to the cape city of Saru Gnarl where they would stealthily take a ship. They would then sail south along the coast to Kalm's Point, where Remtall could safely board. From then on out it would be Remtall's ship, and until they harbored in Enoa they would answer only to him.

"On to bed then—follow me," said Remtall, and he led them all upstairs to their rooms. The last two to bed were Slowin and Adacon, who shared a room. Slowin slept half off his mattress; he seemed comfortable despite the small bed. Before nodding off, Adacon rattled off his last question of the night.

"Is Erol Drunne a free city?" he asked.

"It is Adacon. It is one of the last in Darkin," Slowin answered.

"And what is it that is so dangerous about the route to reach it?"

"That city is only accessible by crossing the Fang Shoals. It is said that more than just shoals, however, stay those waters."

"Fang Shoals, it sounds dreadful."

"It is, and those forbidding shoals must we thank for Erol Drunne's safety," Slowin ended, and he turned over to go to sleep. Adacon's imagination flared briefly, imagining what Erol Drunne and the Fang Shoals looked like; then he thought about his friend Remtall, and his new friend, the gnome father. It seemed that each day passed with more excitement than the last, and though the contents of the days were stained with dark omens, Adacon relished in it, enjoying each new curiosity. He tossed for a short while in hope, and then fell fast asleep.

VI: WEAKHOOF

The morning came fast for Adacon and his party, and Deedle's Inn was alive and bustling in the early hours of a new day. The group had a swift breakfast in the tavern before convening outside the Inn on Rislind's main drag. The slaves—filled with fresh Rislind tea, dough cakes, burnt potatoes, and sausages—decided it had been the best food they had ever tasted. Slowin led a brief council in the cool breeze, and with urgency he pressed the party to move eastward, yet Remtall interrupted:

"I believe I can procure for us three horses," he said, and in the early morning sun he released a flask from his side and drank twice. Remtall, it appeared, was already drunk with liquor.

"Horses! That would be exactly what we need," Adacon replied with glee.

"I expect no horse could carry me," Slowin confessed.

"I know such a steed as might carry you Slowin—indeed I know *just* the steed," Remtall proclaimed.

"But we've never ridden horses before. Besides that, there are five of us traveling," Erguile said.

"These horses will mind you less than you will mind them, so worry not that you have never ridden. To you Slowin, I will give my steed Thunderhoof. To Flaer and Adacon I will give Fablefen; and Erguile, you will have Weakhoof," Remtall explained.

Flaer, Slowin, and Adacon nodded in acknowledgement, but Erguile looked confused.

"Weakhoof? I wonder if he will make our journey, or does his name belie his endurance?" Erguile griped.

"His name more than belies his hardihood; though Weakhoof is old and slow, he is ever full of valor," said Remtall.

"And then what horse will *you* ride to Kalm's Point?" asked Adacon.

"Gnomes have other friends in nature that you have yet to see—Yarnhoot!" Remtall shouted. In a moment a giant black condor appeared, diving down and standing next to Remtall. The bird was half as big as Adacon, and the perfect size for Remtall. He immediately mounted Yarnhoot and ascended, turning his path mid-air for a nearby meadow where horses grazed.

"Astounding!" Adacon remarked.

"Yes, gnomes are curious in their partnerships. I myself would prefer a giant tortoise over any other beast," Slowin chuckled.

"A golem on a giant tortoise—that would be a sight; I think I'll need some of Remtall's liquor before seeing that," Erguile laughed.

"It is odd that he drinks at this early hour," Slowin thought aloud. Flaer nodded in agreement to Slowin.

"Maybe he is celebrating his return to the ocean as a captain of the high seas," Adacon guessed merrily.

"Yes, perhaps."

Remtall suddenly returned in the sky, and just as quickly he descended upon the street, diving in for a landing that thumped, and he bounced off of Yarnhoot with a stutter. In the meadow three horses could be seen galloping in toward Deedle's. Soon the three horses stood before the party, neighing in unison and then hanging their heads in a mellow fashion.

"The saddles, and then we will be off," Remtall said, and once more he hurried off, this time on foot, leaving Yarnhoot with the slaves. The enormous condor eyed the group lazily and diverted its attention to some bugs crawling on the ground nearby. Adacon and Erguile went to the horses and petted them, offering the much needed creatures a warm greeting.

"We're very lucky to have met Remtall's aid here. Without horses we would be delayed almost two days' time," said Slowin.

After several moments Remtall appeared again, carrying saddles. He went about fastening them, introducing each horse as he worked. Thunderhoof was a powerful looking white stallion; Fablefen was an equally impressive brown stallion; and last was grey old Weakhoof, who looked more a mule than a horse. Weakhoof and Erguile began to converse.

"It looks like we have a tremendous adventure in front of us, eh?" Erguile prodded his horse. Weakhoof groaned miserably and looked away.

"A fine partnership already," Remtall poked, drinking from his flask again.

"Let us go then. Vesleathren acts surely as we do, and our hope lies not in Rislind, but across the Fang Shoals," Slowin commanded.

"Yes, yes: All is well now that the sea calls me back and I seek revenge for my son," said Remtall. He was wearing a new pack for his journey; he sat down for a moment, taking off the pack and grabbing from within it a leather flask, thrice as big as the one fastened at his hip. He promptly refilled the smaller flask and drank anew.

"It is unwise, Remtall, to drink so much at this early hour of our departure," Slowin said with concern. "We shall need all your wits."

"Hah, my wits will be kept in perfect order at Kalm's Point, this day at Dusk," Remtall replied. "I have only to tell the mayor here of my going, and then Yarnhoot will guide me away from this village for the first time in ten years."

"Farewell then, Remtall, that we may meet you soon," said Slowin, and the party exchanged farewells and mounted their steeds. Erguile had the most trouble, stumbling and falling off twice before finally finding his seating. They trotted down the main road out of Rislind, leaving by the eastern gate. They waved to a few straggling citizens who gawked at Slowin, and Thunderhoof, whom he dwarfed. Finally the three horses and their riders were traveling east once more, down the path that led toward the emerald foothills.

"I am upset we didn't stay longer, I wanted to meet trolls," said Adacon as they approached the first line of trees.

"There will be a better time for that; the journey we attend is more pressing," replied Slowin.

"I know; they just fascinate me so!"

The three horses worked their way up a steep gradient and to the surprise of all the horses made the trespass appear easy. Every ten minutes the group would wait up on account of Weakhoof, the only horse stumbling on the rocky terrain.

"Come on you bastard!" Erguile yelled. "Who has a whip for this brute?"

"Be patient with him," said Adacon.

"Yes, Weakhoof is doing her best," Slowin added.

The trek up and out of Rislind through the eastern route was surprisingly easier than the path in, and before long they came to another secret pass at high elevation. A boulder among a great many, along the side of a high ridge, blocked the way through. All around was a steep drop, but the horses were sure-footed, even Weakhoof. Slowin dismounted and treaded carefully along the thin path toward the enormous boulder, indistinguishable from the others nearby.

"Remtall said it would be marked," Slowin said, bending down on one knee to look for an etching. In very small print near the bottom of the boulder was a tiny carving that read *'Fare On East.'*

"This is it," Slowin said, and he told the others to back up some, and in a moment he squatted down and began to stretch his arms around the circumference of the massive hunk of rock. Even Slowin's arms looked puny against the size of the rock, and Slowin grunted as loud as he had ever done. With a start the boulder began to roll to the right, and having nowhere to go on the slim ridge it rolled down the mountainside, crashing its way through dozens of trees, sending startled birds into the sky to avoid its destruction.

"How did you know which boulder had the marking?" Adacon asked, stunned once more at Slowin's power.

"Am I not a Metal golem of the Red Forest? I have dwelt long enough in Nature to know when man has restructured her," Slowin answered, ushering them through the passage. "No matter how small the tampering is."

"On the western side the vine wall grew back to block the way in, so what of this pass? Won't the secret way to Rislind be open for all to enter?" Erguile worried. Flaer looked toward Erguile and motioned upwards, and Erguile looked overhead. At just that moment a thunderous crackle echoed from the ridge above, and over its lip another huge boulder began to roll. It seemed to be rolling off at just an angle to drop into the place of the boulder just removed.

"Dear god!" Erguile yelled. Terrified, he smacked Weakhoof's side repeatedly until the old horse trotted on through the hole in the mountainside. Slowin quickly mounted Thunderhoof and fell in line behind Fablefen as they all made it inside just in time, and a loud crash accompanied by an earth shaking tremor let them know the way was sealed once more.

"What strange magic," said Adacon.

The three horses maneuvered through the short cavernous pass and came out on the eastern slope of the mountain, slowly stepping onto what seemed a trail amidst the rooted tangle of the forest floor. The descent was not nearly as steep as the way into Rislind, and it was easy riding for what seemed a long stretch of time, until finally the trees began to thin out and a flat horizon once again appeared. The slaves beheld the golden prairie before them, forgetting fast the mountains they had come through. The sun was high overhead and no dark clouds weighted the sky. Ahead was the Rislind Plateau Wilds: golden straw and emerald-patched grasslands stretching interminably into the distance. The party saw, though very faintly from great distance, what looked to be a road tangling in and out of several running brooks. By all measures it was a beautiful day, and being thoroughly heartened at the sight of blue sky and puff-white clouds, Erguile spoke with cheer:

"How long is it before we reach the Saru Gnarl cape?"

"Riding strong, as I would have it, we'll be there by nightfall," Slowin replied.

"This land is beautiful," Adacon said, reviewing the roving green hills that stretched away in each direction. Each hill was twined with flowers and pink-leaf trees that grew down to the edge of the streams.

"Rislind has always been a pretty place, but it turns to marsh soon, and we must return to the gravel Slave Road of Grelion before long, lest we sink deep into the mire," Slowin warned.

"How are you holding up Flaer?" asked Erguile. Flaer glanced over at Weakhoof and Erguile, and from his expression it looked as though he thought them the oddest looking pairing he'd ever seen. Smiling, Flaer looked to the sky and back at Erguile, nodding approval.

"Alright, time to quiet our chatter and see the mettle of our steeds at last," Slowin said, holding tight his reigns and kicking Thunderhoof's side gently. "Yar!"

Thunderhoof began galloping over the brimming prairie at increasing speed. Fablefen followed at Flaer's command, and finally, bringing up the rear, was Weakhoof. All three horses left the green mountains and sped far from the haven of Rislind. In the west whence they had come was a small silhouette of a distant range.

Before long the horses closed in on the gravel slave road they had spied from afar, and much as Slowin predicted the terrain turned marsh-like. Slowly the grass had turned grey and thin, and the streams ran wider and darker. The trees grew gnarled and hunched, and the meadows turned to treacherous vats of mud. Bugs swarmed the riders as they slowly descended the Rislind plateau. The sky stayed clear and bright, but the air had certainly thickened with a humid stink that ran with a growing wind; the odor became more rancid with each passing moment as they worked deeper into the bog. It had been five hours since they had passed through the mountains, and Slowin brought them to a halt at the side of the road by a clear stream.

"This may be our last source of pure water for awhile," he said. "Have your fill and replace what you've drunk." All the riders dismounted and gathered at the edge of a murky stream. The horses greedily lapped their fill; Weakhoof tried to drink from the same spot where Thunderhoof and Fablefen drank, but they neighed and aggressed on him, forcing him to walk away and find some other place to drink.

"Poor Weakhoof, disrespected as an elder," Erguile sympathized.

"He is a slow horse. I wonder if Remtall could have found no other for you, he weakens our pace," Slowin remarked. Just then Weakhoof shot a cold glance at Slowin, as if in recognition of the slander.

"Mind your tongue, metal brain. Weakhoof is going on as best he can manage, and we should be grateful for any horses at all," Erguile said with a hint of anger in his tone. Slowin didn't respond; he merely completed filling his canteen. Flaer drifted off on his own to survey the land, the scents, and the grey-blue horizon.

"I suppose we should eat something now, given we have two more hours of riding before we reach the city," Adacon said.

"Eat your fill; but I fear we have been delayed by Weakhoof, and three or four hours is more likely now," Slowin admitted.

"Lay off him!" Erguile roared. It seemed Erguile took Slowin's words personally, and that he had formed some strange attachment to his old horse.

"I am sorry, Erguile. As a golem accustomed to slower travel on tortoises I should have more acceptance; it is just that I fear for Remtall if he is kept waiting long, alone, at the Point," Slowin said, fear in his voice for the first time. Flaer turned around at Slowin's words, then walked back shaking his head, and he patted him on his giant shoulder.

"What is it you fear?" Adacon asked.

"Kalm Point. Though it's isolated and abandoned, it is no place for a drunken gnome to camp alone, with no wits about him. Carnalfages are said to hunt its grounds meticulously, and at any cost I would reduce his stay there," Slowin said solemnly. Flaer appeared as if he very much wanted to chime in, but he sighed and hung his head instead.

"What are Carnalfages?" asked Erguile. Flaer shook his head, disapproving of the question.

"Parasites of the sand, flesh mongers of the beach," responded Slowin. "And while they would pose no threat to me, Remtall is made of such stuff as those creatures would reckon a delicacy."

"Or us then, for that matter," Adacon worried. "But, do these Carnalfages only live there then? We have nothing to worry about ourselves?"

"They can appear wherever ocean meets land, but at the Point they hold special abode, and that is the reason the place is so rarely traversed by flesh-draped sentients," Slowin answered, and Adacon quivered for a moment.

"But won't Remtall know to expect them, what with him choosing the Point himself?" Erguile asked.

"He certainly knows of them. It is that he has been stricken by his liquor, that I fear for him—besides that, this is his first trip away from Rislind in many years," Slowin said, growing agitated with the line of questions, deciding that perhaps he should have kept his fear to himself.

Flaer began to prepare a quick meal from the fresh biscuits and dried meat given to him in Rislind, and as fast as possible they all ate. They filled their water from the stream and drank heartily, only to refill again. When not a half-hour had gone past in silence, Slowin looked up.

"Let's move on, the sun falls in the sky!"

The troop mounted their steeds, this time Erguile getting on properly before the others, and Weakhoof led them away from the water and back onto the road. Soon the three horses were in full gallop again, heading fast for the eastern cape-city of Saru Gnarl.

The riders pressed on hard, and in the eastern horizon the sky darkened prematurely before the sun had waned behind them. Dark clouds rolled in the distance, and a clap of thunder was heard before long. The terrain had thickened with shrubbery and hunched trees that hugged the edge of the road. The air grew humid, and the fresh green blades of Rislind were all but forgotten in the mire they now surveyed. The streams that covered much of the land earlier were now turning into wider pools of muck, foaming in spots, abound with slimy stones. Adacon began to notice bugs on the surface of the marsh waters next to the gravel road; bugs that seemed to grow larger and larger the deeper they traveled into the swampland.

Soon, all the land that had been solid disappeared, and the only thing left was the gravel road. At the edge of either side of the road was a steep drop that went three yards down into the opaque marsh. Looking back, Adacon saw no trace of firm soil. Up ahead the sky grew increasingly dreadful as thunder sounded closer.

Stretched out as far as could be seen was dark muck, and the even the trees and plants that had been intermittent in the water were gone now. Around them appeared to be a vast field of tar with no end in sight; it gave the appearance of firmness, but Erguile suspected the putrid water would not hold a man's weight. Occasional bubbles came to the tar's surface when oddly shaped insects would land and take off. An odd mist began to settle on the surface of the swamp, clumping in spots here and there. As they rode on the grey fog seemed to thicken around them, and the various balls of mist welded themselves together to form a sheet over top of the road. Although none of them could see more than ten yards in any direction, Adacon started in terror and halted Flaer and Fablefen.

"Something ahead, on the road!" he wailed. The other horses stopped and came together in a huddle. The road was barely six yards wide, a thin strip of earth amidst the vat, and each member of the party looked in vain through the fog to see something. Thunder clapped loudly and rain poured down; light drops came at first, soon turning heavy and furious. Weakhoof neighed in anxiety.

"I can't see a thing," Erguile said.

"Neither can I," said Slowin. They all looked to Flaer who shook his head, having not seen anything either.

"But it was there!" Adacon said as he pointed directly ahead down the road. Still, nothing but dense grey fog and a charcoal sky filled their view, now accompanied by the cool downpour of heavy rain. Thunder clapped again and for a moment the sky lit up. Only Erguile had been looking directly ahead when the flash came, and in the brief light he had seen a tall striding figure.

"There! There's a man coming this way!" Erguile yelped uncontrollably, much too loudly.

"I still see nothing…" Slowin said peering ahead, straining for any shape in the distance; he did not yet seem alarmed.

"How far away Erguile?" Adacon asked. Flaer wasted no time questioning the validity of the sightings; he drew the Brigun Autilus.

"The orb!" Erguile remembered, and Adacon reached frantically into his pocket and withdrew the orb of light that Slowin had given him. Immediately it shone in a unidirectional manner, and Adacon focused the beam of pearly light into the fog ahead. Against the dense rain and mist the light of the orb reflected back at the group, the glare blinding them. The orb of light shut off, but not before Slowin made out a human silhouette that flickered in the distance. Flaer saw it too, a mysterious stranger closing in on them.

"To the ground," Slowin commanded as he hopped off Thunderhoof with shocking grace. The others followed suit and Slowin bade the horses back off behind them. Next to Flaer Slowin aligned himself, drawing quickly his weapons into his hands—mallet and dagger. Erguile drew his broadsword while Adacon equipped his bow, hoping he could still fire it in the rain with some accuracy. The four stood in front of their horses, forming a wall across the entire width of the road. The ferocity of the pelting rain increased, as did the volume of the thunder and lightning. It was a full blown storm, and the constant lightning gave away the approaching figure: a man's shadow drifting in and out of darkness nearly twenty yards away.

"Brace yourselves," Slowin prompted, and then he roared into the storm so loudly that Adacon and Erguile both trembled: "Who goes there?"

No response came, yet the shadowy figure continued toward them.

Several yards away the dark stranger stopped. He was cloaked in black from his feet to his neck, and a dark bandana covered neatly around his soaking head. There was a momentary pause, and Slowin questioned the shadow again:

"Name your business, stranger," Slowin commanded.

"Is this road not public, for use by all in Grelion's register?" responded a hoarse voice, barely audible over the din of rain. The stranger's face was almost completely concealed by black wraps, leaving only slightly glowing red eyes to look upon.

"Then pass," Slowin ordered, and he gestured for Flaer to step aside so that a gap opened in the road for the stranger to go through. The shadow did not move, it only continued to gaze at each of them. After several minutes, the stranger spoke again:

"I am sorry friend, but it is you who mustn't pass. The way to Saru Gnarl is flooded ahead, and the city is become an island for the time being," the man rasped.

"Then we will survey it for ourselves," came Slowin, and he strode forth toward the stranger. The black man put up his arm, as if commanding Slowin to stop where he stood.

"Sheer might alone will not gain you passage this way, dear Slowin," coughed the dark figure, and his eyes began to glow bright within the veiled visage.

Thunder and lightning echoed, coming in turbulent waves. Weakhoof had taken to excessive neighing, and the slaves feared the horses would run, so they held fiercely the reins. Flaer stood ominously behind Slowin, Brigun Autilus in hand.

"How do you know my name? Reveal your purpose here tonight," demanded Slowin, raising his mallet and dagger slightly.

"Folly would it be to strike with weapons such as those against me, metal golem of the Red Forest. You wander too far from home, on an errand you are not fit for," replied the dry voice. Adacon couldn't believe what he was witnessing, if only because Slowin's might was being challenged; the slaves had now reckoned Slowin to be invincible.

"We shall see," Slowin said. Suddenly the giant golem raged forth, dagger and mallet twisting in a death-thrust at the stranger. A scarlet-orange flash issued from the eyes of the man and Slowin was quaked down by an earth-tremor at his feet; his weapons flew from either of his hands out into the swamp.

"Ughrrr," Slowin groaned, tasting mud as he stumbled to the ground, his knee boring deep into the gravel. Flaer's blade suddenly lit to an extraordinary brilliance; the light transformed into a ruby-pearl hue that blinded the slaves. He leapt toward the stranger; Adacon squinted and saw the strange man attempt to quake Flaer with energy from his eyes as he had Slowin, only this time the blast emanated out only to be absorbed directly into the Brigun Autilus. At seeing his attack fail, the shadowed man drew a sword from his side and blocked Flaer's downward slice; blue sparks flitted.

Adacon fixed an arrow on the black stranger and let it fly as Erguile stood by waiting to strike. The arrow glanced off the robes of the stranger, appearing to stop short at some kind of invisible wall. Slowin slowly regained his feet and stood up once more.

Flaer dueled ferociously with the cloaked figure, working him away from the rest of the group. Slowin prepared to rush forward again, but only stayed at seeing Flaer with the fight well in hand; the Brigun Autilus was throbbing bright as ever with each strike, and the dark figure seemed beaten back almost to defeat.

"Ragh!" screamed the shadow, and an eruption of fire emitted from his dark folds. Flaer fell back but kept his footing, as the Brigun Autilus absorbed most of the blast; still, enough energy shot past, and Flaer stood dazed for a moment. In the lapse of attack, the man raised his arms skyward and issued forth a foreign-tongued command. The gravel road began to shake, and the horses fled away down the slave road, galloping toward Rislind. Adacon and Erguile both fell to their knees on the tremulous road, and soon even Slowin stumbled. Flaer stood strong and raised his sword again.

"Who is it in Slowin's party I have not accounted for—what strange power was missed?" said the vile figure, glaring at Flaer.

"You have not accounted for Flaer Swordhand, erstwhile known as Flaer the Slayer," belted the Brigun Autilus itself as Flaer brought the charged sword down upon the stranger; he was quick to block with his own sword, but this time he fell backwards and to the ground at the might of Flaer's strike.

"It cannot be—Swordhand is long dead, killed in the final blast of the Five Country War," the stranger said in bewilderment, face buried in mud and gravel of the road. Flaer's sword spoke no response, instead readying itself for a death pierce into the head of the cloaked enemy. The Brigun Autilus came down with force after the stranger rolled to the side, barely escaping; he jumped back to his feet and backed away, stammering in anger:

"Be you Flaer or not, it is no matter now. The hour of Vesleathren's assault is at hand, as is the death of all those who might oppose him. Friends of Vapoury, behold your end. Even Lord Grelion will kneel before the true savior soon," rallied the mysterious black figure. He backed farther away as Flaer stood in guard. Lightning streaked across the sky, and the black man spoke once more in his retreat:

"Know that your friend, Krem the Vapour, is dead—and know that he didn't die before giving away your route—so that you could be destroyed." The stranger dove head first from the side of the road into the murky depths of the swamp. He started swimming away on the surface of the water, and before he disappeared he shouted once more to them:

"It is too late for you—I have already summoned Holfog, spawn of Delfog! He issues forth now, so fly away, if you can muster wings." The stranger cackled hysterically with laughter in the swamp, finally diving underneath the water, disappearing. Bubbles rose where he submerged, and an impact tremor distinct from thunder echoed from the road ahead. The tremor continued in intervals spaced several seconds apart. Slowin stood wearily and shouted, "Footfalls!"

Flaer turned and ran back to the others, signaling them into a formation. The slaves retrieved their swords once more.

"Who is Holfog?" asked Adacon.

"The Fire Wyvern that approaches us now," answered Slowin. The group reformed the blockade of earlier, barring the western road. The storm had not lightened, yet amid the thunder Holfog's footsteps could be heard clear. Soon the thunder-steps were paired with scaled legs emerging from the fog ahead; massive tree trunks sprouted up from jetting talons. The enormous wyvern walked stridently towards them, revealing its form to the party. Lightning lit the creature's coat of scales aglow, shiny ocher-jade glimmering around several jagged scars. The head of the creature was as a serpent's; beady eyes were set glossily in the back of deep sockets, and they glared hungrily. A limp tongue flicked from its wide mouth, and hundreds of serrated teeth momentarily showed.

Enormous bat-like wings took the place of arms, tucked sturdily down to its muscular haunches. It eyed the party without slowing its advance, as if choosing its first meal.

"It's a dragon!" squealed a shivering Adacon.

"Not quite, but a much smaller cousin to one," Slowin replied, strangely cool.

"This is smaller than a dragon? I don't believe it," Erguile gasped. The wyvern appeared at least twice as tall as Slowin, and its girth was nearly that of the road's width. The beast clawed toward them.

"Fear not, I have handled a fair share of wyverns in my time," Slowin said confidently, standing with his arms braced to strike, though weaponless. Flaer shot a wry grin at his metal companion. The giant winged serpent hissed in front of them, standing erect, almost five yards tall. An enormous pointed tail swung around from behind the creature as its jaws opened and a stream of fire shot forth.

Adacon and Erguile cowered to the ground, shielding their faces. Flaer jumped in front of the beast, using the Brigun Autilus as a shield, absorbing the flame. It was only at the last second before the poisonous tail of Holfog pierced Erguile's poorly defended skull that Slowin leapt into action, subduing the writhing tail in the harness of his silver vise-arms. Flaer recoiled from the final blast of flame as Holfog's attention was diverted to Slowin; its jaw opened wide and descended to Slowin's head, arriving at its target with fangs that pierced even into the metal skin and muscle of the golem. Slowin frantically released his hold over Holfog's tail and pried in vain at the jaws enveloping his head. Just as Slowin began to work the jaws apart, the freed tail of Holfog struck again at Erguile; Flaer intercepted, and he cleanly lopped the spiked tail with a flash from the Brigun Autilus. Putrid blood rushed from

Holfog's freshly severed tail, and the wyvern whined loudly into the thundering sky. Quickly the serpent unleashed its hold of Slowin's head and bent its gaze upon its wound. Flaer wasted no time, and he swept the Brigun Autilus up through the creature's throat. The head of Holfog fell to the ground and rolled off the edge of the road into the swamp. There it bobbed as the rest of its body slumped to the ground. More oily blood spilled onto the gravel as Slowin felt his head for scarring; his head appeared fine, save for two grape-sized holes indenting deep into either side of his temples. No blood dripped from his metal head, and Flaer steadied the golem as the slaves rose from their cover.

"I'm alright, thanks," Slowin said. Flaer backed off and returned his gaze to the fallen wyvern.

"He said Krem was dead," Erguile said with sadness.

"And he's a liar—it's as rare a possibility as him having given away our route," Slowin defended Krem.

"I heard you speak, Flaer," Adacon cried. Flaer calmly shook his head in disagreement, then nodded at his sword.

"The Brigun Autilus can muster a voice, when heroics so fit one," Slowin explained. "And in your debt, Flaer, are we all." Slowin bowed, and seeing it so did the slaves. The storm let loose a great thunderbolt at that moment, and the sky was lit up. Flaer returned his sword to his belt and smiled, returning their grace. Then Flaer bade them in gesture to stop their thanks so that in urgency they could reassemble themselves and resume their passage in haste. It was then that Erguile started.

"Weakhoof!" he wailed, seeing the horse whimpering up from the western road. None of the other horses followed. Weakhoof trotted to Erguile and whinnied.

"He is no longer of use to us, Erguile. Fablefen and Thunderhoof have fled," said Slowin.

"But we can't just leave him here in the marsh," Erguile shouted between thunder claps. "It's dark, and he can't see this from that!"

The party was sullen and quiet.

"Slowin's right, Erguile. It is not a happy thing, to send him away here. But with him alone…" Adacon trailed off uneasily.

"He can walk along with us," Erguile offered.

"We approach Saru Gnarl now, and a horse will only give us away. Our only way of stealing a ship is stealth. I had planned to send the horses back together; I did not foresee this—this stranger of such power," Slowin said solemnly. Flaer acknowledged agreement with Slowin by hanging his head; he enjoyed the idea no more than any of them, but it would have been done anyway.

"Going to just send him off alone—to die along the way in a thunderstorm?" Erguile argued.

"Weakhoof knows the way better than any of us, Erguile," Slowin comforted.

"Not tonight. Not my horse," Erguile burst. He mounted Weakhoof in all the haste he could manage. Adacon thought that he saw tears welling in Erguile's eyes. A bang of thunder coincided with Erguile's voice for a last time.

"Yahh! Eeyah!" Erguile ferociously kicked Weakhoof's side; with all the strength of a noble stallion, Weakhoof set off, galloping east down the gravel road.

"Come back!" Adacon called.

"Erguile!" Slowin roared as loud as he could. The sound of thumping hooves dissolved into the chatter of rain, and then there were only three.

VII: BLOCKADE RUNNER

"Does your head hurt much?" Adacon asked as the three journeyers marched toward the eastern coast.

"No, I don't feel anything at all," Slowin responded. The terrain changed as they left the bog, and solid earth sprung up along the roadside again. The marsh fog began to wane, and soon the swamp transformed into a system of streams amidst firm grassland. Trees started to appear again, and the road was no longer an island strip surrounded by bubbling mud-water; even the thunderstorm had ceased, its clouds parted, and a cool breeze stole through the air as all but the lightest rain subsided. Moons blossomed above them, and Adacon spoke:

"Erguile! Ach, stupid of him. Who could have foreseen him being so attached to that horse? Now he's gone to get himself killed."

"He seemed to detest Weakhoof at the start, if I recall correctly," said Slowin. Flaer walked alongside their conversation, eyeing the new greenery sprouting around the road. Shrubs and trees grew in bunches, and tall shoots rose moonward. In the distance a low-lying forest wall loomed, beyond which nothing could be seen.

"He did—he hated the old horse," Adacon chuckled.

"Save your worries for the task at hand. Erguile has made a decision over which we are powerless now," Slowin said. "And we might see valor come of him yet, in his flight east."

"I sure hope so. I will miss him, anyway—an energetic force to have among our company."

They pressed on several more miles before deciding to pass off the slave road for an inviting glen, and there the three sat by a tree and fixed a meal as properly as they could manage. The grass was nearly dry, and the very aura of the land seemed shifted from that of the foreboding darkness they had come through. Somehow, Adacon reckoned, the trees and bushes that grew thicker about the land signaled some prevailing hope for their errand; they had made it through the harrowing ordeal in the swamp alive, save for losing two horses and a member of their own. Flaer managed a small fire under an old maple tree by way of a spark that came from the tip of his sword.

"Your magic—I mean—Vapoury, is incredible, Flaer," Adacon stammered. Flaer looked up from the salted piece of meat he was roasting to provide Adacon with a wink.

"Odd as this may come across, I can't wait to get to Erol Drunne and lift your curse, so that I can talk to you," Adacon said, maintaining eye contact with Flaer. Flaer looked away and down, tending to his meat.

"It is not odd, Adacon, to wish to speak with him. Nor is it odd you find the world so wondrous even in the face of mortal danger. You have been so oppressed that everything new is exciting, and better than slavery, I am sure," said Slowin.

"Krem said the rebellion would start with me, that fate had decided it," Adacon said. The fire leaped up while he chewed on a fresh-smoked rind.

"Krem doesn't believe in fate, but in Gaigas—so he must have jested. But I do think he meant it when he said you would begin the rebellion. A slave army to topple Grelion, I think he had in mind."

"But you speak as if the plan has changed from that?" Adacon queried.

"Well, not entirely: It is Vesleathren's return that alters the quest at hand, but a slave army will be required nonetheless. It is, after all, Grelion who reunited Darkin's free people only to later shatter them, leaving them as they were at the end of the Five Country War."

"Please tell me more of the war?"

"No—not now anyway."

"But…" Adacon pressed his luck, but then Flaer looked up and shook his head, glaring icily.

"And the one who assailed us on the marsh, what of him? Do either of you know?" Adacon pushed further.

"I am afraid not," Slowin said, glancing at Flaer, who looked up again from his food only to show that he didn't know either. "I do know of Delfog the Fire Wyvern, whose offspring Flaer slew back in the swamp."

"You knew the fire dragon?" Adacon squealed.

"As he disappeared, did you hear the stranger yell: Holfog, spawn of Delfog?" Slowin asked.

"Yes, I didn't make the meaning of it."

"Delfog was the biggest wyvern to ever live, larger than many dragons, it is said. In the elder age of Darkin, known to some as the Iinder Age, Delfog descended upon this very country of Arkenshyr during the first great war of Darkin. It is told in legend that it was on the plains of the Vashnod that a great Vapour struck Delfog down, causing the crater there known as the—"

"Vashnod Eye!" Adacon said, cutting him off.

"You know of the lore then," Slowin replied.

"Krem told me briefly of Molto and his Spirited Winds magic."

"Then you should know that if the stranger spoke truth, we have slain a descendent of the very wyvern that bore the flame of the Spirited Winds," Slowin explained.

"This is glorious—provided it is no ill omen of more dragons to come…"

"I am wary to believe the stranger's words, but with Vesleathren about, I am apt to have an open mind. Besides that, the sheer power that man possessed; I am afraid that without Flaer, we would have all—" Slowin was cut off this time by Flaer, who kicked at the fire to extinguish it. Flaer sent his eyes to Slowin and bade in gesture that the party should set forth again. Adacon decided that Slowin's grim reflection was of no aid to them now, as they had passed through unharmed.

"Come," Slowin commanded Adacon. "Our errand takes us to Kalm Point."

Adacon harkened and soon the three were marching again east on the gravel road. Along the way Adacon saw several paths cutting away from the gravel road, each one going in a different direction.

"What are those other trails?" Adacon asked.

"They are the different trade routes. North to the country of Hemlin-Auk, and south to Great Uthner Island. In these times only Grelion uses them, and so they have all become known as the slave trade routes, though they were known by different names long ago."

"Grelion has corrupted much in—" Adacon began, but he stopped midsentence as Flaer shot him a glance commanding silence, and it was clear that Flaer had grown stern as the cape drew close.

They entered into the thick pines, and as the road had turned into an island strip amidst swamp before, it now became an island strip amidst dense wood. Woodland creatures began to make their songs heard, and the fresh scent of the pined glade overbrimmed the air. The sky was clean and placid, lighted by the dust of stars and the aura of the moons; the road seemed to offer cheer to the weary travelers, and a dim opalescence afforded by slits in the canopy. Noise grew steadily around them: chirping and hooting, until there was a fuss among the foliage on either side of the road. It seemed the nocturnal animals of the forest had suddenly come to life. Insects buzzed and whistled, and Adacon shooed away a mosquito as it drove for nectar from his skin. On they marched in silence through the wilds.

Just as Adacon was about to ask Slowin if they would reach the city soon, and when they would next sleep, a strange noise broke the choral chirping of crickets. It did not come from the forest at their sides, but from directly ahead; Slowin and Flaer heard it at once also, and recognized it for the clonking of hooves and rolling of iron wheels against the gravel.

"Quick, past that glade," whispered the golem. He ran off the road through a small clearing and into a patch of trees, trying to act furtively against the will of his enormous frame. Flaer and Adacon quickly followed, and soon they found themselves in a tall thicket hidden from the road. Quietly they watched through a tangled knot of branches as a horse drawn carriage clanked along the gravel path heading west. There were three horses, all jet black, tugging a carriage draped in maroon canvas; it had foreign gold lettering stitched down its side. The front of the carriage was illuminated by two small torches. Adacon realized that had Slowin not been bandaged and clothed so heavily, the torchlight would have reflected off Slowin's metallic skin. Still, as it was, they hid unseen, and the carriage rattled on and away leaving them behind.

"Who were they?" Adacon whispered.

"Slave traders out of Saru Gnarl. I think it would be unwise to stay upon the road any longer, especially with the coming daylight. Carriages will increase as we get close to the city," Slowin said, and Flaer agreed with a nod.

"Then what can we do?"

"Take to the forest—seek the golem entrance to the bay," Slowin replied, and before Adacon could ask what the golem entrance to the bay was, Slowin had already hustled deeper into the woods. Flaer quickly followed, with Adacon bringing up the rear, and they cut away from the gravel road on a course southeast through the wilderness.

*   *   *

The forest chattered with life around the travelers, and strange insects thronged about, biting whatever open flesh was available. Slowin, of course, was not bothered by the bugs, and he led them quickly along as if he knew the way. They reached a wide clearing; set like a gem in the middle was a small pond mirroring the stars above. About the rim of the pond were crumbling stone structures that looked ancient, barely visible in the dim light—Adacon thought they could have once been statues of tree-nymphs. Something stirred in the water, and Slowin brought them to a halt.

"Where are we?" asked Adacon.

"This is the golem entrance to the bay," Slowin replied.

"But I don't see any entrance."

"It's underneath the water, through a tunnel pass," said Slowin, and then the enormous golem suddenly dove headfirst into the water. Adacon looked to Flaer who smiled, and then back to the water in apprehension.

"Come on," Slowin splashed, resurfacing like a fountain and spraying mist at them. For a moment Adacon forgot where he was, fascinated that Slowin could stay afloat given his great metal body.

"But I have never swam before; I don't know how to," Adacon admitted with horror. Flaer pointed at Adacon's breast plate and then jumped into the dark water.

"Going to have to leave the armor. Take your sword and bow," said Slowin.

"I don't know if I could even do it with the sword," Adacon worried, taking off his armor.

"Leave it then," Slowin said.

"Let me try first," Adacon said as he ran with a start at the water, tripping in near the edge with a splash. Slowin and Flaer bobbed on the surface watching patiently for Adacon to come up. After several moments bubbles rose to the surface and Adacon burst up gasping for air. Flaer looked to Slowin who made no motion to interfere. Adacon continued to writhe in the water, going under once more only to reappear, swinging pitifully.

"Help, I'm drowning!" Adacon yelped, swallowing a mouthful of cold water. Slowin hesitated no longer and heaved Adacon from below, flinging the slave up on onto the dry earth once more, soaking and in shock.

"Lose the sword," Slowin directed.

"But I'll drown even without it," Adacon coughed.

"No you won't, the pass is short. You'll only be under for a minute."

"But I can't, I'll die…" Adacon whimpered. Flaer appeared irritated.

"Let's go—back in. Leave the bow and arrows too; there will be more where we're going anyhow," Slowin ordered.

Adacon hesitantly dropped his quiver and bow, leaving them beside his sword near the edge of the water.

"Now in, see if you can try holding your breath under the water," Slowin persuaded.

"I don't know—"

"There's no time to spare, unless you wish to be found by the slave traders of Saru Gnarl!" Slowin barked, growing angry as he floated with strange buoyancy in the pool, stars glimmering on his skin. Flaer ducked underneath the surface, disappearing from sight.

"I just can't, you're going to have to leave me here Slowin. I've failed this cause," Adacon cried. As he stood defeated by the brink of the murky water a hand seized his leg from the depths. Adacon was pulled down into the water and held there by hands firmly clamped round his skull. He struggled in panic to free himself for nearly half a minute, until suddenly calm swept over him and he stopped twisting.

Above the surface of the water Slowin laughed heartily, and Flaer grinned thickly the width of his shaggy face. Finally, Flaer let go of Adacon's head, and Adacon burst up to air once more, gasping the same as before. His eyes darted wildly as he regained his breath. After several minutes he felt composed again and looked at Flaer and Slowin. They were both smiling when Slowin broke the tension:

"That was at least as long as you'll need to be under for. So, with thanks to Flaer for proving you can do it, shall we?"

Adacon did not respond to Slowin but looked down, his spirit bruised, his tension boiling. At first there swelled anger at Flaer and Slowin, but slowly it was replaced by a sense of acceptance; soon Adacon felt triumphant, and he laughed at himself for being so frightened.

"Come on lad," Slowin winked, "We will need your orb of light."

Adacon remembered the Orb and drew it from his pocket. Slowin and Flaer descended beneath the surface and Adacon quickly drew a breath and followed. The orb of light worked the same underwater as it did above, Adacon soon discovered. The water was lit green with the glow of the Orb, and Slowin led them through a large aperture in the rock wall of the pond basin. It was only a moment before they all came up for air on the opposite side of the pass, and Adacon quickly peered around at a winding edifice of underground rock. The ceiling was carved granite, stalactites hanging down and walls of smooth green slime. Adacon put his Orb back into his pocket but the cavern became death black, and he brought it back out immediately.

"Do you know the way Slowin?" Adacon asked.

"Surely, boy. Follow me so that I may prove fleet in caves as well as woods," Slowin boasted, swimming forward. Flaer and Adacon fell in behind; Adacon clutched the Orb tightly to guide their passage. It seemed an impossible web of intertwining caves, and he was astounded to see Slowin navigate the maze, which forked every several yards in a new direction. After what seemed half an hour of twists and turns, they finally arrived in a corridor whose end had starlight, and in eager anticipation of getting out of the water Adacon paddled faster alongside the others.

"The exit!" Adacon cried.

"Yes. You see, golems know many tight and hidden passes, though our size belies that truth," Slowin said.

They continued down the tunnel toward the light, and Adacon put his Orb away at Slowin's command. Before them was a starlit expanse of bay, and deeper off under the bright moons towered many anchored ships, each a different color. Adacon gasped in awe at the sight of the port city. It seemed Slowin brought them through to the southern edge of Saru Gnarl's bay; the city buildings loomed like spikes across the water, held up it seemed by an endless string of rose-colored torches. Their position at the back of the bay was cloaked from view; they shook the water from their garments under overhanging trees and tall reeds. A stony shore spread out on either side of them, several yards wide, separating the bay from the forest. Slowin led them forth to its bank and into a huddle behind bramble that grew high on the rocky shore.

"We must follow the shoreline, and take a boat ere the sun rises. We cannot afford to be seen in or around the city streets. We risk much as it is chancing the docks," Slowin said, directing caution at Adacon. Adacon turned to glance at the boats in the distance again. They each had three girthy wooden poles harnessing massive sails, a rainbow of different colors and embroideries, softly visible beneath pearl moonlight; some were pure white, others mixed red and black, and others deep green. Some of the sails had stitchings of strange symbols, foreign to Adacon, and others had common pictures like trees and wolves. Some small boats appeared to be single-masted, and some seemed to have no sails at all. The docks stretched far from the bank into the ocean, and Adacon couldn't make out where the dock intercepted the city buildings. The buildings could be seen among and between treetops; it was a dimly glowing city of mists and spires, the grandest and only Adacon had ever seen. Some of the ships were moving out to sea, others were entering into port, and some too, Adacon surveyed, were still yet alive with movement on deck. Even the city looked to be moving with life, winking with rose and calcite hues that carried high into the night sky. Voices were audible as a faint chorus of chatter that drifted across the low-rolling tide.

"The ocean is marvelous," Adacon exclaimed, and Slowin struck him on the arm to silence him.

"Ow!" Adacon cried.

"Though the city is still on the other side of the bay, know that voices carry fast and far over these waters," said Slowin, and then with great care they picked a trail along the pebble-rich banks of the bay. The course of the bank wrapped in a circular fashion northeast, eventually jutting out to conceal the majority of Saru Gnarl in the distance. Between the trees they caught traces of walking lights, bustling workers coming from the city to the docks.

"Does this city ever sleep?" Adacon whispered as he trailed Slowin.

"No, the port keeps business though all hours of the day and night. Grelion has new slaves shipped in from the eastern countries across the sea—each one allowing him to harvest the land better and build new farms," Slowin replied. As the group crept forward the stone shore turned to sand, and after several minutes its width had doubled. The tree line receded and a bog-meadow of hard reeds took its place. The path became less concealed until almost all cover save the darkness of night forsook them. It was then that Slowin deemed a nearby jetty rock suitable to huddle behind, and there he began to reveal his designs to take a ship:

"We are very close now. After we come to the dock trail there will be no turning back," Slowin warned.

"What do you want me to do?" said Adacon.

"There, beside those three clippers," Slowin pointed to a small vessel with two masts that was anchored next to three tall ships. "I know the markings on that schooner. It's a pirate vessel, and Grelion's forces are less likely to give chase if it is commandeered."

"We're going to steal a ship from pirates?"

"Yes, we will try anyway. I know the red and black flag it bears; it is the property of Smither Govlonks and his gang. They operate a far reaching ring, and their fleet is ever scattered. I think if we could take the ship without event we would be safe upon reaching the point." Slowin said, and he looked to Flaer for approval of his idea—Flaer nodded as one convinced.

"With the greatest swordsman in Darkin it shouldn't be that hard, right?"Adacon poked. Flaer smirked.

"Follow me up the path to the first dock. There will be guards and merchants about, but being past the main city gates already, we should be absolved of suspicion."

"But you are an enormous silver golem—how will you not draw suspicion?"

"I have thought of it, and it helps that many different races of people come through the Saru Gnarl port. Nonetheless, I am of unique magnificence to look upon, and so—" Slowin chuckled, "I have decided that should anything occur it is best to pretend as if I am a captive, a prize of Grelion's being offered to the eastern countries in return for their slaves."

"And how are we to do that?"

"Grip my arms, both of you, from each side; and Flaer, keep the Brigun Autilus drawn, unlit." Flaer nodded.

"But Slowin, you and I have no weapons. What if the plan goes wrong, you didn't say what to do—" Adacon said.

"Worry not about that, lest it happens. In any case, when things turn sour, duck and hide behind Flaer and me, so that we do not throttle you in your own defense," Slowin joked. Adacon wasn't sure how to feel about the plan, but he trusted Slowin. They walked north across the sand to the first dock trail.

"What about once we get to the schooner?" Adacon asked.

"Leave that to Flaer and me."

The sand transformed into a reed-filled meadow with a dirt path cut amidst it. They marched along the dirt path and came determinedly to the first dock; a row of torches glittered, fastened to a rail that led out to sea. All around them, looming bright as ever, was marvelous Saru Gnarl, great port city of the cape. Adacon, though nervous, looked in awe at the magic lights of the city. It seemed there was an amazing number of things all happening at once: on the wide-paved street that ran down to the docks from the inner-city, Adacon ran his eyes over many strange looking figures, each conducting some form of business or revelry.

"Arms now," Slowin ordered, and Flaer and Adacon walked on either side of the hulk holding his hands as if he were shackled.

"This looks convincing," Adacon whispered sarcastically. Soon they were treading out toward the ocean atop the southernmost dock in the port; they walked hurriedly by several humans who appeared to be unloading goods from a small sailboat anchored by the bay.

"Quite a catch there mates!" came a high-pitched voice from one of the merchants. Flaer turned and glared at the men who squatted over their parcel. The Brigun Autilus glowed red for a brief instant.

"Sorry, just being courteous," replied a frightened voice, and the men went back to tending their load. Adacon gritted his teeth at the exchange, sighed deeply, and kept walking without a word. Ahead was a single man near the end of the dock, nearly fifty yards away. Three massive clippers on the left side of the dock appeared abandoned, as did the tiny schooner anchored on the opposite side.

"He might be a city guard," Slowin warned. Adacon wasn't sure if that changed their plan, but he kept walking forward in the best imitation that he was doing nothing unusual.

"Good evening men, how goes your business?" asked the guard as they neared. Flaer brought them to a stop and there was a moment of awkward silence before Slowin nudged Adacon as furtively as possible; he hadn't realized he would be the only one able to speak for them.

"Just off to the East with this shipment—care of Grelion himself," Adacon stammered.

"Personal cargo from the lord himself, eh? Does look rather strange though doesn't it… never seen a golem that color," the guard said, poking Slowin curiously on the arm with his finger. The guard wore brown cloth and chainmail with a thin brass helmet that covered half of his face. On his side hung a broadsword, similar to the ones Adacon and Erguile had once used.

"Yea—he's a present for one of our best traders," Adacon bluffed. The guard eyed Slowin from top to bottom and then turned his glance to Flaer.

"Where's your crew?" the guard asked.

"Ehm—actually staying in port; they say the Saru Gnarl Cape offers many pleasures. To be honest, I couldn't convince them to return with us," Adacon lied.

"Strange to think after being through so many times they'd still enjoy the place so much."

"It's a new crew," Adacon fired back.

"Right then. What country of the East are you faring back to?" the guard asked.

"Actually I can't say, sorry."

"Always with his secret business," the guard muttered to himself. "Well then, sounds important—papers and you're off..." the guard said, looking at Flaer as he spoke. Adacon coughed and drew the attention from Flaer back to himself.

"Papers?"

"You've got your papers right?" the guard reiterated, directing his question at Flaer. Slowin had been keeping his head hung, acting inconsequential, but now he lifted his gaze.

"Well—" Adacon said, buying time to think.

"Does talk, doesn't he?" the guard said, glaring at Flaer. Flaer stood motionless, looking past the guard to the ocean. "Hey, I'm asking you a question. Where are your papers?" the guard asked Flaer again.

"We've lost them in the swamp," Adacon finally answered.

"The swamp?"

"On the way in there was a storm, and they were blown away," Adacon made up.

"How have you have been to the swamp and back, your ship has only been anchored but an hour now?" the guard said with growing suspicion. "Matter of fact, I didn't see anyone coming off dressed as odd as you two." The guard drew his sword. "I'm going to have to detain you until I can get my captain down here to check your—"

The guard couldn't finish his sentence, for Slowin head-butted him with the might of a Metal golem; blood ran down the guard's forehead as he slumped to the wooden floor of the dock. Slowin frantically looked about for sign of anyone else on the dock, as did Flaer and Adacon; it was still abandoned, except for the crew at the entrance who were still sorting their packages. It looked as if they hadn't noticed the brief scuffle. Flaer urged them forward in haste toward the schooner.

It was a small red-black wooden vessel with two masts and enormous lettering on the hull that read "Blockade Runner." Adacon saw through the portside window a dim candle flickering in the cabin, but nothing else on board moved. Adacon followed behind Slowin and Flaer, running across the ramp that brought them on deck. Once aboard, Slowin rushed to the cabin to make sure it was empty—the candle alone occupied it.

"Clear," he called to them, returning to the deck. "Raise sails!" Adacon watched helplessly as Flaer and Slowin set about raising the sails on the ship, wishing he knew how to help.

"Adacon, keep your eyes on the docks, not us," Slowin commanded while maneuvering about the rigging of the ship. Flaer had already ascended the second mast, and soon five sails were open to the night wind. Adacon couldn't help but wonder if Flaer and Slowin had used some magic to get the sails open as fast as they had. Two wide sails were fastened to the base of either mast, a smaller square sail rested at the cross atop the forward mast, and two more triangle sails extended over the bow. Each was colored red and black, embroidered with an emblem Adacon likened to a fish caught on fire. He kept a close watch on the dock and the street beyond that led to Saru Gnarl's well lit center; it appeared all was routine there, and there was no sign of anyone advancing toward their position.

"Alright, she's full-stretched," Slowin yelled up to Flaer on the mast, where wind was catching the sails and causing the ship to lurch from its anchoring. Slowin ran to a pulley and called Adacon to his aid; together they hoisted the anchor of the small ship onto the deck. The vessel heaved into the moonlit bay.

"What a success," Adacon whispered.

"No need to keep quiet; just don't shout and we should pass out of port untraced," Slowin said with a deep sigh. Adacon realized how close they had come to disaster, but the danger had felt exhilarating to him. The Blockade Runner drifted away from the dock as Slowin and Flaer guided the ship. Adacon stood idle, content to watch the sparkling city from afar until his shipmates needed his help. It was only after Flaer and Slowin seemed to relax that Adacon started up with alarm:

"Look!" he said, pointing toward the main street of Saru Gnarl, a wide strip of gravel that ran downhill between buildings toward the docks from the inner heart of the city. There at the bottom of the street Slowin spotted what Adacon had started over: a ruckus of smoke and light. Just where the street spread out into a paved platform before the dock, a figure could be seen on a horse, riding away from a trail of pursuers. The pursuers rallied with arms and torches, chasing from where the fire and smoke rose, and the man on the horse galloped hard in a direction toward the last dock, the one from which the Blockade Runner was taken. Adacon focused on the fleeing horse that bore a flailing rider. "Erguile!" he exclaimed.

"Could it be?" Slowin said "Can't be him—he couldn't have made it through the front gates of the city." Flaer focused on the scene now too, and he smiled broadly, recognizing the old grey horse; it was Weakhoof. Adacon soon heard wailing coming from the fleeing rider, and all of them strained to hear.

"You will not take me alive! I will have all your heads before I give mine!" came Erguile's furious voice. He menacingly brandished his broadsword while turning Weakhoof about; there atop his bucking steed he faced his troop of armed pursuers. Five men braced themselves, and Adacon thought they all looked much the same as the guard Slowin had knocked out on the dock.

"Turn back, we've got to get him," Adacon ordered, but Slowin and Flaer had heeded the command before it was given, and the Blockade Runner turned on the open ocean and sped toward the dock.

"Erguile!" Adacon and Slowin yelled together as loudly as their throats could manage while Flaer waved his arms in the air. At once Flaer unsheathed the Brigun Autilus and held it aloft; a soft red glow turned abruptly into a vibrant glare, and the sword became as a lighthouse in the bay. Adacon winced, shielding his eyes from the tremendous charge of the sword. Erguile spotted the light and heard the calls of his friends. Weakhoof turned again from his pursuers, only in time to narrowly escape the strike of a sword. The Blockade Runner closed in on its mooring post once more, and Weakhoof galloped full speed toward the ship as the light of the Brigun Autilus went out. Adacon was alarmed at the strange speed of the ship and called for them to halt before it crashed into the dock. Weakhoof bore his rider with great speed onto the dock and out toward the returning schooner. Erguile twisted his neck to see the guards still following.

"Bit faster now—come on," Erguile called to his friends, reaching the water's edge before the ship.

"Jump in the water, we'll pull you aboard," Adacon urged. Erguile ignored him. "They're coming, hurry!" he yelled again. The guards were halfway between the start of the dock and Erguile, chasing at a full sprint.

"I won't leave Weakhoof for the slaughter, I'll go with him should it come to that," Erguile stubbornly replied. Finally the Blockade Runner drew up along the dock and Slowin threw down the boarding ramp. Weakhoof scampered on board and Slowin withdrew the ramp, but not before two of the fastest guards had managed to sneak across—they tumbled to the deck floor; a third guard dove across but missed and fell to the sea. The last two stood glaring from the dock, helpless to assist their comrades.

Flaer wasted no time on the guards—he relit the Brigun Autilus and shone it directly at their faces so that they stumbled back in the blinding light. The guards regained their footing near the starboard rail in time to look up as Slowin rammed forward with his right shoulder, knocking them both over into the bay.

"Well done!" Erguile applauded. The guards on the dock had been joined by reinforcements who worked to rescue the three men who fell; each was struggling to free himself from armor underwater. An archer came to the dock too late, and his arrows missed the Blockade Runner as it picked up wind, speeding out upon the great Kalm Ocean. Weakhoof whinnied at the rolling motion of the ship as its course drew them away from the dock, and Erguile dismounted.

"It's great to be back with you—I have been blessed," Erguile proclaimed, hugging each of them.

"You are a true fool, Erguile, and mad—risking the front gates of Saru Gnarl," Slowin scolded.

"Was no easy task, but had you not come for me those guards might have met a worse fate yet," Erguile boasted, smiling.

"Hah—surely I won't doubt your valor again. But I am glad you have returned to us, and that we have accomplished our task so quickly," said the golem. "And to Adacon and Flaer do you owe thanks: Adacon spotted you, and the Brigun Autilus called your gaze." Erguile offered his gratitude again as Flaer extinguished the last glow from his sword and sheathed it once more.

"We are on course to Remtall?" asked Erguile as he tended to Weakhoof, still quivering with fright at the small waves that hit the ship.

"Yes, due southeast to the Point," Slowin replied. "And thanks I owe to you Weakhoof for keeping our friend in safety. You have proved a steed worthy of noblest recognition—no doubt is left that your name belies your character." Slowin placed a hand on the grey horse's mane and stroked. "This horse has shown us intrepid hooves this day. I am sorry, Erguile, for doubting him." Weakhoof neighed at the compliment, and Adacon laughed merrily; it seemed the old horse had understood and replied to Slowin.

"See—he has already forgiven you!" Erguile laughed.

The Blockade Runner sailed on into the night, and no ship came in pursuit of her from Saru Gnarl. Slowin ordered that they should get some sleep, and that he himself would steer the ship as they regained their strength. It had been a long time since any of them had had any rest, and Adacon heartily welcomed the repose. It was not long before he was asleep on the floor of the cabin upon a soft fur rug, dreaming of Erol Drunne. Erguile lay nearby, and

Weakhoof stayed near the cabin door, tied to a small post. Flaer sat mellowly on the deck, gazing at the stars while Slowin commanded the helm. Soon, even Flaer sprawled out to find comfort and sleep. Many peaceful hours passed, until finally dawn rose in a meandering pink line from the East, turning its color ever so slightly more golden, as Slowin kept awake, guiding them all.

VIII: AGAINST THE KALM

"Wake up," Slowin said, nudging Adacon.

"Ugh," Adacon complained as he turned over, squinting up at Slowin through rays of morning sunlight. "What time is it?"

"Late enough in the day. We are soon to be upon the Point. Come out on deck," he said, then left the cabin. Adacon sat up and rubbed his eyes. Looking around in the light of day he noticed several elaborate maps and sea charts that hung about the walls, and detailed paintings of strange ocean monsters. There was a loud neighing from the deck, and Adacon forgot his preoccupation with the maps and stood to head outside.

"Adacon—missed much you'll find," Erguile said proudly. Adacon looked in awe at Erguile: he stood dressed in shining silver-gold armor and held aloft a beautifully engraved long sword.

"Good sword for riding Weakhoof—I can grip it with one hand, but on foot, I can grasp with both," Erguile said. He gripped the sword firmly with both hands. "Like this," he said, demonstrating by swinging the sword wildly. Behind Erguile stood Slowin and Flaer, gazing at the turquoise sea over fresh mugs of steaming drinks. They leaned over the stern as wind kicked into the sails above, pushing the Blockade Runner away from dark clouds that hung in the distance behind.

"Where'd you get it?" Adacon exclaimed.

"Secret booty, of course," Erguile quipped, and he continued to practice with his new sword, slicing through the morning breeze.

"Secret booty...treasure on board?" Adacon resounded.

"Flaer found it this morning, under those planks," Erguile said; he paused his phantom strikes to point his blade at some upturned deck floorboards near the starboard rail.

"Is there anything left? Why didn't you get me up?" Adacon panicked as he ran to the floorboards, rubbing cobwebs from his eyes.

"Maybe; I thought I saw some more weapons, a suit of chain mail..." Erguile replied, returning his attention to his new sword, absorbed by it. His old broadsword lay discarded on the deck near Weakhoof.

"Good morning," turned Slowin, watching Adacon fervently search the yard-wide gap in the deck. He looked within the dark space below for any more shiny armor or swords.

"Morning..." Adacon replied, distracted.

"You'll find there's another—" Slowin began; he was cut off by a shout from Adacon:

"Ah! What a sword," Adacon said, lifting a black-tinted great sword from the orifice. He held it high, his face aglow with the excitement of a small boy. "And I thought I'd be out of arms."

"I didn't want it—too bulky for riding with," Erguile scoffed.

"Should serve you well, I'm sure, provided you build up strength for her," Slowin remarked. Adacon noticed Flaer turn to give a nod of approval for the quality of his new sword.

"Amazing—it's so light for such a massive sword," Adacon observed. Slowin turned toward him to touch the blade.

"Odd engravings on the blade, as you can see. No telling where it was stolen from," Slowin said.

"So this is a real pirate's ship then," Adacon replied.

"Absolutely is," Erguile beamed. "Go on and grab your chain mail so we can spar." Adacon briefly relinquished his sword, setting it down in its sheath. In an instant he returned to the treasure stash to look for armor. Under the floor boards were scattered jewels, gold coins, several small daggers, metal boxes, several bottles of what looked like liquor, and two coats of glossy chain mail. Adacon grabbed one of the mails and stood to try it on.

"Fits," Adacon smiled.

"And you were so worried to leave your things at the pond," Slowin laughed. Flaer smiled widely and drank deeply from his mug.

"Tea, Adacon?" Slowin offered.

"Tea?"

"Pirates had a great stash of it, a fine blend too, invigorating…" Erguile explained from across deck. Weakhoof whinnied, and Erguile put his new sword in its sheath to tend his horse.

"Still brewing some," Slowin said. Flaer left for the bow of the ship toward an iron stove propped up against a mast. "Of course there's fresh porridge as well, and thick bread—some exotic fruits I've never tasted before too."

"What about the Point? You said we were closing in," Adacon asked, peering into the horizon and seeing the Kalm Ocean spread uniformly in each direction, no signs of land. The sun was almost halfway up in the sky, and in front of the ship there wasn't a single cloud.

"As Flaer has it, we make a sharp turn west in a few moments time. That should bring us right up on the Point. We have been sailing parallel with the coast for some time now," Slowin replied. At that moment Flaer returned with pirate food and tea for Adacon, who sat quietly near Weakhoof and ate hungrily.

Before long they were filled with porridge, fruit, and bread, and wide awake from strong tea. Adacon felt replenished from the sleep he had finally regained; he wondered whether Slowin had ever gone to sleep, but decided he probably didn't require sleep as much as the others, being a silver golem. Flaer and Slowin worked together in steering the ship; soon the schooner turned hard and land sprouted from the sea.

"Thank Flaer for his nautical skill; without him I'm afraid I wouldn't have known how to navigate, and led us perhaps to be swallowed by the great Kalm," Slowin declared. Flaer humbly smiled and hung his head, then squinted into the distance; he smacked the rail of the ship to draw their attention to the Point. In the distance a strip of grassland jutted out from the coast, a natural jetty; near to the very end of the low-lying strip sat a gnome by a fire.

The ground where Remtall had made camp was barely solid, just firm enough that he could keep his weight there. The rest of the strip stretching inland was mud and rock that dissolved rapidly, descending deeply on either side into the depths. In the cramped space at the end of the jetty Remtall had built a small fire, and even managed to build a thatched shelter of vines and shoots; it looked like a dirty organic mat he had used to sleep under. Soon the Blockade Runner treaded the shallower water surrounding the jetty, and in the calm surf Slowin threw down the anchor. Remtall stood nearly seven yards from the schooner, separated by ocean, but the ship could come no closer.

"Good morning friend," Slowin called.

"The morn is good and sweet, fair golem of the Red Wood," Remtall replied lazily, extinguishing his fire. "Shame you all can't come in and stay awhile." They laughed as Remtall broke down his camp, heaving his shelter of roots into the ocean. "Think she'll take me across?"

"You're joking right?" Erguile said.

"You think that gnomes can't swim, do you?" Remtall responded. The midmorning sun coursed down upon them, and suddenly the day had turned dreadfully hot.

"Where's Yarnhoot?" Slowin asked.

"An important errand, he'll be needed for awhile yet in Rislind," Remtall replied, and turned to scoop up his few possessions. In his belt there was a dagger sheathed, and on his side he fastened his pack; next to it he hung his flask. "Alright then, I'm coming along now—and well done, she's got the right colors for our task I'll admit." Remtall said in appreciation of the stolen ship. He staggered toward the end of firm grass, leaving the solid earth behind. Each step encroached farther upon the loose rocks and mud that merged into sea.

"Careful," Adacon called, watching Remtall wobble on the loose ground.

"Never mind a gnome's footfalls—nor his burst in water," Remtall replied. He stood still, slowly sinking into muck, only so he could release his flask. Remtall squinted at the sun as beads of sweat rolled down his face; he looked up at the sky and drank heartily from his silver flask. Still wobbling, he took off his green cap and used it to mop his brow, then returned it to his greying mess of brown hair. "Alright then."

"Careful now," Slowin cautioned the gnome again. This time Remtall ignored the remark and instead plopped sideways into the water. He began throbbing about helplessly. After a few suspenseful moments, Remtall seemed to straighten himself out and propel his small frame forward in odd looking bursts, kicking his legs high and splashing in all directions.

"Little farther," Adacon cheered as Remtall lunged toward the rail of the schooner where Flaer was dangling a rope.

"Got it!" Remtall coughed, spitting saltwater as he gripped the end of the rope with both hands. "And hoist mate!" Flaer tugged Remtall aboard. The gnome sat soaking wet, coughing up the last of the sea he had swallowed.

"Clearing that awful taste ought to help, eh?" Remtall spat, and he drank his liquor.

"Easy, Remtall; there is much ocean to cross, and no other man do we have to cross it for us," Slowin advised.

"No man fit for the task? How about a woman fit for my ravaging? Besides, spirits haven't the effect on gnomes they have on men," Remtall burped. "Or golems—be you a golem at all, you silver heap!"

"Alright then, enough," Slowin replied. "Good to have you back Remtall, either way."

"Captain Remtall," Erguile added.

"Captain Remtall Olter'Fane—now there is a missed title. I've not been captain in a great many years."

"But isn't it true you were once among the greatest seamen in Darkin?" Adacon queried.

"Sea-gnomes, good sir—but yes, I won't deny. I was once in command of many ships, a battalion of the north country Hemlin-Auk, a gnomen Fleet in service to Grelion."

"You served under Grelion?" Erguile recoiled.

"Indeed. I daresay I was one of his most trusted captains. This was a time when he was not yet corrupted, you see. Grelion possessed many great qualities in his unspoiled youth, before passing to greed and obsession. Alas, it has been a long age since he withered to madness."

"I can hardly believe it—Krem told me that since I have been alive Grelion has ever been the great oppressor," cried Adacon.

"And right your friend was, young boy. But remember that I have lived more than five lives against your one, and I can recall the shadow that befell his soul, the great loss that took Darkin's chance of lasting peace after the war," Remtall replied.

"When your son—" Adacon began but was cut off:

"Speak not of my son!" spat the gnome, and he drank anew. "Our quest is now apart from the fate of my son save a lingering hope for blood-filled revenge. It was long after my exile that Grelion's law ran afoul and turned to such evil measures as calling the aid of Zesm the Rancor, sickest plague of Arkenshyr—all for greed of gold," Remtall seethed. He spit into the wind and cursed loudly.

"Our purpose now is to cross the Kalm Ocean safely and reach Erol Drunne. Let us keep our minds on this task alone, before anger stays our good judgment," Slowin advised.

"I'm sorry, Remtall," Adacon whimpered.

"We'll leave it be. But each of you know this. . ." Remtall said coldly, and he glared at each of his crew, "I journey again upon open water in pursuit of a single end, one purpose at mind; I go now from Rislind for revenge, and throw my life to the whims of Gaigas. It will be my life or Zesm's in the end—there can be but two ways this crusade closes." A silence came over the party, and Slowin waited for the tension to rest so that he could set his captain upon his proper business. Soon Remtall seemed to calm. He took the helm of the Blockade Runner, guiding her sharply around the jetty and toward the eastern horizon.

Slowin pored over sea charts that Remtall had brought in his pack, while Flaer sat idly by the aft mast, gazing westward. Erguile and Adacon sat alone, musing together over their new weapons and armor. They talked about Grelion more, and of the elusive Zesm.

"This Zesm—Remtall really hates him," Erguile said.

"Yea" Adacon replied.

"You saw him that night . . . you said he was glowing at first?"

"He was like an aura, red and yellow swirling light, and then his voice changed. He looked like a man, but all hunched. He was covered in grey rags, and he had a bloody sword."

"Must have been my sword, but why would he steal it while we slept and not kill us?"

"Who knows? Following orders from Grelion perhaps," Adacon sighed. "I hope we see Krem soon."

"Perhaps he'll be in Erol Drunne."

"Maybe. Slowin won't tell me anything about Krem's errand. I'm still unsure of our real purpose in Erol Drunne."

"I believe we're to find counsel for a course to war, against whomever our greatest enemy is," said Erguile.

"It's unclear now whom that is; I left the farm with no intention but to break away from the horrible existence there so that I could kill the lords, but once Krem told me of Grelion, and that Grelion was the only one, I think I focused all my hatred upon him alone. Now with Zesm and Vesleathren, I'm not sure who we should wish to kill more."

"I fear none of them," Erguile exclaimed, clasping his long sword. "Perhaps it's a question of which of those three we should kill first."

"And the Feral Brood—with his dark magic Vesleathren is turning creatures into those foul beasts. We both witnessed it; Bulkog didn't look like what I could call a troll."

"Yea, and what a waste that fool was. I'd like to have another go at him," Erguile said, rubbing at the newly formed scar on his neck where Bulkog had struck. Just then Remtall approached, staggering slightly, edging his way along the rail of the ship toward them.

"Talk of women, eh?" Remtall chuckled as the slaves put their arms aside and stood to properly greet him.

"Captain," they both chimed, nodding down to Remtall.

"What have you got in the way of women on the slave farms, boys?" Remtall asked, turning his gaze out to sea toward a patch of dark clouds hanging in the southeastern horizon. The sun was beginning to descend slowly in the West, and the clear blue sky of morning had turned into a veil-knitting of streaked clouds.

"Women, er—you know we haven't truly ever met a wom—" Adacon spoke, but was cut off by Erguile:

"Speaks for himself! I had ways to find women, experienced in their trade I might add," Erguile said, winking at Remtall who turned back to them from the sky.

"Never had a woman?" Remtall gasped, staring at Adacon.

"I haven't," Adacon said sadly after a long pause, "and how could you have?" Adacon glared at Erguile. "I don't remember even so much as a whisper about women coming past the farm."

"There were times, boy, trust me. And I had an eye for it; knew when they were in the wagons, and how they were disguised," Erguile explained. Adacon doubted the validity of the boast.

"So then, Adacon boy, you've at least *seen* a woman?" Remtall continued.

"Sure, I've seen plenty of drawings, quite a lot actually," Adacon replied.

"Only ever seen them clothed then," Remtall surmised.

"Well, of course—" Adacon answered shyly.

"Poor boy," Erguile sympathized, patting Adacon on his back.

"No worries son. Surely you'll meet one soon, now that you're free and roaming east, keeping company with Captain Olter'Fane and his crew," Remtall cheered. Adacon smiled, not realizing he was blushing.

"You think I could meet a woman in Erol Drunne?" Adacon asked.

"Perhaps, son, perhaps," Remtall said between gulps from his flask.

"And what should I do next, after I've met her? I don't know what they're like, or what they like—what are they like Captain?" asked Adacon.

"Easy son—a woman is like the nurturing part of your soul you've missed to notice, a part that cares for you, attends to all bits of clockwork, cherishes your mold," Remtall explained. Erguile stood quietly listening, nodding as if he already knew what Remtall was talking about. "Course they can slaughter you too. But you'll be fine, young and stout as you are."

"What would I do when I," Adacon began, but stopped midsentence as he watched Remtall look wildly about, then to the eastern sky. "What's wrong?"

"Where's the pirate store? There's a fine squall coming in," Remtall spoke loudly.

"Pirate store?" The slaves asked in unison.

"This is a pirate ship you stole, or do my eyes deceive me? The pirate store—the rum!" Remtall exclaimed.

"Oh, there were some casks under the deck, look there," Erguile said. He pointed at the wooden planks that protruded near the rail. Remtall hurried off to look for the hidden treasure he sought.

*　　　*　　　*

The Blockade Runner sailed forth amidst increasing swells, and soon the sky turned deep grey all around her. The winds grew strong, as Remtall had forecasted, and soon a clap of thunder sounded just as the schooner gathered real speed.

"Captain, the waves are getting bigger. Is there anything to worry about?" Adacon asked nervously, creeping up behind Remtall at the helm. The gnome calmly steered the wheel, showing all signs of one supremely at ease.

"Surely not boy. I haven't been on the Kalm in some time, but I can say she offers much worse than this," Remtall reassured. Just then Slowin came suddenly to them from the other side of the deck, his footsteps causing the deck to creak. The thunder had picked up considerably, and a light rain began to patter his shoulders as he spoke to them:

"Erguile has fallen sick."

"Sick? He was just fine a moment ago," Adacon replied.

"His lunch has gone over the rail," Slowin replied.

"He'll be fine; sea sickness is all. The bigger swells will do that to those with fair stomachs," Remtall replied. Adacon realized the rising and falling of the ship had increased violently over the last few minutes.

"Are you sure? I am not the most knowledgeable in matters of human sickness," Slowin asked.

"Of course I'm sure, silver fool of a giant; count your blessings again, for I am Olter'Fane of the Auk, Captain of the gnomen Fleet—and in Gaigas's bosom was I made seaworthy!" Remtall roared into the wind against a flash of lightning. He took a drop of his flask and turned to see Erguile running toward them from the bow.

"Are you alright?" Adacon asked as Erguile came within earshot. Erguile held his stomach with one hand, a sour look on his face, gasping for breath. He pointed to the bow where Flaer stood.

"I'm fine—but there's a ship," Erguile moaned before diving for the rail of the ship, throwing up again.

"What?" Adacon replied. Slowin left immediately for the bow. Remtall stayed put and in the light rain he withdrew his pipe from his pocket; he began to stuff it with tobacco. Adacon looked toward the commotion at the bow, searching for a sign of the ship. The grey distance offered no shapes.

"Captain?" Adacon said.

"Go have a look—bring me the verdict," Remtall said calmly. Adacon ran from the helm toward the bow. Slowin and Flaer scoured the eastern horizon for a silhouette while the captain watched from afar, puffing on his pipe, trying to cover it from the increasing rain with his tunic.

"What is it?" Adacon asked as he reached them. Flaer seemed to be searching deeply in the grey, and Slowin too appeared in great concentration.

"Looked like a ship—it disappeared behind the fog," Slowin said.

"You both saw it then? Definitely a ship?"

"Looked like it," Slowin replied, and Flaer nodded yes.

"Tell Remtall; we'll stay and watch," Slowin said. Adacon acknowledged and returned swiftly to the helm with the news.

"It was a ship. They all saw it. It's disappeared in the fog," Adacon reported.

"It's no ship," Remtall uttered between puffs from his pipe.

"What do you mean?" Adacon asked, stricken with surprise. At that moment Erguile composed himself and trudged over to join them.

"I've known this presence before. Though it looks like a ship, rest assured she isn't," Remtall answered. Adacon shuddered.

"What's going on, did anyone see it?" Erguile asked.

"Slowin and Flaer did, but it's gone now. They're keeping an eye out for it," Adacon answered. "What is it Remtall?"

"It's a phantom—a vision of a ship that sank more than three hundred years ago," Remtall said.

"What?" Erguile recoiled.

"Don't fret; she'll be of no harm to us. There's the Fang Shoals for fretting."

"A phantom ship," Adacon's eyes widened as the wind picked up, rocking the ship violently. Remtall grabbed the rail while Adacon grabbed the side of a mast, but Erguile went tumbling onto the deck. Thunder came at its loudest, and a great whine reverberated from near the cabin.

"Weakhoof!" Erguile cried, rushing to his feet. In his sickness Erguile had forgotten about his horse. Weakhoof had braved enough of the storm quietly, but as it worsened the steed could remain fearless no more. An eruption of neighing sounded from the cabin, and as Erguile came to Weakhoof's side he saw that the horse had nearly loosed its rein.

"Easy girl," Erguile comforted. "We'll be through this soon." Adacon and Remtall watched Erguile quiet the horse; he seemed even through his fit to be courageous.

"How can you be sure we're in no danger of attack?" Adacon asked Remtall as he steadied the wheel.

"Fool...Complex answers I do not give for simple questions. Have a draught," Remtall responded. He offered Adacon his flask. Adacon took a sip and coughed, handing it back to Remtall.

"Much harsher than Krem's wine," Adacon complained.

"We will have much time to discuss phantoms and shoals when the Kalm has regained its namesake; until then, fetch yourself to help your friend. Weakhoof looks distressed," Remtall commanded. Adacon nodded, leaving the captain alone at the wheel with his smoldering pipe.

The Blockade Runner jogged eastward into the storm, and the weather worsened. Adacon tended Weakhoof with Erguile, and Flaer remained on the bow searching the fog-ridden sea. Slowin had retreated to the stern, standing next to Remtall, discussing something. The swells increased and Erguile fell sick again. Several hours seemed to pass, and finally the rain slowed. The sky cleared, revealing an early cluster of moons. Tired from the storm, the crew retired after a quick dinner without conversation. Adacon had been eager to learn more of the phantom ship from Remtall, and he wanted to ask Slowin if he knew where Krem might be, but fatigue won out. Soon they were all asleep, even Slowin, save for Remtall who somehow kept awake and guided the ship onward under the still night sky.

Time passed quickly for the crew on their second day at sea. Both slaves apprenticed under Remtall, learning what they could about the rigging of the schooner. The weather remained fair throughout the day, and Weakhoof seemed to be especially enjoying the lack of waves. He stood shaded underneath a tarp Erguile had raised for him. The sun waned and nightfall crept upon them once more, and near the cabin Flaer made a dinner of food from the pirate store: biscuits, gravy, jerky, tea, and sweet rainbow-colored fruits served for dessert. The cool night air wrapped around them as they sat eating; the stars shone bright, piquing Adacon's imagination.

"How many days until we arrive?" Adacon asked Remtall, sitting across from him puffing on his pipe.

"Three weeks, I suppose, at this rate," Remtall replied.

"Who would know an ocean was this big?" Erguile chimed in, lighting his own pipe; it was filled with the last remnants of Krem's tobacco.

"The Kalm is greatest of all the oceans, and surely the sweetest to her patrons, save for the Fang Shoals," said Remtall.

"How many oceans are there?" Erguile asked.

"Four that are known; legend tells of uncharted seas deep in the West, beyond Arkenshyr. No one can know for sure, as the Carnalfages hold too strong a patrol on the western rim of the Angelyn peninsula. Not even Grelion dares trade upon those waters."

"Carnalfages—did you see any on the Point?" asked Erguile.

"Unfortunately—I had to lay several to rest during my stay," Remtall chuckled.

"Our captain boasts, and drinks too much," Slowin laughed.

"Boast?" Remtall said; he quieted in seriousness, unsheathing his dagger: the once smooth edge of his blade had a serial lining of nicks running its entire length, the serrated signature of teeth bites. "I wish I had utility to boast on a journey such as this, silver golem. But I can't wholly blame you for doubting me, seeing how much a gnome's stature belies his valor in combat." Remtall gulped from his fresh-filled flagon of pirate rum, apparently offended by Slowin's sarcasm. "We'll face our share soon, I think."

"What do you mean by that?" Adacon asked.

"I *mean*, don't be fooled into thinking this trip will be all glorious fun, because where we purpose to go holds a greater danger than any of you yet realize," Remtall foreboded.

"The Fang Shoals?" Adacon asked anxiously. Flaer shook his head, tired of hearing Remtall's rants.

"Yes, the Fang Shoals. But much worse is Karabden, the black tidal kraken who calls the Fang Shoals her home," Remtall warned.

"Kraken?" Erguile questioned. "You mean, the great whirlpool monsters?"

"Quite learned for a slave, aren't you boy?" Remtall replied. Slowin lay back against the rail, and quick to follow was Flaer; they both closed their eyes as Remtall began tales of sea monsters that lasted deep into the night. Both slaves hung on his every word, constantly inquiring about the frightening lore their captain spun, until finally Slowin advised that they should all get some sleep. As Flaer retired to his portion of the cabin floor, followed by Erguile, Slowin turned to Remtall, who continued to drink from his flask and puff on his pipe.

"Don't you think you should get some sleep, Captain? You haven't slept since coming aboard," Slowin urged.

"Never mind sleep—not for a gnome. The need for sleep does not burden a gnome as it does a man, or a silver golem for that matter," Remtall snickered. Slowin smiled, and decided not to press Remtall further, although he felt troubled by the gnome's vigilance. Slowin walked to a part of the deck near the starboard bow where he kept a rug. Adacon trailed him, asking another question before the golem lay down for the night:

"Slowin…"

"Yes, Adacon, what is it?"

"Krem—is there anything you haven't told us? Do you know any more about what he's doing or where he is?"

"Ummph" Slowin sighed. "He was very vague with me that day in the forest. He only told me that a great evil had returned to strength, and he was off to halt it before it might strengthen further."

"When do you think we might see him again?" Adacon asked.

"I cannot say, Adacon, but rest assured: Krem will return, just as I will return home to my forest."

"You're not going to keep traveling with us once he comes back?"

"Once I have fulfilled my favor to Krem, I intend to return to the peace I have ever enjoyed in seclusion," Slowin replied, emotionless.

"But how can you do that? You know what is at stake for the world," Adacon gasped.

"There will be a great council of Vapours in Erol Drunne, perhaps we will learn more of Krem's actions there. Perhaps—perhaps he will be there. For now, however, it is good night," Slowin answered. The hulking silver mass lumbered away leaving Adacon rabid with more questions. Slowin lay down on his mat to sleep. Adacon surveyed that everyone had gone to bed except Remtall, who had drifted up to the stern. Saddened by

Slowin's desire to leave them as soon as he could, Adacon trudged to his own spot of cabin floor, wishing Krem were back.

*　　　　*　　　　*

Adacon awoke the next morning with greetings of furious wind and rain, accompanied by the loud whinnying of Weakhoof. It was barely midmorning, and already the sky was blackened with thunderclouds. Adacon slowly stood to his feet; he saw Erguile huddled under Weakhoof's tarp and sprinted under to find shelter with them.

"Good morning Addy," Erguile grunted, trying to keep Weakhoof calm. Rain pelted heavily upon the tarp in rhythmic waves. A cold chill whipped underneath the weather shield.

"Morning—this is unbelievable—what weather; I thought the Kalm got its name for being a calm ocean," Adacon replied.

"So did I. It's been like this for nearly ten minutes. I don't know how you managed to stay asleep," Erguile said.

"It was strange—I was in a dream talking to Krem, and he was telling me about my true quest: *our* true quest," Adacon recalled. "He was telling me that from Erol Drunne we must again return to the West to meet our final destiny, and that before the end a great tragedy will come to pass."

"Strange indeed, but I don't heed silly dreams—nor should you pay it much mind. For all we know Krem is dead, just as the dark stranger told us," Erguile coldly replied.

"Don't say that! Even Slowin says he lied!" Adacon replied defensively. He sulked in quiet for several moments pondering Krem's fate. "What of this storm? Have you talked with Remtall?"

"When I first woke I did. He thinks the storm will only worsen as the day goes on."

"I'll go and speak to him. Do you need help with Weakhoof?" Adacon asked before walking across the deck and into the rain again.

"She'll be alright. She's been very brave through all this. I don't think she much approves of sailing though," he chuckled. Erguile returned his attention to Weakhoof as Adacon struck out into the rain toward the cabin where Slowin, Flaer, and Remtall were standing.

"Good morning Adacon, and a fine one at that, eh?" Remtall greeted. The others turned to say hello.

"This weather is awful, and Erguile said we should expect it to last?" Adacon probed.

"As sure as I am a gnome we should expect more. And I think we will be delayed a day or two if these winds stay easterly," answered the captain. Though the gnome had not slept in the past few days he seemed oddly rejuvenated, and Adacon marveled at his vigor. Flaer returned to the sea-chart he had been poring over, examining their course. Slowin asked how Erguile was dealing with the waves.

"Surprisingly well I'll say, compared to the other day. What's more surprising is how well Weakhoof is handling the weather," Adacon answered.

"There is more to that steed than meets the eye," Slowin replied. "Help yourself to some tea, and there's something to eat over there."

"Thanks."

Remtall and Slowin joined Flaer in his study of the chart. Adacon surveyed the horizon in all directions, seeing nothing but thick grey clouds and occasional flashes of lightning. The rain had lightened since he first woke, but it seemed colder, and Adacon longed for a place that was warm and dry. The steady pour of drops increased again while Adacon fetched his cup of tea, and got a second for Erguile. Returning to Weakhoof's tarp, Erguile thanked him heartily for the hot brew.

"Should do me well, I didn't get much sleep last night," said Erguile.

"Maybe you'll get rest this afternoon if the weather breaks and the air warms."

"Perhaps. I am weary though. Much like your dream with Krem I had a dream, but with a darker note—mind you I pay dreams no mind, but they linger when dark: the phantom ship had come back, and it sieged our vessel. And just as death came I envisioned Karabden rising from the sea, coming to swallow us all in its thousand-teethed mouth." Erguile trembled as he relayed his nightmare.

"I'd tell you your own advice again—as you pay my dream no mind, do the same for yours. We truly are safe as long as Remtall keeps his wits."

"That's another thing—sometimes I doubt that little man's composure. He's always drinking liquor at the oddest hours of the day, never sleeping. I wonder how long he can keep it up."

"I guess we can't worry about it until the time comes, can we?"

"I suppose you're right…"

As the two slaves finished their conversation, the loudest clap of thunder either had ever heard sounded. Adacon looked upon the eastern sky for the source to the noise; there he witnessed a sight that shocked him more deeply than anything he'd so far seen on their journey: cutting down from the heavens, a league in front of the Blockade Runner, was an enormous lightning bolt, impossibly thick and bright—and rather than dissipating in a flash, the bolt drilled down into the ocean ceaselessly. Through the grey and rain it was perfectly visible; the two slaves stood as if paralyzed, witnessing the writhing light that seemed to thicken. Just then a clap of thunder came again; the noise did not fade but lasted, growing louder, just as the bolt of lightning that lit the sky in the distance. The slaves covered their ears in response to pain, as the thunderous note sustained, unwaning, increasing. With his ears covered, Adacon felt pain vibrating deep into his skull. The thunder loudened in furious spats. Erguile saw Weakhoof begin to panic; he frantically tried to calm the wild horse, but the noise was too much for the old stallion to bear. He broke from his post and began to gallop wildly about the deck in panic. Erguile gave chase, releasing his hands from his ears and allowing the pain of the thunderous noise to throb deep into his brain.

"Erguile don't!" Adacon tried to yell, but his shout was useless amidst the terrible volume. He turned his glance to the cabin and saw Flaer and Slowin both covering their ears, staring out at the terrible apparition in the sky; they stood motionless, awestruck by the force of light and sound. Adacon suddenly jerked into action, seeing Erguile struggling with Weakhoof, who was attempting to throw himself from the portside bow.

Looking at the lightning bolt once more, it seemed to be growing wider at a faster rate—it had sprouted branching rays from its stem, and before being blinded Adacon took hold of a sight that disturbed him most deeply—though he couldn't be completely sure, he thought he was seeing ice rocks; giant chunks of white bobbing in the water near the spot where the bolt funneled into the ocean. Adacon momentarily forgot his pursuit of Erguile as he stood in shock, watching a floor of ship-sized mats of ice spread rapidly in every direction away from the lightning, covering the sea underneath. The tendrils that forked out from the main bolt began to grow erratic and far-reaching; it seemed that it would not be long before a league-long tentacle would reach out and scorch the tiny schooner where it fought the violent swells. Adacon remembered his urgency and looked to Erguile, who was still trying with all his power to keep Weakhoof from jumping into the sea.

Speech was useless against the piercing thunder, so he didn't try to communicate once he reached them; he only gripped the horse's mane to keep it from going overboard. Both slaves were losing strength, and Weakhoof readied to finally break free; the pain of the noise had strengthened such that it was too much to bear. The horse stopped struggling. Adacon and Erguile both looked at him, wondering why she no longer fought: Weakhoof was looking calmly at the lightning bolt, as if she had suddenly been petrified by it. Adacon traced the horse's stare and saw what had transfixed it—there in the distance where the ice-floor spread toward them, undulating from its pulsating center, a great wall of ocean rose, tall as half the height of the lightning. Adacon froze, realizing that the ice was in fact no wall; it was a wave, driving toward them, devouring the grey of the horizon. The great mountain wave powered on toward the helpless Blockade Runner; it grew higher with each passing second, taking more of the sky for its own. Adacon could no longer see the bolt of lightning, only the rolling wave that drove to cover the whole horizon in white bergs. Adacon and Erguile looked at each other, farewell in their eyes, then back again to their final vision. The schooner rocked and rolled, somehow remaining afloat; it was a surprise of luck that the ship had not yet flipped from the turbulence, or had a lightning tendril reach out and take it.

In a final moment of acceptance, as ice crystals showered his face from the sky-destroying wave overhead, Adacon looked about the ship; time was dilated by some strange force, and he took it as a chance to be comforted by the sight of his friends one last time before they shared in death. Flaer and Slowin had not moved in the slightest since last he saw them; they stood helplessly staring, the same as Weakhoof, awestruck by the fury that had so suddenly thwarted their quest. The next moment came, the wave finally ready to overtake them, and Adacon caught a most startling image—Remtall stood against the starboard rail, calmly smoking his pipe, shielding his tobacco from the downpouring ice crystals, smiling; then the gnome winked at him. Adacon decided the sight an illusion, and being filled with powerlessness he turned at last to meet his fate. The mountain-high wave of icebergs crashed, drowning everything in white, and the numbing chill of death forsook the crew of the Blockade Runner.

*　　　　　*　　　　　*

Adacon opened his eyes and began to rub his head. An awful pain coursed through his temples.

"Terrible dream," he said to himself. He recalled a terrifying storm where a lightning bolt had stayed in the sky, thunder had roared unwaning, and a wave of ice and light destroyed the Blockade Runner. Slowly he rose, his senses unclouding, and he looked around: he was no longer on the Blockade Runner; all about was endless ocean and a scorching sun, half-risen in the center of the sky. Adacon realized himself to be in some kind of translucent boat; in shock he saw the ocean through the floor where he lay. Frantically he rubbed his eyes to be sure of what he saw. The sight remained the same, and around him hugged the rim of a tiny vessel that he could see through. At the opposite end sat Remtall, looking away toward the eastern horizon.

"Remtall!" Adacon squealed, forsaking his grogginess.

"Morning," Remtall replied. The gnome turned to face Adacon, pipe in hand, lighting his tobacco.

"Where are we?" Adacon said, standing up to survey their surroundings, looking at the half-invisible boat that was separating him and the gnome from the depths of the sea.

"I expect we are fifteen leagues from the Fang Shoals, dear boy."

"What happened? The storm from my dream was real?"

"But of course. I'd just as soon have stayed on the schooner had it not been sundered by that damned magic." Remtall spoke without apprehension, as if it had happened long ago.

"What about the boat—the others?"

"Calm down some, boy. We are three days from land."

"Three days?"

"Yes, and you have slept two long months as we drifted across the Kalm. Give yourself time to settle into the waking life once more."

"I don't understand."

"It's alright to not understand, boy. It was a terrible thing—that cursed bolt. Only thrice have I seen worse things come upon a ship at sea."

"Are the others dead?"

"I cannot know for sure, but we are truly lucky to have been saved," Remtall said, puffing continuously. He was sitting near a small store of food and drink, piled by the front of the boat. "Vesleathren must have come to know of our quest, for I know no other conjurer capable of such a spell. Lucky for us, the phantom ship had been trailing us—in fact, it trails us still..." he explained. Adacon glanced behind but saw nothing but blue sky and gentle water; then suddenly a flicker of color appeared, the outline of a hulking ship of old, grand next to their own small boat. As soon as Adacon saw its outline, the phantom ship disappeared, and there was again nothing there.

"I can't believe it—and what about this boat, it appears to be made of air," Adacon said, staring at their transparent floor, flickering in and out of existence, at times seeming like nothing was keeping Remtall and Adacon afloat.

"After the wave came down, they preserved us in a net of magic—phantom magic—but they could not protect the others, or our poor ship, for the storm came too quickly," Remtall told. "There is some hope that they survived, though my heart warns me against such romantic thoughts; you see, a month ago, as you slept, Yarnhoot paid us a visit. In his beak he held a parchment—from Krem the Vapour."

"Krem!" Adacon gasped.

"The same who first journeyed with Erguile and you from the Solun Desert into the Vashnod Plains. Here—read for yourself and find what hope may be afforded by it," Remtall said. He fetched a yellowed scroll from one of the bags at his side, unrolled it and handed it to Adacon. He read the handwritten ink on the parchment:

'Dear travelers,

I must write vaguely, for as much as I trust Yarnhoot's hardihood, recent news has made it clear that this letter may never reach you, and I must account for the chance it will fall into their hands.

Know that the hermit of Molto's Keep lives, and goes about aiding you in ways unseen. Sorry I am for the abrupt departure, A. and E., but a severe matter darkened our world—such that it grew blacker than I could have foreseen. You know this now, I am sure.

Know also that phantoms trail you, keeping watch for your safety. They repay a favor of old. Be not saddened either, for my magic is with the rest. Press on, brave journeyers, and seek your destination still. Farewell.

Sincerely,
~Solun Hermit'

"I must be the abbreviated A, and Erguile the E," Adacon realized, regaining spirit.

"When he writes *be not saddened*, I take him to mean the loss of Slowin, Flaer, and Erguile," Remtall responded.

"Yes, it must be," Adacon replied, overjoyed. "And Weakhoof as well, let's hope."

"It won't be long before we pass through the Fang Shoals and reach Erol Drunne. In the meantime, we must think of some great thanks to pay the phantoms for keeping us alive."

"Have they been with us since the storm?"

"They have," Remtall answered, taking a drink from his flask. "Since the moment they set us to sea in this boat, they have watched us, keeping us with food from the wrecked schooner."

"Then I will attempt to repay them in what way I can once we arrive."

"Try as we might, part of me thinks they will disappear as soon as they have guided us as far as Krem asked them to," Remtall guessed.

"Either way, we remain in their debt," Adacon said, and he turned to the phantom ship behind them but saw nothing; he waved with glee at the blank sky.

"It is perhaps through some magic of theirs that you were sustained through your sleep," Remtall said. "For as I tried to force feed you, you would never take what I gave, save for some rum I managed to drizzle past your teeth." He cracked a wry smile.

"The debt I owe for being kept alive—be it to Krem, the phantoms, or Gaigas—I will try to repay somehow," Adacon proclaimed. Remtall ignored him and set about making a small meal of stale bread and dried meat.

The two sat under the hot sun, drifting atop the half-invisible floor, eating and discussing their fate.

"Should we still fear the Fang Shoals with the phantoms aiding us?" Adacon asked in between bites.

"We do not need to fear the shoals themselves, as this dinghy seems to glide above the water. We might take her into the surf and onto the sand if we needed to. But Karabden is a different story," Remtall muttered.

"Does it lurk in the waters we head toward?" Fear trickled into the back of Adacon's consciousness.

"I have been told as much by all the captains of the sea I ever knew. I know that if maneuvered right, the whirlpool of Karabden can be wholly avoided. I have also heard that the maneuvering needed to avoid her is a tremendous feat, even for a sea-gnome," Remtall explained.

"But it's the phantoms who move our ship, isn't it?"

"It is boy; this vessel has no sails, as you know, nor any oars or rudders," Remtall replied. "Relax—you think too much already, and you've only just got up. Enjoy the peace of the Kalm, for we are upon the shoals in two days time."

"You want me to rest after I've been resting for two months? You're right though, there's nothing I can do. Why did I sleep so long?"

"As I remember it, a great brick of ice clipped your head, just before that net of the phantoms formed. Lucky you survived at all, I think." They had their fill of bread and meat, and then the gnome and human stretched out to find as much comfort as possible on the tiny boat floor. Remtall erected a tarp he had made from one of their food sacks, shielding them from the scorching rays of sun.

"And Remtall," Adacon said.

"Yes?"

"You looked so calm, I remember, just before the wave hit us. You were even smoking your pipe still…"

"As I said before boy, I have thrice seen worser things come upon my ship at sea, and thrice have I survived. A gnome knows his end when it nears, and I knew that wasn't it. Enough about that forsaken storm—let us talk of women, boy, and the ones you'll soon meet when we come ashore," Remtall said, changing the topic. Adacon laughed, sighed, and lay down under the makeshift canopy. Remtall began a long treatise on how to properly treat, and seduce, a lady.

The next two days passed slowly, and the waters of the Kalm Ocean remained friendly to the phantom dinghy. Adacon and Remtall talked much, and when they weren't talking about women the conversation would turn to Remtall's son. Adacon relayed all that he could remember about his friend, and considering that Remtall, the son, had taken action against the tyranny of Grelion first, Adacon credited him as the true starter of the rebellion. Remtall drank and listened, smoking occasionally, and when Adacon's turn for story ended, the gnome told endless tales of the great gnomen fleet he once commanded. He detailed the service he had rendered to Commander Grelion Rakewinter in times before the name bore ill omens. It had been more than a half century since the Five Country War came to pass, and Remtall spoke of it as if it had happened yesterday; he told of great naval battles, and of the final blast that ended the war. He offered a shocking new truth about the Five Country War—Flaer Ironhand himself had commanded an army, alongside a great king of the south, and in the final hours before the end of the war, Flaer himself had dueled against Vesleathren.

"Flaer dueled with Vesleathren?" Adacon repeated in surprise.

"Sure as I drink ale, boy, he did—and that is how he came to possess the Brigun Autilus," Remtall replied.

"The Brigun Autilus was Vesleathren's sword?"

"Yes—you might see his traces when it glows, speaks, or conjures other sources of devilry unknown to me," attested Remtall.

"I wonder why there was so little protection over the sword—Slowin took it from the tower so easily; he didn't break a sweat."

"Hahaugh!" Remtall laughed heartily. "A metal golem sweating!" He violently coughed at the image, choked some, then finally resettled. "I cannot say why Grelion took so little care in keeping it safe; I daresay he did not know the full power of that sword, nor its origins."

"How old is Flaer?"

"Much older than me, young boy. And *I* am much older than any ordinary man could hope to live," Remtall replied. "A great and ancient enchantment courses through his veins, though he will not speak of it. It keeps him young and fertile—but it is a curse, for he is doomed to live longer than even elves."

"Elves? Tell me about them," Adacon begged.

"Now is not the time," he replied, turning his head sharply to watch the crash of a soft wave against the transparent hull. In the distance ahead, waves churned in a circular motion. Though they foamed violently, they were still far off. Adacon could make out the frothy lips of the rough water, crashing on top of itself as it spun in a wide circumference.

"Is that..."

"Karabden."

Remtall shot a glance back at the phantom ship that trailed them, but he saw nothing flicker or appear. He returned his gaze to the whirlpool that already drew them steadily toward its center.

"Looks like this one is going to be all us, boy—I fear the phantoms have finished their task and left us," Remtall said.

"What can we do?"

"Not much more than hold on." Remtall rummaged through one of the bags at his side and pulled out what looked to be two tiny pans with long handles. "No time to talk boy," Remtall said as he put the two pans into Adacon's hands.

"I've never rowed—" Adacon said as he stuck the make-shift oars into the water. "They're too small. . ."

"Never mind how small they are—keep us south, row that way," Remtall instructed, pointing for him. Adacon began to row, and the waves circling in the distance grew closer, larger; soon the white fury of a mid-ocean surf was rocking the small phantom boat.

"It's too strong, it's pulling us in!" Adacon said, struggling against the tow of the whirlpool. Rowing as hard as he could in the opposite direction seemed to only speed them toward their doom. He could do nothing as the boat entered the waves at the rim of the spinning surf; soon the boat was lost in the ferocious grip of the spiraling waters. White foamy water splashed over the boat, its speed increased, and Adacon gave up rowing; he looked to Remtall for help.

"What are we going to do?" Adacon barked over the thundering crashes of the Karabden's whirlpool. The boat bobbed up and down atop the gyrating surf—the churning suction throttled the boat, slamming Adacon and Remtall to the floor. The whirling vortex spun them round, dizzying them, drawing them closer to what appeared to be a depressed center of blackness: Karabden.

"Nothing we can do—except hope the phantoms didn't bring us this far to let us die now," Remtall answered as the boat rode the roaring foam in ever-quickening circles.

"I see the phantom ship! It's sailing away!" Adacon cried. When Remtall turned to his side he saw the same sight: the great phantom ship had set a course westward, abandoning them; its stern flickered out, several hundred yards away.

"Blasted Phantoms! Ghosts of devilry and half-valor!" cursed Remtall as he realized their new fate. The boat now traveled the circumference of the whirlpool every thirty seconds, losing time with each pass. The black center grew large before them.

"Look!" Adacon grabbed Remtall, still furiously cursing the phantoms, and forced him to look upon the center of the whirlpool. Together they watched the dark eye of Karabden: from its abyssal heart rose a scaled head, followed by a serpentine body the color of coal, glistening under the glare of midday. The serpent's eyes were pure white; it had no irises. It rose twenty yards into the sky before opening its jaw; it whined a great piercing howl down at its victims. The creature's tongue slithered from its gaping mouth; its tongue was forked, gliding over a jawline set with thousands of crooked-hook teeth, jutting out to either side. From the Karabden's scaled worm-body protruded a mane of thorns running down its back, ornamented with rows of sickle spikes. A high-pitched scream emitted from the beast; suddenly the glistening serpent was diving straight down, its mouth poised to swallow Adacon and Remtall whole. Karabden's jaw engulfed the entire boat just as Remtall pushed Adacon overboard and jumped himself into the white foam. The serpent lurked under the water. Adacon looked at Remtall as they struggled to stay afloat in the surf. The black center drew them in.

"I'm glad to have met you, boy—a fine pleasure to share your company—now let us meet our deaths with the honor we meant to have in life," Remtall said, dipping underneath the waves and taking a gulp of water, only to cough it up. Adacon didn't know how to reply; he felt scared of death for the first time since his journey began. Even the ever-brave Remtall had resolved to give up, and all hope was lost.

"Yarnhoot!" Adacon shouted with the enthusiasm of witnessing a miracle. "And another bird's with him!" Remtall struggled to look up; he saw diving toward them his giant condor, Yarnhoot, and its mate. Karabden resurfaced next to Adacon; the giant serpent wasted no time rising into the sky to screech before attacking: it rose only to eye-level with Adacon. Karabden opened its jaws wide. Inside the serpent's mouth row after row of hooked fangs gleamed. The giant sea monster made its fatal strike.

"Here!" Remtall shouted from the heavens. As Karabden's jaws pounced forward, Adacon looked up to see a hand hanging from the sky. "Hold fast friend!" Remtall exclaimed. Adacon grabbed on to his hand just in time to avoid the lightning strike of the serpent. Crashing into the waters with an empty mouth, Karabden rose quickly, angered, striking ferociously into the sky; its black body shot straight at Yarnhoot, who somehow held

Remtall and Adacon by its talons. The other condor flew underneath Adacon as he slipped free from Remtall's grip; Adacon plopped squarely onto the back of Yarnhoot's friend, who ascended immediately. Karabden bore his strike down upon Yarnhoot; the powerful bird had been unable to gain enough altitude to escape the length of the uncoiled serpent. Remtall looked down and saw the whole of the whirlpool: from its center the black slimy length of Karabden had jumped, racing through air to swallow the great condor. The serpent lunged in a final effort to eat both bird and gnome in a single gulp.

Remtall railed against the sky, cursing the cruel irony of their near escape. As if in response to the gnome's final cry, Yarnhoot's companion swooped in, gouging out the left eye of Karabden in mid-strike. Milky white pus streamed forth as Karabden once more emitted a piercing scream, so loud that vibrations knocked Remtall's green hat from his head; it twirled in flight to its doom below in the swirling waters. The condor loosened its talons from Karabden's face, and the monster shrieked all the way down to the dark sea beneath the vortex. Remtall rejoiced, as did Adacon, and they exchanged weary smiles from atop their condors. The great birds flew in close to one another; Adacon's condor bore his human weight as gracefully as Yarnhoot bore the gnome's.

"Adacon, meet Wester," Remtall introduced Adacon to Yarnhoot's mate.

"Pleased to meet you, Wester," Adacon squealed, and he smiled in relief, petting Wester's neck. "And it's very nice to see you again too, Yarnhoot." Adacon glanced back over to Yarnhoot, who carried Remtall. Just then the two great condors let out a song of happiness, chirping sweetly, as the mellow air of the Kalm returned with a cool breeze.

"To Erol Drunne!" Remtall exclaimed, and the birds turned to fly east, and soon, much to the delight of Adacon, there were small grey and green bumps in the distant horizon, and together, gnome and slave shouted: "Land!"

The Country of Enoa spread out below Yarnhoot and Wester as the two great condors glided on a strong westerly wind that took them over a dotted white shore. Adacon looked back at the ocean behind him, and with relief he thanked Gaigas for having come across the Kalm safely. Remtall stared straight ahead and took in the beautiful scenery of the Enoan landscape: the beach led to dense groves of broad-leafed trees, which multiplied into a vast jungle of luscious emerald shades and dewy canopies atop which many foreign birds were making happy song. All beneath the condors sprawled the blanket of living vegetation, through which no floor of soil could be seen. The birds flew higher above the jungle, and deep in the distance Adacon saw blue-grey mountains looming like luminous needles in the sky. The weather was calm, and only a few clouds hung about either side of the travelers; the jungle stretched so far that Adacon could not see anything else, and he presumed the entire continent of Enoa to be verdant forest. After almost half an hour of flight, Adacon spotted what looked like a break in thick canopy, up and to their left. The birds redirected their flight toward the clearing he had seen, and soon Adacon made out what appeared to be a cloistered collection of vinethatched buildings, built from the bowels of trees that stood within the bare spot of low-grassed earth.

"What's that there?" Adacon shouted as Wester flew in close to Yarnhoot's side.

"I believe that's the post of Carbal Run, farthest civilized point from Erol Drunne," answered Remtall.

"Are we going to land there?"

"I should hope so—these birds have flown across the sea, aided by what force I cannot say; and though they are still strong in their wing stroke, they need rest."

The condors descended swiftly upon the secluded post, tucked in a circle of thick jungle wall. As the birds came within several yards of being level with the tree canopy, Adacon felt a fine spray envelop him.

"What in Darkin!" Adacon exclaimed as the birds dipped beneath the highest layer of trees; the fine mist seemed to dance all about them: tiny shimmering droplets that hung in the air, reflecting light spontaneously as if a spray of radiant stars. "What a curious place!"

"I've only been to this jungle once before in my life, and I was just a child then, but I do remember the mist; one always remembers the mist. It hangs about the air year round, giving vitality to the lush greenery that is so plentiful here," Remtall recalled. "Ah, I can't wait for a drink of elven ale…"

"Elven?" cried Adacon in childish excitement. "How I have longed to meet elves, and hoped that they were not only fable!"

"Hah—wait till you meet some elvish women, boy," Remtall chuckled as the condors descended lower and lower until finally there was nothing surrounding them but the girth of enormous trunks. The birds set their talons to rest on the earth near one of the thatched buildings that jutted as if a carving from a massive trunk, the body of an especially mossy jungle tree. The elf buildings were constructed of branches and leaves that seemed still attached to the trees themselves, alive; each house possessed vertical hallways, passing through wooden floors every ten yards or more, progressively higher, directly toward the sky, eventually terminating somewhere in the mesh of canopy above. Misshapen windows of amber-colored glass speckled the houses, and through the nearest one Adacon saw many faint glints sparkling, candles perhaps, producing on the amber glass fractals upon which the dew seemed to clump and respond, as if alive. Despite the mist, Adacon noticed it did not feel humid, much as a hot day at the farm would feel, and he could breathe as easily as ever. Yarnhoot and Wester unloaded their passengers, and soon the two birds were stepping together toward a nearby babbling stream that cut through the heart of the village.

"I've never seen so much green in my life," said Adacon, stunned by the colorful vegetation that sprouted round the bases of the elven houses; flowers and plants danced amidst the floating droplets: deep crimson; bright purple; magenta; sapphire; pink and orange. Erect in front of the house closest to them was a wall of scarlet flowers, bent with dew in the cool midday air. Next Adacon noticed the noises; all around he heard not only chirping, squawking and squeaking animals, but songs: melodies emanated from the houses. From a distance, Adacon made out foreign chatter which he guessed to be elven speech.

"Music—it's beautiful—twice before I experienced it, but never this sweet," Adacon rejoiced. Remtall turned to him and smiled; sighing he released his waterproof pipe-satchel from his side, inspecting for damage.

"Good thing we've made it to the post," Remtall uttered. A stranger, tall and lightly clothed, came out of the nearby brush.

"Because it is elven?" asked Adacon, alarmed by the sight of the figure who strode toward them.

"Because Enoa has few peoples that would care to harbor man and gnome in peace—and you seem to have lost all your weapons to the sea," interrupted a booming voice, accented, deep and gravelly. Surprised, Adacon and Remtall looked to the stranger from whom the words had come. "We are pleased to welcome you to our fertile home, distant travelers."

"Indeed as much as we are pleased to be on dry land for a spell," Remtall eagerly greeted the tall elf. Adacon stood speechless; as customary of Arkenshyr he offered his hand to be shaken. The elf took and shook Adacon's hand, and Adacon used the moment to study the elf's foreign appearance: he had leaf-color stained skin—Adacon realized with a start—as if his skin was meant to blend with the foliage. The elf wore little clothes: a thin russet tunic hung loosely, falling as low as mid-thigh. To Adacon's shock the elf was barefoot. His hair was raven black, like the whole of his irises, and his face was deeply carved from a slim symmetrical nose that ran its length equal to a scar along his cheek. His eyebrows were thin but long, and they curved a sharp point near their middle. Adacon looked to the elves ears, searching for the characteristic points as he'd seen in books: to his surprise the ears were barely pointed. Exaggerations, Adacon thought—though his ears were distinctly drawn back and away from the head, giving the illusion of a point.

"Forgive him—he was a slave, and has never seen an elf in his life, as you might have guessed," Remtall said, covering for Adacon's rudeness in having stared so long at the elf.

"Adacon, I presume," the elf said.

"Yes! How do you know my—"

"And Remtall Olter'Fane, fair captain of the gnomen fleet," the elf said, interrupting Adacon. Remtall and the elf embraced in a strong hug.

"We are greatly appreciative for your welcome here, though we've lost any offerings of gratitude to the Kalm, as you may already surmise," Remtall said. He gripped up his flask and took a celebratory drink.

"Forget excessive pleasantries, as Krem the Vapour has enlightened the elves of Carbal Run to your task and purpose. And know that we, the jungle elves of Carbal, embark astride the task of sustaining your errand," the elf replied. "I am Iirevale of Tuhrn Falls, son of Tuhrn."

"Glad to meet you, Iirevale," piped Adacon, finally breaking his paralysis. Just then, from behind Iirevale, strode forth a young elven woman, carrying yellow-white fruit. Once again Adacon stood dumbfounded—this time more so than before; he could not believe the beauty of the elven woman: her raven hair hung long, streaked of silver light, about her supple frame; glimmering bits of gold sparkled on her skin, faintly reacting with dew-streaked rays of the sun—but even bits of gold sparkled in her eyes, he thought, as he pored at her through hanging particles of starry mist. She was as loosely dressed as the male elf, yet her body was pronouncedly different: Adacon stared at her strange curves, running from her muscled thigh to where they climbed the arch of her lower back; her shaped chest drew him from there, and led him to her serene face, more elegant than any Adacon had ever seen. Her nose was like the man-elf's, a smaller version thereof, more slender, rolling down to stop before pink lips.

"A bit unrefined, this boy—pardon him," Remtall chuckled, noting Adacon's odd manner of staring at the elven woman's body. "Was a slave of Grelion's, my dear—forgive his wandering eyes." The elven woman stood next to Iirevale and returned Adacon's crippled gaze.

"Welcome to Carbal Run, freed slave of the west," the woman placidly greeted Adacon with an accent like Iirevale's, but more refined, nurturing.

"And…" Adacon tried to respond, slipping off momentarily before regaining his composure, "and you too, sweet lady." Adacon struggled to recall the courtesies Remtall had taught him to use in the company of women.

"You will find your stay here enjoyable I hope, though it is much different than your home country," the elvish woman said. "I am Calan of Tuhrn Falls." Adacon extended his hand as he had with Iirevale; Calan shook it, but Iirevale laughed, and Remtall burst out as well, looking up for a moment from his flask.

"Have I done something?"

"No," Iirevale replied. "It is just in the difference of customs we find humor."

"What do you mean?" Adacon replied nervously, distracted by a sweet fragrance that rolled from Calan, or perhaps the fruit she carried, some mixture of dew and sugar.

"Carbal elves embrace in meeting, while men of your country are formal and shake hands," Iirevale explained.

"Elves hug, Adacon," Remtall filled in. Suddenly, seemingly unprovoked, Remtall fell over; his small frame collapsed hard onto the grass. The elves watched in bewilderment; Adacon cringed. "Pay me no mind, it's just the liquor," the gnome immediately reassured. All of them laughed, and suddenly Calan promptly hugged Adacon to put him at ease, as he appeared tense, as if he had done something egregious by shaking hands. As she touched him, her warmth flowed through him, and he was made to feel as water; wobbliness momentarily overtook him, and he thought he might follow Remtall to the earth, but as quickly as the warmth came, it disappeared, and she released her embrace.

"Though we wish to keep your presence and honor it with greetings and celebration, your task does not allow it—the Feral

Brood march south from the North Country, and already at the border is war," Iirevale grimly proclaimed.

"War, already? And here?" roared Remtall, reinvigorated, bouncing up from the ground where he had been lying with his flask.

"Sadly; it is Enoa's greatest city, Erol Drunne, that the Feral Brood ravages this dark hour," Iirevale said. "None dare enter that fair city—not before the front is pushed back, and the Enoan road made passable once more."

"But how goes it at the border then?" Remtall railed.

"As you know, our jungles stretch many miles north, and cover hills and mountains alike. Where the great Teeth Cliffs meet the border of our country, a great army of Feral Brood has forsaken our peaceful land. Even across the ocean in your homeland, Vesleathren's forces march down through the Angelyn pass, once again, as they did nigh a century ago," Iirevale said. "This time, I'm afraid Vesleathren has managed war on both sides of Darkin."

"What about our friends? Have you heard news of anyone coming across the Kalm besides us?" Adacon asked.

"I am afraid not, young human. The great Vapour, known to you as Krem, sent word that we should be expecting you and your friend—no others were mentioned."

"Was Krem here?" Adacon asked, brimming with hope of more information about his magical friend.

"No. A message he sent us through the tongues of the birds of Carbal," Iirevale replied, and Adacon's worry over his missing friends renewed.

"How goes the front then?" Remtall demanded, impatient with the elf.

"It is not good, friend Remtall," Iirevale solemnly proclaimed. "We were unprepared for a war; we have lived in peace too many springs—even the corrosion of Grelion had not darkened our fair country, so far from his oppression are we. Very last of our concerns here has been Vesleathren, whom we thought to be long dead. The Feral came upon us without warning, and sacked our northernmost city Therenglade. From there they took south the Enoan Route, our greatest road, which runs the entire length of Enoa. Since the invasion several days ago, they have hastily advanced. Twice we tried to waylay them, but were forced to retreat."

"To try and waylay them without Remtall Olter'Fane, high captain of the gnomen Fleet?—there was your mistake; but no more! Let's be on to them! To the front!" roared Remtall with a fiery passion, and he drank again from his flask with restored thirst.

"The Feral Brood is heavily armored, heavily armed, magically veined. We have not numbers to counter them: even as free men of our country unite with elves, and dwarves of the eastern ranges, we may not stand up to this great force," Iirevale foreboded.

"And what then? What are your plans, pitiable elf? Will you flee to the South? To the beaches of the Persh Wale, so that you may fly from worldly sorrow? We march north—for it is the only task left us," Remtall fired, and suddenly, several nearby elves came to take notice of the hostile gnome.

"It was our intent, Remtall, to do just that. The beaches of the Persh would provide a haven—but as I said, Krem has contacted us and asked a favor. Be it that we owe him more than is repayable, we honor his demand. It is our task to find safe passage for you to the near front, the Wall of Dinbell, past the great Dwarven city of Oreine. It is there where Enoa's greatest convergence of hope shall form into an army against evil—the last chance to slow the invasion."

"Iirevale—when do you leave?" Calan suddenly spoke up.

"Morrow morn, dear sister."

"Who will go?" she asked, looking to Adacon distractedly. Adacon looked back vacantly; though he was enamored of her, the grim news of war had shadowed his heart.

"All who muster the courage to do so," Iirevale answered.

"Then I will go, and help in the ways I can," she replied.

"I cannot stop you, nor can I change your mind—but know that the road is perilous, the destination more so."

"I understand," she answered.

"Good. See that our guests are given warm food, and rest. I believe this friend would like some elven ale, so that his vile drop of the West can be discarded..." Iirevale said, finally drawing a smile again. Remtall winked in agreeance. "Be comforted friends; you have in Carbal Post found one more night of rest, before marching north, through all veils of safety. . ."

"I would prefer to leave now—but I suppose a rest would do us well—restock the nerves," Remtall decided reluctantly.

"Iirevale..." Adacon spoke up as Iirevale departed.

"Yes?"

"We lost all our weapons and armor at sea. What will—"

"Your new weapons and armor shall be ready for you in the morning. Now follow Calan and feast. Enjoy the comfort of safety while you may." At that moment Iirevale left toward a corner of the small village where two houses twined together into a giant trunk. Calan led Remtall and Adacon toward the floor of tubular house that ran high into the trees.

"We will have a delicious meal—have either of you tasted elven food before?" asked Calan.

"I've had more than elven food!" Remtall exploded, thoroughly embarrassing Adacon.

"Excuse him, he is drunk—too much at times," Adacon said, trying to excuse the gnome's belligerence without offending him.

"He's right, excuse my tongue fair dryad. It's been a trying journey, and I long for your elven drop."

They followed Calan into the leaf-fringed houses; inside Adacon took a moment to look around: It seemed everything in and around the house was built of living plants—some small and round, some ropy and vine-like, and some very strong, flat and broad. Small tables made of yellow wood centered the room, low to the ground, and intricate sculptures and engravings lined the walls: the carvings appeared to be of weapons, armor, elven symbols, and flora. Small birds and small furry beasts inhabited the house; they went about their business unobtrusively. Soon Calan led Remtall and Adacon to the foot of a vertical hall. Looking up through the mist-clumped air, Adacon could see no summit to the ladder that ran interminably canopy-ward. They stood encased in broad leathery leaves, dressed with dew, preparing to embark up the sky tunnel: Calan climbed first, and fast, showing deft familiarity; Adacon followed, smooth in his own right; Remtall climbed last, clumsily. Sweet greenery ensconced them as they beat up past floor after floor, witnesses to a deluge of colors and mist.

Before long they arrived at a small platform that had an outcrop, and the three took a short rest before continuing higher. Adacon peered out from the ledge, over broad leaves, and already he guessed that they were a hundred yards up. A shudder traced from his spine through to his fingers, and he stepped back.

"Beautiful!" he exclaimed in between gasps for air. Remtall didn't bother to say anything; he panted meekly, concealing the effort it took him to catch his breath.

"Look there, in the distance: the Pouring Fountain of Granwyn," Calan pointed out. Adacon strained his eyes, peering deep into the distance; his eyes glanced over the encampment, then farther into the jungle, unable to catch sight of a fountain. Finally he saw a bubbling stream near where Calan had pointed, and Adacon stuck out his finger at it.

"Is that it?" he asked.

"No, here," Calan responded, and she touched his hand and guided the tip of his finger to the fountain which lay hidden between two small groves amidst tall shoots of grass. Adacon felt a rush of sensation when her hand had grasped his. He beheld the Fountain of Granwyn: a starward plume of water reflected bluish-gold sparkles in its stream, glittering determinedly, dancing somehow clear against the shrouding mists that clouded the air.

"It's beautiful!" Adacon exclaimed, and suddenly he realized he was grasping her hand firmly, only to be embarrassed and pull it sharply away.

"Yes it is. I hope you will eventually have the chance to see the whole of our land, as there are a great many wonders to marvel at," Calan smiled, and she led them back to their climb, but not before looking to Remtall, still heaving for air.

"Shall we wait a little longer?" she asked.

"Pah! Never mind a gnome's wind—nor his stamina as it concerns upward thrusting; on elf, on!" Remtall barked, and finally they were all climbing up again, higher toward a nestled room, safe in the canopy of the Carbal Jungle.

IX: THE ENOAN ROAD

Remtall was the last to reach the summit atop the vertical hall. He came into a leafy room with several beds carved right out of the walls, which were actually the interior of the tree's trunk. There were several small stools and a table, along with a stove already burning with fire, a pot atop it in one corner. The shiny droplets of mist were still in the air, but inside the room were less than outside, and Remtall could see more clearly. Adacon and Calan were already fast at work preparing some kind of elven feast that Remtall had been smelled for the last leg of his climb.

"Smells like a fine supper coming, what are you making?" Remtall blurted out, trying to catch his breath without appearing winded.

"It's Miew meat, stewed with many different fruits and vegetables found here in the jungle," Calan explained.

"What is Miew?" asked Adacon, as he helped Calan withdraw utensils from a nearby wooden chest.

"A galloping rover of Carbal Jungle, an animal much like wild deer in Arkenshyr," she explained.

"It doesn't concern me what kind of meat it is, just as long as it's meat all the same. Now where to the elven ale?" Remtall said.

"Ravenous, aren't you?" joked Calan. "There." She pointed to a wooden keg in another corner of the capacious room.

"Think I'll fix a drop for myself—either of you two interested?" Remtall asked, able to breathe without trouble once more.

"No thanks," Adacon responded, and Calan simply shook her head.

They continued making the meal, with Adacon repeatedly asking what to help with as she went about it. All the while Remtall sat drinking his ale, where he had found a spot on a balcony ledge, extending out from the trunk-room's exterior, high amidst the jungle canopy. On the balcony outcrop Remtall lit his pipe, and far down below the Carbal Post seemed alive with lights and movement, shimmering hazily through the mist droplets.

"Wonder where that Yarnhoot has got off to…" Remtall said to himself, glancing back inside the room to see how the meal was coming along; he saw Adacon and Calan laughing merrily.

"Be falling in love soon enough, I expect," Remtall chuckled to himself. "Course that'll bring the boy his share of lessons." The gnome sat ponderously and continued to drink his ale, puffing on his pipe when the mood for it struck him. The smell of Miew meat grew stronger, and soon the delicious scent was calling Remtall back inside, but not before Wester unexpectedly appeared, followed by Yarnhoot. The two birds surprised Remtall, and he nearly spilled his mug of ale. Gracefully the birds affixed themselves to the carved wooden branch that served as a guardrail for the balcony, and Yarnhoot chirped.

"Good to see you too, friend," Remtall smiled. "And you, Wester." Remtall stroked their feathers graciously. "What's this?" Remtall saw a scroll in Yarnhoot's left talon. "For me?" He picked up the crunched paper and unrolled it.

"I'll be damned, another letter from Krem," Remtall exclaimed, and had Adacon heard the commotion he might have come running out to read it as well, but Calan drew his attention from the noises of the world.

'Dear Travelers,

The Feral War has begun, and our crusade against Grelion's slavery is stayed, as this greater evil now attempts once more to sack the whole of Darkin. I battle at the front, at the Wall of Dinbell, and the great armored centipedes of war known as Gazaran breach our lines. We hold their dark force at bay this day, but I cannot descry tomorrow's fortunes, not even with all my powers of Vapoury. Iirevale will guide you both, as far as he might, to meet me here at the wall. Also, Remtall—I have asked Yarnhoot and Wester to perform a task for me, I hope you won't mind.
Sincerely,
~Solun Hermit

P.S. I have sent a summoning stone. Use it once you are upon the road. An old friend of mine will bring you aid.'

"A summoning stone?" Remtall gasped. Just then Yarnhoot opened his beak, and inside was a tiny green and red marble. It was not bigger than a pebble, but the colors inside the glassy sphere swirled about, mixing then dispersing as if alive.
"Remtall, come on, it's time to eat!" Adacon called. Yarnhoot sung merrily and bowed his head to his gnomen master, and after Remtall showed approval with a nod, both condors took flight, off to perform Krem's errand. Remtall returned to the elven room carved from the jungle ceiling, feeling saddened at having

had the company of his condor friends for such a short time. Adacon and Calan laid out huge wooden bowls filled with Miew stew, elven bread, and a light honey-fruit tea native to Carbal.

"Krem has sent word again," Remtall said as he sat down.

"Just now?" Adacon cried.

"Yes, by way of Yarnhoot, and he has also asked both the condors on a mission, and so I let them go," a solemn Remtall proclaimed. He handed Adacon the letter, who quickly read it while Calan sat patiently.

"A summoning stone?" Adacon said with wonder.

"Here…" Remtall said; he held aloft in his hand the tiny green and red stone, alive as the colors swirled around inside, mixing and separating.

"What on Darkin?" exclaimed Adacon; Calan and he moved to peer close at the summoning stone. "What is a summoning stone?"

"Beautiful," gasped Calan. "I have once before seen such a stone, used by an elven druid who lived amongst the Carbal elves several years ago. Though he never used it, he claimed it could summon a giant creature of the wood—though his stone was gold and black."

"This is all too much, too much to think about before a proper meal has been eaten—let me refill my mug, and we will eat before we are consumed by such mischievous pebbles," Remtall commanded, regaining his tone of captainship.

Soon the three of them were feasting, and when they finished, seconds were served. Adacon drank heartily the honey-fruit tea that he learned was called *Ebper Froth*, a restorative blend the Carbal elves consumed often to refresh body and mind. Remtall stuck with his elven ale, and before long he was acting foolishly drunk.

"It's just a matter of time before I meet my end, and face in heroic valor a Gazaran, taking its life whilst it takes mine!" Remtall coughed, puffing quickly on his pipe.

"Remtall, gnome of Rislind, mind to our quest and its prosperous outcome alone. We do not need talk of worthless martyrdom to spoil these last hours of haven," Calan interrupted. Adacon marveled at her strength and bravery, both required when confronting the drunken gnome.

"Certainly right, my dear, and I am sorry. It is for my son my sorrow spills out, and ever is it renewed when the foul Zesm, kidnapper of my only child, aids the villain we march against," Remtall said, reclaiming his calm.

"I wonder what those centipedes of war look like, and how big they are," Adacon thought aloud.

"I have seen them before, never wearing armor though," Calan attested. "They are as tall as five elves, and have the girth of four dwarves. They do not bother us as we do not bother them; though if they are corrupted with black magic, and turned Feral, I do not guess what evil they might be capable of."

"I dread to think," Adacon replied. "Hah, look!" Calan turned to see what amused him: it was a sleeping gnome, upright in his stool, lit pipe dangling from his mouth. Suddenly Remtall toppled from his stool, where on the wooden floor he promptly began to snore. Adacon walked over to extinguish the smoldering pipe, and together he and Calan lifted the old captain onto a nearby carpet, plush enough to serve as a bed.

"Well—serves him right I guess," Adacon said.

"Does he always drink with such abandon?" Calan asked.

"He has since I have known him."

Adacon drifted off, forgetting Remtall, staring at Calan: her attire clung loosely around her fragrant body, and she appeared moist with the dew that hung about the trunk-cabin air. Her jet hair shone with silver brilliance that seemed to radiate its own light, and her deep eyes drew his attention even from her curved body.

"Adacon?" Calan spoke after an awkward pause; they had both been staring at each other.

"Sorry, I was thinking of tomorrow," Adacon lied.

"Would you come out to the balcony with me, and see the stars before sleep?"

"Sure," Adacon replied with delay. He became excited, yet sick with nervousness. He stared at her from behind as she led them out onto the balcony. On the balcony the stars glittered wildly above them, twinkling through sections of broken canopy; every few moments a shooting star trailed through the luminous night sky.

"It's beautiful," Adacon replied. "In my country, the stars aren't so visible. I can't think what to blame for it except Grelion and his destruction."

"I don't know if this will be troubling for you to answer…" Calan said.

"No, please—what?"

"Was being a slave—it must have been so awful…" she trembled. Adacon did not respond at first, and Calan felt as though she had overstepped a boundary; her face contorted with a terrible anxiousness. Instinctively Adacon touched her hand to ease her, and she looked up, startled.

"It's ok—it was awful—I never really gave it much thought until after I slew all the men that kept me there."

"I'm sorry," Calan offered. Adacon clasped her hand in his, she tightening her own grip.

"Don't be. I have come to accept it for what it was, and what it is—and now, though our journey is grim, I am much happier—just for each moment of freedom, even if the consequence is death." Calan smiled in response, and they both looked up to the starry cutouts in the canopy; from the branches surrounding them emanated subtle night songs, and it seemed all the birds of evening had come alive to sing melodies of love. The mist that hung static in the air shimmered in combat with the light of the stars, and so it appeared the forest was filled with glistening jewels, bright as the night above. Far down, at ground level, Adacon could see fires roaring, where masses of elves carried on in revelry amidst the sparkle-checkered air.

"You know, you're really the first young human I've ever met; I have met old Vapours, and most other races of Darkin as well. But there are few men in Enoa, compared to your country. It is a new experience for me," Calan expressed. Adacon thought to tell her that she was the first female he had ever met, human or otherwise, but out of embarrassment he did not; instead he leaned forward and kissed her. Calan recoiled, and Adacon looked away, feeling sorely mistaken, loosening his clutch of her hand. Suddenly she gripped his head and turned his jaw back on her, and they kissed once more under the starbrimmed heavens.

* * *

The morning came fast and with quite a start, as a great bell sounded throughout the entire post, and soon Carbal Run was alive and bustling with the coming day. Already gathered about the center of the post was a great congregation of elven men, and several elvish women. Adacon and Remtall awoke atop the jungle in their high room. Adacon thought immediately of what had transpired the night before: Calan and he had kissed, he remembered; it hadn't been a dream. Adacon looked around the room and found they were alone; she must have left after they had lain down together and he fell asleep.

"Up with the sun, boy. What, no energy of youth? Get up! Have a drink to raise your spirit," Remtall said, kicking Adacon's ribs; once stirred, Remtall filled his mug for a morning drink.

"No thanks," Adacon muttered, rubbing his eyes, slowly rising to his feet. He thought for a moment about telling Remtall what had happened, but then thought better of it, considering how unpredictable Remtall had been acting lately. Soon the gnome had polished off four mugs of the elven ale, and had somehow discovered a vial of elven sap liquor.

"This will do us well on the Enoan road," Remtall explained as he filled both his flasks up.

"Haven't you lost enough of your wits?" Adacon asked wearily.

"Never mind a gnome's wits, boy. Know that Remtall of Rislind marches north this day, to the beat of vengeance," Remtall said. After they were both awake they descended the long tree cut ladder to the jungle floor.

Adacon reached the floor of the jungle first, and through various twining plants and high grasses he rushed toward the congregation forming at the center of Carbal Run. Remtall was quick to follow in the mist-filled morning, and soon they both stood before a pooling of elves. Each man-elf wore armor that shone a deep hue of jungle bark. Two of the elves spoke while the rest listened reverently; they spoke in a foreign tongue that neither Adacon nor Remtall could understand. Adacon recognized one of speaking elves as Iirevale; the other was a much older elf, covered in long greying hair, with a thick beard protruding from his jutting chin. Calan spotted them and came to Adacon's side amidst the clamor.

"Good morn," she whispered.

"And good morn to you fair lady!" Remtall said loudly, without restraint. Suddenly the elves of the congregation turned to see who had interrupted them: the whole of the elven council brought its eyes to Remtall, who withdrew his pipe and began stuffing it with tobacco.

"Never mind a gnome when it is the first hour of the morning," Remtall instructed the staring elves. None of them turned back to Iirevale and the old elf. "Go on, back to your council." Finally the elves dismissed the rudeness of their guest, and Iirevale began to speak again with the old elf in the foreign speech of the Carbal elves.

"Remtall, you must whisper, everyone is on edge..." Calan said. Remtall winked at her, and walked off to a nearby tree trunk, plopping himself down to puff on his pipe in peace.

"What are they saying?" Adacon asked, speaking in the faintest whisper.

"Iirevale is speaking with our chieftain, Gaiberth. Word came early today that Carbal Run's sister village, Nightwink, was destroyed," Calan said with sorrow.

"But, I don't understand—the war is being fought many miles from here, in the North, I thought?"

"It is," Calan replied. "But black magic is far reaching, and it is said that Vesleathren himself is launching great ranged attacks, deep into the heart of the jungle."

"What kind of attack could span so many miles?"

"I dare not say—I only hear rumor and conjecture—but Gaiberth believes the magic to be darkfire, *Artheldrum*: a sun-shaped flame cast into the firmament that sails many leagues in the sky before finding its prey."

"That sounds horrible."

"Worse news has come today: it is being said now that Aulterion, greatest of black mages, has risen from his grave to aid Vesleathren once more."

"Krem spoke of him once—he said that Aulterion had ended the Five Country War."

"It's true. They direct all their warmongering on our continent, much as they did yours in the last Great War. We are ill prepared for this, Adacon," Calan said in despair; they touched hands for a moment, then let go.

"What is it then—what's all this business about?" Remtall said in a quieter voice. Adacon and Calan turned in surprise to the small gnome who had snuck up behind them. As Calan was about to reply, the congregation broke up; some formed into marching ranks, while others returned to their houses. Iirevale rushed over to them.

"We depart now, sooner than expected—you are thanked for your understanding," Iirevale said quickly.

"I'll gladly bring aid sooner to any cause that might bring me revenge for my son!" Remtall piped.

"I am coming," Calan said sternly.

"I cannot protest it, not at this hour, our time is too precious. Quickly, gather a sword and shield each from the store, there is no time for anything more; we march north along the Enoan road, on to the Wall of Dinbell," Iirevale commanded, and he left them for the ranks of elves that stood waiting, Gaiberth at their head.

Calan led Adacon and Remtall to a nearby hollowed trunk, wide enough to fit several men; therein was a narrow underground tunnel leading several yards underground. Inside she led them to a small room where thin elven blades and wood-shields clad the walls. They each grabbed a sword and shield, and in a hurry they returned to the elven formation just as it was about to leave. Among the elven men were several woman-elves going to war; behind the troop gathered the women and children of the village, alongside several elders too frail to travel north, all of whom were to stay behind. The elves remaining at Carbal Run wept openly at the departure of the strongest in their community. Calan said hasty goodbyes to loved ones she left behind, and Remtall and Adacon followed behind the company of elves as it began to march along a small trail cutting northeast from Carbal Run. Soon the post was out of sight behind them, and only thick droplets of mist could be seen hanging everywhere about the air, intertwined with thick jungle terrain. Many wondrous thickets of trees crowded the trail once the troop exited the jungle clearing of Carbal Run, and they marched at last into the heart of the jungle. The shrubbery and foliage was denser than anything Adacon had imagined possible, and constantly the forest seemed to be moving, making noise, breathing; every few seconds some kind of mysterious critter could be seen scurrying by, many of which were colored very strangely, with vivid stripes and spots, and Adacon couldn't place a name on any creature he saw. The trail the company followed was well carved from the jungle, though it was only four yards above them that the jungle closed in, sealing off the sky, none of which could be glimpsed; only a spectrum of green hues, the rising trunks of the canopy, sprouted with tremendous vines, branches, leaves and trunks.

"How long of a march do we face?" Adacon asked.

"Pipe down boy. Never mind the length of the march, it matters not in the scheme of things!" Remtall riled.

"Sorry—I was curious."

"Curiosity thwarts valor, young slave," Remtall chided as he drank his elven sap liquor. As does your drink, Adacon thought to say in response, but he kept his mouth shut.

"It's a week long march to the end of the jungle, and another day to the dwarven city of Oreine. The Wall of Dinbell is just a day's march beyond that," Calan said, ignoring Remtall's harassment.

"A fine journey, I might say. I hope they have brought enough food for us," Remtall said, coughing between gulps.

"We elves of the Carbal know ways to find nourishment from the forest, and there is hardly a stretch on the road where the jungle doesn't lend herself to our appetites in some way or another," Calan said.

"Are there many fruits along the way?" Adacon said excitedly.

"Certainly, a great variety of them: some delicious, some healing, some fatal."

"And what of ale on the journey?" Remtall asked, calculating that he had not brought enough now that he knew the length of their march.

"I am afraid we have not had the time to secure such a luxury for this trip, as haste has become our greatest ally now," Calan explained, winking at Adacon. Adacon smiled, and Remtall fell suddenly silent as the three marched on at the tail end of the elven troop. For many hours they continued on without any event.

Late in the day, when the golden rays of sun finally stopped lightening the shades of green above, Gaiberth brought the company to a halt. In elven speech he addressed the assembled troop, which numbered fewer than thirty.

"What's he saying?" Adacon asked.

"We make camp here tonight," Calan answered. Soon all the elves were rolling out mats of fuzzed moss that had been strung to their satchels. Adacon, Calan, and Remtall squeezed onto the end of one of the largest mats, sharing the company of several elves. Fires were started in spots along the length of the troop, running down the middle of the trail. A small meal was prepared for everyone, and to Adacon's delight, there was Miew stew again. Calan went off to speak with Iirevale, and Remtall and Adacon sat alone after their meal. The sun had nearly set, and a darkness enveloped the forest in shadow, save for the flickering illumination offered by the small fires. The flames crackled softly, harmonizing with the nightly beasts that awoke for the night to sing or chirp or squeak or hunt.

"Remtall, I long for news of the others," Adacon moaned.

"As do I, boy. But Krem made no mention of them in his letter, and I fear the worst now. But don't let it weigh you down; we still carry the mission, and our purpose has grown more important."

"I know, but I am saddened—I don't know of anything that could kill Slowin or Flaer, if only they had made it to land alive. I daresay the two of them together are invincible." Adacon smiled in fondness of the memory of his friends.

"I know, I think the same as well. Let us hope in our hearts that we meet them again, and Erguile and Weakhoof; but we cannot dwell on what has come to pass. It makes me sadder still that just as you had acquired your new weapons from the pirate stash, they were lost to the sea," Remtall grumbled. "And now we are given these flimsy elf blades."

"I think there is more to these wooden shields than meets the eye—the odor alone I have never smelled from a wood," Adacon responded.

212

"It is the smell of rotting!" roared Remtall, and one of the nearby elves eyed the gnome in disgust before returning to his own conversation. "Forget all that, and let's sleep soundly tonight." Remtall borrowed some flame from a nearby fire, and soon they had their own small fire going beside where they sat, on the edge of the trail, beyond which was interminable darkness. Adacon noticed that, strangely enough, the mist that clumped near the fire seemed unaffected by the heat and smoke. Instead it shone brightly, not being dissolved to vapor, but dancing in reflection of the leaping tendrils of flame.

"I don't like sleeping at the end of the line, so close to the darkness," Adacon said, filling with fear at the many strange noises emanating from the jungle.

"Pay those noises no mind, boy, and know that you sleep next to the most feared gnome in all of Darkin," Remtall said; strangely, Adacon felt safer. He looked up the trail in the hope of catching a glimpse of Calan, but she was nowhere to be seen. He assumed she was talking to her brother. Tired from marching all day, Remtall and Adacon both stretched out on the moss bed; they found the mats extraordinarily comfortable for things that looked so scratchy and moist.

"Good night Remtall," Adacon said, his eyes shutting with heavy fatigue.

"Night boy." The gnome sat upright a few moments longer, puffing on his pipe, before joining Adacon in the realm of dreams.

*   *   *

"Get up, both of you—quickly!" shouted Iirevale. Adacon and Remtall stirred slowly from their sleep, until Iirevale began to slap them hard. "Now!" Iirevale commanded. With much groaning, the two sleeping outlanders got up from the moss; the mat was quickly tugged from underneath them.

"What's the intention of smacking a gnome, rude elf?" stormed Remtall. Adacon looked about, sad to be awakened from a pleasant dream in which he had been cradling Calan in his arms. He noticed it was the middle of the night; the camp fires were still strong, speckling the trail with orange-yellow glow.

"In the sky!" Iirevale pointed, and then he rushed off to rouse the others. Adacon and Remtall turned to look where he had pointed: in the sky, seeable through the tree tops, the sky was ablaze with red fury; between the trees it appeared that part of the jungle behind them had become a lit furnace. Despite the late hour in which they stared, the trail behind them shone as if it were day, as if a storm of red light overtook all the path they had thus far traveled. Adacon felt a terrible heat, and his skin began to burn. A loud eruption of cracking sounded, several thunderous pops, and in the southwest a great plume of fire went up into the sky, visible by all despite the thick canopy, where an explosion had scorched from the earth a mile-wide section of jungle.

"Carbal Run!" shouted several of the elves. Calan rushed to join Adacon.

"We must move!" cried Calan, and the whole troop began suddenly marching again northeasterly, leaving the flaming jungle behind them. Adacon couldn't help but stare back at the enormous fire that transformed the sky, high above the trees, a burning sun of conflagration where Carbal Run had once been.

"Vesleathren…" Adacon wailed as the troop pressed on with their greatest speed yet.

"No—only Aulterion could conjure such a devastating force of magic," Remtall said.

"But the post—what about the families, the children?" Adacon cried. Calan could not respond; she wept openly into his arms.

"Come on," Remtall called back after they'd stopped moving for a moment. "There will be time for grieving once the head of that black wizard rolls." Calan continued to weep. Adacon stood holding her in his arms, unresponsive to Remtall's command, despite the heat that began to sear them both.

"Now, move!" Remtall roared with all the vigor of a gnomen captain, and as such he was finally heeded. Calan wept as she walked again forward, and Adacon held her, as the company of elves jogged away with increasing speed. No words came for a long time—not elf nor man nor gnome spoke. The night wore on. Soon dawn came, barely noticeable through the canopy, and slowly the weak rays transformed into morning's full blossom. Adacon thought he heard noise from the elves for the first time since they had escaped the fire; at first he dismissed it as his imagination, and he looked to Calan, whose tears ran lighter down her soft emerald cheeks. Suddenly, a mysterious tune carried through the ranks, and Adacon knew he had not been mistaken. A song of sorrow had been taken up by the troop of elves. Adacon could do nothing but listen as the song wavered and peaked, ascending ominously in the morning sky: a lullaby for the departed. The words were as if hummed to the human ear, but Adacon could tell the language was elven, though he could understand none of what was being sung. It did not matter, as the song was as beautiful as anything he'd ever heard. Soon, surprisingly, Remtall joined into the song. Though the gnome did not know the words, he appeared with a gift for music, and kept his tongue in key, adding various harmonies where he could. Even Calan began to sing with the party, and soon a great melancholy set into the forest, as the song of mourning bore its noteful fruit to the waking creatures of Carbal Jungle. Adacon was still unnerved, but he couldn't help but join in; he entered at the level of a whisper, and he knew then that all of the loved ones of Carbal Run had been lost to the *Artheldrum*.

It was nigh a week before any of the elves spoke comfortably again, and Adacon did not notice how quickly the days had passed. Since the fire explosion there had been no signs of danger, and the march had gone smooth enough. Remtall had run out of liquor, and as a result was becoming increasingly irritable. The nights passed calmly enough, and Calan had started to sleep by Adacon's side. It became known to the elven company that the two were entranced with one another. Adacon did what he could to comfort her, but it mattered little; Calan's spirit had changed. She seemed eager to battle, as much of the elven company did, and spoke of little else. Remtall and Adacon joined the company's hunger for war, feeding deeply upon a spirit of revenge. No longer did the elves simply pay a debt to Krem, and no longer did they march for anything other than vengeance. On the seventh night after the explosion, a vitality that Adacon had feared to be lost in Calan's spirit returned.

"I am sorry, Adacon," Calan whimpered, as they lay close to each other near their fire.

"It's alright. I have known loss all my life. I understand your pain, but I cannot console it," Adacon said, holding her tighter.

"We will continue on—we will overcome this great evil, it must be so. Gaigas still aids those who care for her," she said. Adacon warmed with hearing the first words of faith from her in many days.

"Yes, we will," Adacon replied, and he leaned at her; they kissed, lying twined upon the jungle floor. A loud snore startled them, echoing from Remtall who slept nearby. They laughed together; Adacon's heart rejoiced at the healing of laughter, and he felt at ease for the first time in days.

Morning overtook the troop, and a brief breakfast was prepared for the company. Remtall managed to procure additional sap liquor from one of the elves in the troop, through some secret bribe of which he would not speak, and he was in better spirits once more, though still belligerent.

"One more day of marching and we'll be out of this blasted, sweltering jungle—and good riddance to it I say," Remtall complained, drinking freshly from his refilled flask and eating a stale elven biscuit, along with a purple fruit that Iirevale had gathered from nearby brush.

"Yes. And then we go to the legendary city of Oreine," Adacon exclaimed, forgetting the sorrow of days past with renewed hope of seeing the fabled dwarven city.

"The Blue-Grey Mountains are beautiful," Calan smiled; Adacon stroked her arm.

"Quite the strange couple you two make—elf and human, an odd combination—though I must admit my wife was human. I am most proud of you Adacon," Remtall said.

"Thanks," Adacon laughed.

"Don't hold his inexperience against him, fair lady elf," Remtall replied.

"Much as I don't hold your leering eyes against you, master gnome," Calan retorted.

"Pah! Never mind a gnome's age; though you're elven, know that gnomes live almost as long as your race, and in some instances longer," he boasted.

"Well, the day I think of you as young will be the day—" Calan began; she trailed off as Iirevale rushed up to the three of them where they sat eating breakfast.

"What's wrong brother?" Calan asked.

"Our scouts have just returned—they've spotted a rogue warpede ahead on the trail," Iirevale informed.

"Warpede?" asked Adacon.

"Gazaran: the armored centipedes of war, corrupted with Feral magic. This one is without rider—it's thrashing about unchecked, eating wild boars of North Carbal, and likely us if we get too close," foreboded Iirevale.

"I'll have at it, just stay back and wait for me to clear her out," Remtall said with great seriousness, and he drank heavily of his flask before extinguishing his pipe. Suddenly, Remtall drew forth his dagger in one hand and his elven blade in the other, and leaving behind his shield, he rushed down the trail at a sprint.

"Remtall—wait!" called Iirevale, but the gnome had caught a spell of madness, and could not be stopped by words. Iirevale began to chase after him, but Remtall cut madly into the wild bush surrounding the road with an uncanny burst of speed. Iirevale stopped his pursuit and returned, unwilling to leave the company; he was saddened that Remtall had deserted, but he knew he must remain with the elves and work with Gaiberth in commanding them—for if they did dare approach the warpede, they would have to do so in a carefully orchestrated ambush.

"I am sorry Adacon," Iirevale said as he returned to them. Adacon sat still in shock.

"I can't believe it—he's run off to kill himself! What good will that do to avenge his son?" Adacon said, standing up; Calan sensed he was about to run after the gnome.

218

"I fear he's lost his wit from too much drink," Calan restrained Adacon, now ready to spring off and chase down the errant gnome.

"Then we must not wait; we have to run on and save him!" Adacon pleaded.

"We will march on, but we must first form a plan of attack; and Gaiberth ultimately commands this company—he would not have us wander recklessly to our collective doom," Iirevale replied.

"Please brother, send a party ahead to save him—there has been enough needless loss already," Calan asked.

"I am sorry, but the approach of such creatures is grave. A small party, let alone a single gnome, confronting a warpede is certain death. Even with the might of thirty Carbal elves, we must be thoughtful beyond error in our approach," Iirevale explained.

"Then nothing can be done? We forfeit his life?" Adacon cried.

"It is not my decision—it was the decision of the gnome, and the choice he made shall bring him to suffer his chosen fate," Iirevale said coldly.

"Then I cannot stay. Remtall saved my life upon the sea, and I owe him at least the same. I am sorry Calan, I must go," Adacon said. He turned and kissed her sharply; it smarted upon her lips, and then he faced Iirevale.

"Go—but know what fate awaits you alone in foreign jungles, young traveler," Iirevale said, making a last effort to deter Adacon from succumbing to the madness of Remtall's flight.

"Farewell—Gaigas let us meet again soon," Adacon grunted, and he sped away up the trail, much to the bewilderment of the company of elves who watched, patiently awaiting word from one of their commanders. Iirevale looked to Calan and knew immediately he was to lose his sister also.

"I know there is nothing you can do, but please—at least let me go unhindered," Calan said gravely. "All our family is dead." Iirevale glared at her; a dilated moment slipped by.

"You must not go!" Iirevale roared, and the others of the company quieted to witness the confrontation.

"I am gone," Calan whispered. In a flash she vanished into the brush, too fast to be grabbed. Iirevale ran after her, forgetting his better judgment and duty. The company of elves turned toward a disheartened Gaiberth, who, at once accepting the loss, began to instruct them with a course of action against the warpede.

Calan ran north as fast as her strong legs would carry her, parallel to the trail. Trying with all his strength, Iirevale could not catch her, though he ran only yards behind. She flickered in and out of vision: he caught sight of her, only to lose her again behind a bend of thickets or branches. Ahead in the distance Iirevale could hear another noise on his right, coming from the road. He glanced in that direction to witness a man running along the main trail—it was Adacon. Suddenly, Calan cut out of the dense jungle and onto the trail, alongside Adacon, surprising him, and they ran north together. Iirevale manifested a fiery burst of energy from his spirit, and cutting back onto the trail he caught up with them.

"At least let me join your miserable rank then!" Iirevale shouted. "So that we might kidnap this maddened gnome and return him to our company alive." Adacon and Calan continued running at human speed, and Iirevale took the lead.

"You know you're both mad—completely mad," Iirevale chided.

"Not as mad as Remtall, at least," Adacon said, smiling at the company of the elves. "Who'd have guessed he could run so fast?"

"I feel the quaking of the warpede," Iirevale said, and Calan nodded, though to Adacon's dull human senses nothing could be felt.

The three pressed on fast, rounding a sharp corner that led them to a vine-girded stretch of road. Adacon finally felt the vibrations; noises of thrashing, and the cracking of tree trunks echoed at them from ahead. Another bend came in the trail, circumnavigating an outcropping hill of thorns. After the road wrapped back around, the runners beheld Remtall, standing in a cleared field of splintered trees. The trail disappeared where the warpede-strewn carnage of mangled branches and felled trees buried the road—and directly in front of Remtall was an erect monster, glinting in shining gold armor: there upon its many-legged haunch stood the warpede, a *Gazaran*. It reared its head, and down its abdomen, on either side, ran a thousand-spiked row of wriggling feet. It looked to Adacon like a horrific worm, covered in armor, several yards in girth, countless yards long. The creature's face undulated with writhing mandibles of pus-ridden needles, the frightening teeth that protruded from all sides of its armored head. Remtall stayed his feet before the giant centipede's uncoiling body, and the two locked into a stare of death. The warpede dove toward the tiny gnome, mouth gaped, and several pincers seized Remtall to feed him into its jaw.

"No!" Adacon shouted, rushing forward, tackling Remtall out of the grip of the pincers; in confusion the warpede struck its armor-plated head into the earth, burying itself several feet down. All about them the jungle was destroyed, leveled by the rancor of the centipede, and a Feral slime coated the trees wherever the creature brushed against them. In a frenzy the warpede struggled to withdraw its head from the earth; Remtall broke from Adacon's grip and plunged his dagger into a slit between the beast's armor. Putrid black ooze coursed from the wound; the warpede shot up from the earth with a high-pitched squeal, again facing its attackers. The centipede launched itself high, opened its jaw, and shot down for another strike. Adacon drew his elven sword and shield; Remtall stood with a dagger in one hand and his elf blade in the other.

"Drive home to my spike, foul worm, and be glad I give a better fate than has become you!" screamed Remtall at the armored face of the creature; its body was nearly covered in golden plate mail, so that its skin revealed only at several spots. Its eyes were unguarded, and Remtall angled his blades to pierce the warpede blind.

Unexpectedly, mid-plunge, it swung around its whip-like girth, using itself as a tail, surging forward; from the sides of the warpede's frame, which erect stood thrice as tall as Adacon, barreled its legs encased in armor, needle sharp: the swipe of its body landed quick, knocking Adacon and Remtall to their feet. The centipede returned its jaw to its fallen victims and lunged again where they lay collapsed.

"Meet the jungle's own!" Calan shouted. Iirevale launched her atop the back of the warpede; as she landed on it she shoved her sword deep between two pieces of its armor. The warpede loosed a terrible whine and flailed violently, bucking Calan from its back. Remtall regained his feet, followed quickly by Adacon; not a moment was wasted as together they stuck their blades deep into the unarmored belly of the warpede. It screeched again its high-pitched cry, and suddenly the Feral beast went berserk, contorting its worm-body wildly, knocking trees down in every direction. The ancient bark cracked and fell in every direction, and Iirevale jumped, narrowly avoiding heavy debris. Calan rose from where she had fallen, ready to finish the evil beast; the warpede seemed unfazed by its leaking wounds. The warpede tempered its fury to strike at her with its right row of dagger legs; quickly she drew up her shield, just in time, and several of the centipede's legs bore through the elven wood, scratching her chest. The warpede withdrew its body, dragging Calan's shield away with it. Defenseless, she jumped behind Adacon where he held his wooden shield high. The warpede rose above them again to glare down before an assault, wiggling its gold-spike feet, dripping the black sludge of its blood upon their heads.

"Stand back!" Remtall cried, stepping in front of them as the warpede shot down, jaw wide. Adacon and Calan fell back at Remtall's push, and the Gazaran smashed directly on top of Remtall; the tiny gnome vanished from sight.

"No!" shouted Adacon. Iirevale joined them as the warpede lifted itself up, preparing for another attack; to their amazement, Remtall clung to the underbelly of the centipede. It appeared that the tiny gnome had managed to dig both his sword and dagger into the belly of the warpede between armor creases, and slowly the creature drained of its gelatinous blood; underneath, clinging, Remtall became a faucet of pus. Despite its gushing wounds, the warpede showed no signs of relinquishing its life-force; it used the girth of its plated form again, its body acting as a whip, catching everyone with great force, knocking them each to the debris-covered ground in a cloud of dust and leaves.

"I'll teach you—maggot-fiend—to tread upon my road—demon of the forest—meet the demon of the sea!" Remtall stammered, struggling to cling to the belly of the beast. Quickly he released his right arm, thrusting his dagger again and again into the belly of the warpede, dangling by his elven sword from its underside. The beast rose up on its back legs, high into the treetops, still unhurt from loss of blood. It shook violently as the tiny gnome struggled to stay on, mercilessly piercing its gut over and over, showering the fallen comrades below; finally the monster shook so violently that Remtall was thrown from a height of fifteen yards, crashing to the earth upon a pile of upheaved foliage. Grabbing his head where it throbbed, Remtall tried to open his eyes, half-consciously, but he felt overcome by a grey dimness. Calan, Adacon, and Iirevale did not move from where they lay. The warpede shot down toward its paralyzed victims; it dove at Remtall with all the power it had, intent to destroy the gnome that had stung it so many times.

Remtall surrendered—his body was ravaged; it ached from every pore—he decided that he had produced a valiant fight, one worthy of song. Suddenly a flash of clarity overtook the strengthless gnome—something flashed before his mind's eye: was it Krem? He remembered the summoning stone; with energy not his own, he reached into his pocket and removed the tiny globe, and unknowing of how to use it, threw it at the warpede blazing down on him: the stone shattered, cracking upon the armor of the warpede. A choking cloud formed instantly, suffocating smoke of red and green that erupted from the stone's point of impact on the gold armor. Out of the smoke a miraculous apparition overtook Remtall's eyes, and soon it was no longer an apparition at all but a drake emerging from colored fog: a dragon the size of two grown men. It immediately belted a blue flame in the direction of the warpede, which had recoiled away from the smoke. Shades of green and red smoke were lit blue-white by the power of the drake's fire, and the warpede began a dreadful hiss.

"Amazing," Adacon said, awakening to the sight of the drake attacking the gold-armored centipede. Soon Calan and Iirevale were up next to him, and together they rushed to Remtall, well back from the scorching flame. The drake streamed its torrent of blue flame at the centipede; the Feral beast dug its head defensively into the ground to face the brunt of the fire with its armored back. Its gold plating shone red from heat, and then became a blinding white.

"Can we help it?" Adacon shouted amidst the crackling of flame.

"No, keep back," Calan said, grabbing his shoulder.

The drake appeared in deep control of the battle, and the warpede made one last effort to defend itself, as its blood poured out from every orifice only to crisp into ash: being scorched by its molten armor, the centipede thrashed against several trees, setting them ablaze, trying in vain to break away from the dragon's assault. The drake finally relented when the warpede writhed no more. Though the smoldering pile of centipede lay unmoving, the drake strode forth and began to gut the inside of the creature with its talons; soon the drake stomped atop the centipede's armor, crumbling the once brilliant gold metal into piles of grey ash.

"Praise to Krem," Remtall said, finding new energy to stand on his feet again. The others stared at him in awe as the realization set in that they had, every one of them, somehow survived.

"Praise to Krem, Remtall—but not to you," Iirevale said in disgust.

"Iirevale—his valor was great," Calan defended her new friend, as each of them inspected their bodies for wounds.

"If reckless abandon is valor," Iirevale returned, but then went silent. He left the matter alone, deciding to be grateful that they had lived, and that a path was cleared for the rest of his company. Soon the fires of the nearby trees died out, Adacon guessed as a quality of the mist that hung everywhere, and the half-mangled four tried to clean themselves of the tarrish blood they wore. The drake, having finished its business with the centipede's carcass, walked slowly over to them. Remtall bowed to it, and the others mimicked him.

"I have never met a drake before," Calan rejoiced, "We are honored." To all of their astonishment, the drake responded:

"As am I, to have defended free creatures of Darkin; it was too long that you waited to call me—I had been waiting for you to summon me. I was eager to help," the drake said, its voice deep and slow.

"You speak!" Adacon said with glee.

"Forgive our looks of bewilderment, friend—we are not accustomed to talking drakes, or summoning stones, for that matter," Iirevale explained.

"Never mind their poor manners," Remtall joined, fishing for his pipe. The drake stood back: he was a small dragon, colored bright green, though darker shades trimmed the tips of his scales. In places his scales turned red, and eventually bright red at the end of his tale. His head was similar to the fire wyvern Adacon remembered from the swamp, only much smaller, and more cheerful in color. The drake's eyes were yellow with black irises, and its nostrils still smoked from battle.

"My name is Falen, and to the enemies of Darkin I am known as *Death Claw*. I am glad to join your war against Vesleathren, even if it means I am a world away from my home."

"We are heartened to have you with us, Falen," Iirevale smiled. He kneeled to the drake, who though small for a dragon, still towered over them.

"Truly," Calan mimicked, kneeling; Adacon knelt after her.

"You weren't quite necessary—I had already mortally wounded the beast," Remtall boasted. The exhausted gnome attempted to kneel, but wobbled and fell to the ground.

"Hah! Poor gnome, your burden is great, rest awhile," Falen replied. The group laughed at Remtall, who lay unmoving, apparently asleep, and then the drake continued to speak: "I think more of your friends approach us—I feel footsteps. Rise, all of you, and tell me your names, for I bow to you as readily as you do for me," Falen said, bowing, his voice a deep, rich timbre.

"I am Adacon."

"Calan."

"And I, Iirevale."

"And he is Remtall," Adacon said, smiling toward his sleeping friend.

The troop of elves, led by Gaiberth, filed into the thrashed clearing and took sight of the pile of ash that had been the *Gazaran*. They looked in awe at Falen and the warriors who stood dressed in black gunk. A great commotion spread through the elven rank. Gaiberth silenced his men and walked up to Iirevale and the others.

"How is it that the warpede has been destroyed?" Gaiberth asked.

"Thank Remtall and Falen for it was their valor, without which we would all be dead. The warpede was Feral. It had grown terribly strong," Iirevale told.

"My thanks then—but who is Falen?" Gaiberth said as he surveyed the sleeping Remtall.

"I, am Falen, good elf of Carbal Jungle," spoke the fire drake in a deep belly-growl.

"I am pleased to meet you then, Falen, for you are truly a friend to us, to have saved two of ours," Gaiberth said in thanks. "We are in your debt."

"Pay it no mind, and know that I am marching now alongside your warriors. I will lead your path to Dinbell, I think that is your destination," said Falen.

"Yes, it is. There we will face a great many warpedes—I can only guess that they will be as strong as this one was," Gaiberth foreboded. Suddenly Remtall roused from his slumber, and immediately he sat upright.

"They won't be a problem, not while the captain of the gnomen fleet is in your midst!" Remtall shouted. He stood, shaking the dirt and debris from his body.

"Well then, no time for questions and answers that stay our journey—we must march," Gaiberth commanded. Falen began to clear some of the foliage that had covered the Enoan road. Soon the path was unearthed, and the company began to march northeast once more. Falen led the group, followed by Gaiberth and Iirevale. Bringing up the rear was Remtall, and Adacon and Calan walked side by side slightly ahead of him. A weird song drifted from the back of the marching line of elves, and Adacon was first to realize that it was Remtall who was singing.

"Warpede of the forest,
How it does compel us,
To hurry on our way!
Send it back to Gaigas,
That something good may pry
It from its misery!"

Soon the whole company joined Remtall's chant, and for a great number of hours the company marched forward peacefully. Once midday came and passed, Gaiberth stopped the party so that they could eat and rest for a moment, but it was not long and soon the march continued. After several days of marching with no event, the jungle began to dissipate around them; the Enoan road jutted north, turning from soil to a mighty granite streak, set deeply between fields of tall grass, running as far into the distance as the eye could see. The aged grey road roved up a hilled pasture of emerald green, flecked in places with white and purple flowers that caught in their petals rays of the failing sun, and the path was overshadowed by enormous blue-grey mountains, tipped in snow that capped its eastern face. The troop walked the wide valley, nestled between the dark seclusion of the Carbal Jungle and the sky-reaching rock of the mountainside. The road eventually left the jungle behind entirely, and no trees ran along its side any longer; the elves marched with the forest at their backs, the blue mountains on their right, and shaded green hills as far as the eye could see on their left. Directly in front were fields of prairie pearl, and away in the distance could be seen the dark silhouette of a tremendous wall. The wall was several days' march away, yet it loomed as grand in the horizon as the blue-grey mountains. The wall appeared to be built of ashen stone; its strange presence thwarted the rolling meadows that ran to its feet, and veiled whatever land the north held.

"Who built this granite road, and the wall itself?" asked Adacon, his curious nature returning.

"The Oreinen dwarves. They are a magnificent people, but unlike their gentler cousins in the West, they still regard all who are not dwarves to be foes, or at least *almost* all others," Calan answered.

"Is that their home?" Adacon asked, pointing to the blue-grey mountains.

"Yes. Carved within those mountains is their city, Oreine."

"It's astonishing that any people on Darkin could build something as massive as that wall," Adacon said with wonder.

"Yes, and wait until you see it as you stand up against it…" Calan smiled. Remtall snuck up from behind to interrupt their conversation.

"Gnomes have been known to outbuild dwarves," Remtall said. "In fact, it is said that the gnome mine of Palailia is the greatest wonder in all Darkin, a marvelous underground city."

"Say what you will to belittle the dwarves, but they are masters of their craft," Calan replied.

"I mean not to belittle them, princess—but see Palailia, and you will see true beauty," Remtall boasted again.

"Where is it? Have you been there?" Adacon asked.

"It's in the southernmost country of Darkin, the Isle of Aaurlind, and no, I have never seen it with my own eyes," Remtall confessed.

"Then how do you know it rivals the Dinbell Wall?" Adacon questioned.

"Because I have heard the tales and descriptions from the elder gnomes all my life, and every detail of the place has been relayed to me in utmost detail," Remtall replied.

"Isn't Palailia haunted?" Calan asked. "I remember hearing tales of it—that it is possessed of demon magic, and necromancers dance through its halls."

"It's true—an age ago, it was: Palailia was lost to a dark necromancer, and no sane adventurer of Darkin will go there, save with a wish for death—or something worse," Remtall said. The sun began to sink, dimming the valley, and for miles in each direction the company was surrounded by open grassland with not a single tree to rest under. Gaiberth made the decision to march into the night toward the blue-grey mountains, off the road, toward the dwarven gates of Oreine. Under light of stars the company marched away from the Enoan road, heading directly for the mountains. In several hours' time Falen had guided the elves into a narrow valley of rock that cut between two steep schist faces, and the plains were all but left behind. The boulder-ridden path widened, and there were many small shelves of rock to climb, but soon the gate of Oreine was in sight. It felt to Adacon as if the whole troop was crunched together, unmoving in a pitch black crevasse, somewhere underneath a giant slab that bridged the rise of two mountains. Directly before them was a high door carved from the mountain, cut in the flowing grooves of dwarven art.

"How do you suppose we get in?" Remtall shouted, irritable from long hours of marching. Adacon and Calan moved up near the front of the line to watch as Gaiberth and Iirevale approached the giant door of stone. Adacon surveyed the mysterious carving of the dwarves: foreign writing ran the length of the door, and odd glyphs of beasts shaped it. Gaiberth drew his shield and knocked on the stone in an odd sequence, and Adacon noticed that as he knocked, the stone began to glow about its rim.

"A magic door!" Adacon exclaimed.

"No—the light of the city is leaking out, it's opening!" Calan rejoiced. "I was unsure we'd gain entrance. The Oreinen dwarves have grown more fearful lately, even of their neighbors."

Slowly the door slid aside and bright light from a glowing corridor poured out, lighting the cavernous path where the elves stood cramped together. A silhouette strode forth from the at-first blinding light, and soon Adacon's eyes adjusted: for the first time in his life he laid eyes upon a dwarf. The man wore a thick beard, much like the books he'd seen had illustrated them, and there was a dull armored cap atop his wiry mane. All about the man's heavy frame hung locking squares of silver chain mail. He stood shorter than a man, but his girth was that of nearly two men; Adacon also noticed quickly that the dwarf was not unarmed—at his side hung two small axes, loosely clipped to his belt. There was a bright red marking on the dwarf's chest plate, drawn on a piece of hanging leather.

"Ulpo!" Gaiberth resounded. The dwarf quickly embraced the elf chief and turned to see the whole of Gaiberth's company: suddenly, without warning, the dwarf fell backwards, stumbling over his own feet. Falen apologetically bowed for having so startled the poor dwarf.

"I am Falen, and not be to be feared, dear friend of the mountain," the drake said, his voice echoing twice.

"A speaking drake?" said Ulpo, gaining his feet once more. "Goodness, come in, all of you. Krem has just left, and he told me to expect you." Ulpo led them into the lit corridor, stretching interminably straight. Adacon became overwhelmed at hearing Krem's name and he pushed past all the others to meet the dwarf.

"I am sorry to interrupt, my name is Adacon, freed slave of Grelion, and…" Adacon blurted out, startling the dwarf for a second time. "Krem has been here?"

"He has just left. And it's on his word alone that you and your friends have gained entrance into Oreine in these dark times. Save for the bond between Gaiberth and me, you stood little chance at seeing our fair city," Ulpo said, turning to Gaiberth. "And not many dwarves share my kinship with elves, and other *unkindly to look upon* peoples of this world."

"But why did Krem leave?" Adacon asked, desperate for the Vapour's whereabouts.

"He could only stay briefly, for he is too needed at the battlefront. He came to tell us that Aulterion has begun assailing the southern jungle with fire spells from afar, and that we should expect the scattered elves of the Carbal to come to us for shelter in their hour of despair. We of the stone do not share the fear of fire magic, as our home is impregnable, but we are good enough to offer shelter against such rank villainies as Aulterion's," Ulpo said, leading everyone farther along the corridor. Gaiberth caught up to Adacon, tailed by Iirevale.

"What of the dwarven sentiment?" Gaiberth joined.

"We have heard of the Feral centipedes, the Gazaran, and that their numbers grow. We also have heard of the marching Feral Brood trolls, and we don't forget their love of caves; do not worry, son of Carbal: I believe counsel will be taken, and that the dwarves will go to war with you," Ulpo said. "There is, however, something that troubles us deeply, apart from war—an ancient dwarven prophecy has woken from scripture long sleeping. It is unfortunate that Krem didn't stay for but a moment before leaving, for we had many questions for him…" Ulpo said. He trailed off in thought before Adacon immediately prodded in:

"Prophecy?"

"Do you mean the Prophecy of the Key?" Iirevale said.

"Yes, tree dweller, the same—the most read letters in all of dwarven history," Ulpo said.

"What does the prophecy say?" Adacon stammered, hardly able to contain himself. Suddenly Calan and Remtall joined the front of the troop, along with Falen, listening to the conversation.

"Well, if you don't know, then I guess I might offer you a very brief telling," Ulpo said, and he cleared his throat. "There is an ancient scripture, written in times before men or elves or

233

dwarves—even before your kind, little one…" Ulpo told, referencing Remtall who had walked up beside the dwarf.

"Tell on, dwarf lord, and know that I am not angered at your presence, though your race betrayed ours, even as we stayed ever loyal in the darkest times…" Remtall said. As they continued he released his flask as he had done so many times before, and drank deeply of his elven sap liquor.

"Friend, may I taste a drop?" Ulpo said, catching sight of the flask, and Remtall handed over the liquor. Ulpo drank his fill, and when his thirst for spirits had been quenched he returned the elven stock. "An invigorating blend! Elven sap liquor, I think."

"Indeed, but now the favor must be repaid, stout smith—tell your damned prophecy," Remtall said. Ulpo laughed, as did all others nearby, and a happy union was forged amongst the many different races of people; the idea of a company of strangers forming friendships, each different race accepting the other, surprised Adacon.

"The ancient scripture, called the Waln Parchment, was unearthed from the deep belly of the Blue-Grey Mountains by the Oreinen, many centuries ago. It is said that the scripture was written long before even the first great age of Darkin. The scripture foretells of the returning of a people who departed Darkin long ago, an alien race of yore—and that these refugees will return as soon as their key is found upon the fertile forests of Darkin."

"Hah, gibberish!" Remtall exclaimed. He lit his pipe as they walked.

"Would you mind?" Ulpo asked, again borrowing from Remtall, this time a pinch of the gnome's tobacco. Ulpo filled his pipe and puffed alongside the gnome, as Iirevale, Calan, Gaiberth, Adacon, and Falen all followed quietly, awaiting further lore of the prophecy. "The key is said to be extremely dangerous to all who are not the alien people, or "the departed race," I should say, as it is written."

"Why is this tale of such concern?" Iirevale prodded.

"We have found the key!" Ulpo cried.

"What?" Adacon said, fascinated.

"Pah! What do you mean you found the key?" Remtall snickered.

"He was running through a field, alone, heading south, just yesterday," Ulpo said.

"He?" they all replied at once.

"Yes. You see the key is not actually a key at all, even though the scripture names it as such. The key in the Waln Parchment is entirely curious: in the ancient text the key is described as a tall man—some might mistake the description for a golem but for a single trait never found in their kind—that it be built of star-finished metal, some matter foreign to our world. This key, or silver beast, serves as a beacon for the departed race, calling them to Darkin..." Ulpo could not finish his sentence; Remtall and Adacon cut him off:

"Slowin!" they cried.

"What? We're moving quite slow as it is—don't be alarmed, the key is being kept under careful guard, caged deep in the underground. He has been bound, this omen of evil, and he cannot move his legs or arms. We've trapped his mouth so he cannot speak, lest some awful toxin spills from his throat into our fair city—or worse than that, that he calls the dark race here so that they reap our souls."

"We know him—*Slowin* is his name. Didn't Krem tell you about him?" Adacon railed, stopping Ulpo dead in his tracks.

"What? No—as I said, Krem had a grave task before him, and he rushed off without spending more than mere minutes here." Ulpo replied.

"Well, take us to your key then!" Remtall exclaimed.

"That would be far too dangerous. The prophecy portends the danger of the silver golem—not danger just to dwarves, gnome friend, but all people of Darkin," argued Ulpo.

"Pah! Never mind your prophecy, dull-witted dwarf; he is our friend, and a friend of Krem's," Remtall charged.

"A friend of Krem's? But I can't believe that…" Ulpo trailed off.

"These are honorable allies Ulpo, and true friends of Krem's. I place my trust, and the honor of the Carbal elves, on their word," Gaiberth said.

"I am not sure what to—gnome, please, your drop," Ulpo said, bracing himself on the arms of Gaiberth.

"Captain Remtall Olter'Fane, my liege," Remtall corrected, and he withdrew once more his flask for Ulpo.

"I cannot make the judgment myself, but some strange feeling compels me to believe you…I can grant you an audience with the king immediately; not before that could I possibly bring you to the key—beast—er, what did you call him?" stuttered Ulpo.

"Slowin," Adacon quickly filled in.

"We must make haste: a darkness approaches, not very far from here," Falen said, and the party regained momentum. In a moment the troop was marching briskly again. Ulpo restrained his wonder, leading them deep into the mountains with new urgency. Adacon could do no such thing, and his mind raced; he thought of the eon-old Prophecy of the Key, and how it could possibly mention Slowin.

Soon the bright corridor abruptly emptied them into a wide hall, carved from crimson rock, impossibly high, filled with vast square pillars that reflected up their lengths torchlight, bracketed on corners of man-high plinths. The ceiling rose tremendously, and Adacon noticed the sweet aroma of a fire burning, and all about the great hall could be seen various stone houses, cut directly out of the rock walls. Light emanated softly from within each house, flickering into a pattern of amber glow. The pillars that stood throughout the hall were engraved with dwarven art, intricate designs that appeared as old as the stone itself. Adacon walked on, in awe of the underground fortress. Though the place seemed blander in color than he had he expected, a uniform slate-red, the magnificence of the hall belonged to its grand size. The underground city seemed to run on endlessly into the mountain deeps, and the dwarves of the Oreine went about their daily business, for the most part ignoring Ulpo and the odd elven troop marching in his wake. Once in awhile, Adacon caught dwarves staring at them, mostly the small curious ones, what he took for dwarf-children.

The great hall led to a house, much the same in appearance as the others though far bigger, and Ulpo marched them directly inside. Once inside, Adacon realized that the house was a mere gateway to yet another hall: this one was smaller, though still fairly wide. Engravings wrapped the walls more elaborately than before, and there were no longer houses jutting from them, only marvelously colored armors, weapons, and gems of an infinite variety that hung everywhere. Adacon thought he even saw piles of gold, shimmering behind chests that were strewn about in dark corners, but he kept his eyes on a massive iron door that was fast approaching. Four dwarves stood at its entrance, each fully armored, unlike the rest of the dwarves they had so far seen about the Oreinen city. Ulpo approached the guards, and spoke to them in a guttural tongue.

"Dwarven?" Adacon whispered to Calan, who stood at his side.

"Yes, the dwarves are said to use the *common tongue* least of all Darkin's civilized peoples," she responded in a hushed tone, awaiting Ulpo's return. Ulpo seemed to be finished discussing the matter with the guards, and he returned to speak with Gaiberth.

"Four may enter, and no more. I am sorry, but it is the law of the Oreine," Ulpo explained.

"Four is plenty enough," Gaiberth replied, and he turned to Iirevale. "You, you, and you," Gaiberth said; he picked Iirevale, Remtall, and Adacon.

"Alright then, follow me," Ulpo said, and he walked back to the guards who each in turn went to four small pillars nearby, and it seemed for a moment that they chanted something while moving hidden switches. Adacon stared on in amazement, wishing he could be closer to see what magic they were working. A great creak reverberated in the hall, sounding a delayed echo. Calan turned to Adacon, and as their eyes met she smiled and whispered him good luck. The iron door swung open, and an intricate stairway carpeted in plush scarlet fur bore the chosen ones higher, up into the King's chamber. Adacon kept close to Remtall's side, and though he felt safe, he kept his hand on the handle of his elven blade. The staircase led them to a tiny hallway, still carpeted in plush red fur, and the walls too were covered with it, as was the ceiling, ensconcing them in a pillow of red. Walking forth, the light became less and less, the red a deeper shade around them. At the end of the cramped hallway, in a dim glow, two more armored dwarves stood guarding another iron door. They stood with axes in hand, blocking the path, protecting the way from intruders. Ulpo told the others to stay as he approached the guards alone.

"Quite a damned procession, isn't it?" Remtall muttered to Adacon. "Come to any gnomen city—see if we raise this kind of stink! Gnomen kings live among their people!" he complained loudly, and Adacon saw the dwarven guards begin to give the gnome glares of suspicion. Adacon gulped, smiling nervously at the dwarf guards, hoping they would be merciful toward a disgruntled gnome.

Finally, after more mysterious lever pulls, the last door before the king of the Oreine opened; Ulpo led the man, gnome, and elf into the royal chamber.

*   *   *

The dwarf king sat atop a gem encrusted throne, lined with pillows made from what appeared to be the same plush fur the carpets were made from. All about the small chamber of the king were more dwarves: some examined various artifacts, while others were standing in armor as guards. The walls of the chamber were covered with portraits of fattened dwarves, each one Adacon guessed to be a dwarf king of old. Shocked, Adacon saw one etching that looked as if it resembled Slowin. It wasn't quite right, but the basic structure implied the silver golem, and underneath the etching was carved a key. Adacon realized how prominent the prophecy had to be for it to adorn the wall of the king's chamber. Suddenly the dwarf guards spoke:

"Have you no courtesy? Bow before King Terion!" said the two foremost dwarven guards. Each of the visitors immediately dropped on a single knee, mimicking Ulpo's lead; as if in worship, they bowed their heads to the king, who sat still and speechless.

"Kiss my feet now, so that the dirt may be cleansed from them!" commanded King Terion, his booming voice sending shivers down Adacon's spine. Iirevale looked to Gaiberth desperately, filled with reluctance. Gaiberth appeared willing, and slowly they approached the king's feet, except for Remtall, who began to stand up, as he was tired of praising the dwarf king. Suddenly, to the astonishment of them all, every dwarf in the room broke out in tumultuous laughter; even Ulpo joined in. Finally, the others began to laugh too, unsure of what was so funny. After a long spell of riotous laughter, the clamor died to quietness, and Terion cleared his throat.

"Forgive me. You didn't think dwarves were without humor? Kiss my feet—hah!" And the room was engulfed with laughter once more, and this time Adacon and his friends joined, feeling relieved at the easing of tension. After the second spell of laughter died down, Terion decided to assert with seriousness the matter at hand, and he spoke directly to Gaiberth:

"I am brought word, brother of the forest, that our captive is a friend among elves?" Terion asked.

"It is not entirely as you say: the prisoner is a friend to the friends of elves, namely Krem the Vapour—as well as these who stand with me, and before you, now," Gaiberth informed.

"A grave thing it is, to befriend the prophesized one, as grave darkness is portended to come from him," Terion shuddered. "But a claim such as friendship with Krem, our greatest ally, must not be taken lightly—and so you have this audience."

"It's true! Slowin is a friend of Krem's," Adacon said.

"Slowin, did you say?" Terion asked.

"Yes, Slowin is your prisoner's name. He is a golem of the Red Forest, a place near the slave farm I have escaped from. Krem first befriended him there, and did some favor for him. In return,

Slowin has repaid his debt to Krem by coming west and guiding us," Adacon explained.

"Guiding you? But to what end?" Terion replied with faint shock.

"We set out to rid Darkin of the enslavers, Grelion and his under-lords. It was not until Krem suddenly departed from us, in the Vashnod Plains, that Slowin came to guide us to Erol Drunne. We hoped to find counsel there for fighting the greater evil," Adacon continued.

"A noble feat—to break the bonds given you by Grelion Rakewinter—but indeed the greater evil is Vesleathren's return," Terion stated. He laughed maniacally, "but I see not how a mere slave could aid in any fight, be it against Grelion *or* Vesleathren…"

"Believe him, old dwarf—Slowin *is* a friend to the cause of good, though he is a strange golem to look upon. Your prophecy leads you astray," Remtall railed, angered by Terion's doubt.

"What is your name, little gnome?" Terion asked, agitated by Remtall's boisterous intrusion.

"None other than Captain Remtall Olter'Fane, commander of the gnomen fleet," he said with pride.

"Hah! And where is this gnomen fleet today, good sir?" Terion chuckled.

"Destroyed, complacent dwarf, in the Five Country War," replied Remtall.

"Well, we shall unbind the prisoner's mouth, and hear its own tongue," Terion said. Two of the nearby guards rushed off to follow the command of their king.

"Pardon me, good king, but what news have you of the war? How goes the front? And what of Erol Drunne?" Iirevale asked, using the moment of silence as an opportunity to speak.

"Erol Drunne is now occupied by the Feral Brood. The Feral army came upon the city too fast, and without warning. Our dwarven diplomats there are lost, and I know not what the true state of that city is in this dark hour," Terion told.

"We meant to reach Erol Drunne to find counsel, and an army to march on Grelion, back in Arkenshyr," Adacon said with sorrow. "But now it seems Vesleathren is invading your country as well as mine, attacking from both sides of the Kalm Ocean."

"You speak the common tongue well for a slave, I am impressed—indeed you speak the truth, he does just that, and the hour is grave. In the Five Country War, the Feral army descended upon Arkenshyr alone. Now, enough force has he gained, he launches two assaults. And that is why we dwarves are sending out our great force tomorrow morning—so that at the Wall of Dinbell the Feral Brood might be pushed back enough to reclaim Erol Drunne."

"You leave tomorrow morning?" Iirevale sparked up in surprise.

"Yes, there is no more time to wait, at least that much did Krem tell us in his brief visit. If we continue to sit idle in the mountains, it will only be a matter of days before the Feral Brood breaks past Dinbell and marches down the Enoan road, toward our home," Terion foreboded.

"We will march with you, with what force we have. Though we lack numbers, our valor is absolute," Gaiberth said.

"And we shall be most honored to march at your side, friend," said the King. "We have had our differences in the past, but when utter destruction comes upon our homelands we are bound by kinship of good to defend against what is evil."

"Has there been any good news from Dinbell?" asked Iirevale.

"Krem did not stay with us for but a moment, and he only stayed to tell of the attacks on the jungle, and that we should expect and welcome the elves as they strayed from their homes," Terion said. "Other than that, there has not been much in the way of information, save some curious bit floated along by the wereverns."

"Wereverns?" Adacon said, dumbfounded.

"Reptile creatures we dwarves befriended, dear freed slave of Arkenshyr. Terribly magnificent spies of the land, though cowardly at first they may seem," Terion explained.

"What is the curious bit then?" Remtall demanded.

"According to the wereverns, the only reason the Feral Brood hasn't already come through the Wall of Dinbell is due to the heroics of two swordsmen. It is quite silly, though, that the wereverns would take to such a ridiculous rumor—usually their information is reliable—but no two swordsmen alone could ever make a difference in a battle of this scale."

"Flaer and Erguile!" Adacon burst.

"Pah! You're sorrow stricken, boy," Remtall said.

"Who are those you name?" Terion asked.

"Our friends whom we lost at sea, after a spell rent the ocean into a wall of ice, and it crashed upon our ship," Adacon recounted.

"My goodness, it seems for a slave you've had more than your share of adventure in such a short time of freedom," Terion replied in amazement.

"It was nothing I couldn't fetch us from," Remtall boasted, forgetting to mention the aid of the phantom ships.

"In any case, we do not recognize the story of the two fabled swordsman to be anything more than a myth of fancy, and for it our trust in the wereverns information has lessened," said Terion.

"The prisoner approaches," remarked a dwarf guard from the front entrance of the king's chamber. Suddenly Slowin appeared, hands bound, mouth gagged with white cloth. Two guards led him in. Adacon thought of Slowin's tremendous strength when he saw the flimsy shackles binding the metal golem. Surely Slowin could have escaped at any time, but why hadn't he? Adacon wondered. At King Terion's command the guards removed the cloth from Slowin's mouth so that he could speak. Slowin glanced around the room at the company of the king. He smiled immediately at the sight of Remtall and Adacon, who returned the gesture, though they kept silent.

"As you may or may not know, the dwarves of Oreine believe you are the Key, as prophesized in the Waln Parchment. This is a powerful omen of ill fortune for our race, as the Key portends great evil, as written in the scriptures. This is the reason why you have been bound, and are soon to be destroyed in the fires of the Brolsrind Chasm. However—by a most odd stroke of fate—new information has come to light. It seems you have the best friends imaginable, those who would vouch you to be a close friend of Krem's, and an ally in our battle against Vesleathren," Terion said, looking directly at Slowin.

"Had you allowed me to speak when you first captured me you might not have had to wait so long to realize that," said Slowin with coldness in his voice. It sounded strange, as Adacon was used to a measure of warmth in everything his golem friend said.

"Sorry, I am, for the abrupt magic that bound you, that kept you from speaking your peace from the first. But that is a matter I cannot reverse. I can, however, make amends to you, by freeing you here and now. Of course there is one condition, for the

Prophecy lives too firmly in our culture for me to completely overlook the fact that you so resemble the Key..." Terion went on.

"What is the condition?" Slowin asked, displeased.

"March with us tomorrow, to the Wall of Dinbell, to aid the failing militia of Erol Drunne, who single-handedly defend us now. Prove to us in battle where you truly stand in this great struggle of good against evil," Terion said.

"That is exactly what I had planned to do—how strange that is," Slowin lied, as he had heard nothing about the situation at Dinbell. After another moment of silence, he seemed to calm down from a state of inner fury. "Free me please, now that you know I am not your prophecy..."

"Guards! Fetch good Merol to release his bonds," Terion ordered. "And one other thing Slowin, which I presume you wish to be called. . ." Slowin did not speak, only grunted. "Once the war is over, and Vesleathren is defeated, you must grant me an audience, so that I might obtain all the information I can about you, so as to truly invalidate you from the Prophecy, for no reason other than the security of my kingdom."

"Once this war is over, I shall be returning to the Red Forest in peace, to live among the wilds. Follow me there, and you may then ask all you wish to learn," Slowin replied. At that moment, a short dwarf draped in a black robe and a tightly fitted black cap walked into the King's Chamber. The dwarf held aloft a cane that looked somewhat similar to Krem's, though less extravagant. The dwarf's face was filled with black and grey hairs that shaped a thick beard and mustache.

"Merol, please release the spell upon our prisoner's shackles," Terion ordered.

"But, your kingship, *he is the Key!*" Merol retorted defiantly in a high gravelly voice that cracked in pitch.

"Do as I say Merol!" Terion commanded, scorn in his voice for the public questioning of an order. Merol groaned, but did as the king said, and Slowin once again was able to move unrestricted. Adacon realized it had been the black dwarf's magic staying the might of Slowin.

"Now if you don't mind, good king, I have a bit of catching up to do," Slowin said. "We leave tomorrow morning, correct?"

"At first light, new friend," Terion responded.

"Then you won't mind if I go off to spend some time with my old friends," Slowin said. Swiftly the silver golem stomped out of the chamber before Terion could answer, and Adacon and Remtall quickly followed after him.

"Pleased to have met you, King Terion," Adacon called back. Remtall paid no such courtesy, and the three left of their own accord, out through the king's corridor and into the main hall. Ulpo stood with Gaiberth and Iirevale, respectfully waiting for instruction from the king, who stood up from his throne. Merol waited patiently along with the others for Terion's orders.

"Gaiberth, tomorrow we march to perhaps our doom, but I am heartened to have your valiant company with us," Terion exclaimed. "Go, make use of my kingdom, take whatever you need so that your troop is ready for the journey to Dinbell, and the battle that is to come."

"Great thanks, good lord," Gaiberth said, and together with Iirevale he bowed. A dwarf guard came to escort them from the chamber. Once all the visitors were gone, Merol looked to the king, and after a brief moment of silence he spoke.

"Forgive me great Terion—but have you gone to madness? The scripture describes him perfectly, he *is* the key!" Merol pleaded.

"It would seem so, conjurer, but trust in your king is all that I ask from you in our hour of darkness," Terion answered.

"Certainly I trust you, lord, but also in the Prophecy I trust," Merol cracked.

"Me too, Merol, me too, but the situation is such that a greater priority is pressing us, and that is the invasion of our country," Terion reflected.

"Some would say both matters equally concern the safety of our people, master," sulked Merol, but the king did not respond, and Merol limped out of the chamber.

X: THE DINBELL WALL

Slowin, Adacon, and Remtall sat together at a slate table in a dimly lit tavern that was carved from the rock wall of the main hall. In the tavern were only two other patrons, and a lone dwarven bar tender who stood nearby cleaning mugs. Slowin had chosen a table as far as possible from the other customers, both because it was the only table big enough to seat Slowin, and because the other patrons would not overhear their conversation.

"Alright then Slowin—out with it," Remtall said between gulps of dwarven ale. Adacon had decided not to drink—wishing to keep his wits sharp—as the coming day brought with it a great march, and possibly battle with the Feral Brood. After two painful hugs, Slowin began to tell his tale, and how he had come to survive the Kalm Ocean shipwreck:

"At the very moment when you and Adacon were thrown from the ship, it appeared as if time had frozen for Flaer, Erguile and me," Slowin told. "I can't say how it happened, but the entire ship was enveloped in a kind of bubble—just as it was cracking apart—but not before you two were both thrown from the rail. The next thing I knew, the ship was whole again, floating on calm waters."

"Impossible!" Adacon cried.

"Not even Weakhoof was harmed. We talked for a long time afterward, whether we'd hallucinated the lightning and ice—only did your missing bodies tell us it was no trick of the mind," Slowin went on. "Next thing we knew, we had anchored at a beach, set underneath massive cliffs, and we had no idea where in Enoa we were. A jungle was to our south, massive cliffs to our north, and a small trail that curled into a meadow formed between. We didn't know that you two had survived. In fact, we mourned your deaths…"

"It must have been Krem! How else could that bubble have happened?" Adacon said.

"I wouldn't doubt that…so we set forth on the trail, leaving everything behind but our weapons and some food. And then it happened," Slowin said with a deep tremor of dread in his voice.

"What happened?" Remtall asked, as eager as Adacon to hear more.

"Trolls—Feral trolls—they sprang on us, completely surprised us. We had no idea that Vesleathren was already at work mutating them, let alone on the opposite side of the ocean! There was a whole legion of them, and we just walked right into their path. Some were riding enormous centipedes coated in gold armor—" Slowin said. Adacon cut him off:

"Warpedes—we fought one in the jungle!" Adacon cried. Everyone in the tavern heard Adacon and looked over at the strange congregation. Slowin shot them a cold stare, and they returned to their own business.

"Tell it later Adacon, let him finish," Remtall chided.

"So being caught by surprise, we were scattered. Once we were separated, there was nothing to do but run. There were simply too many of them—I saw Erguile galloping away toward

the cliffs, and I saw Flaer head straight into the meadow, slaying all
that were in his path. I stood my ground as long as I could, but I
was swarmed. I was forced to flee, and I was able to hide high atop
a tree at the edge of the jungle. After the troop of Feral Trolls
passed, unable to find me, they marched into the forest. I came
down and took to the meadow, searching far and wide for Flaer or
Erguile. I found no one, and so I ran south and found the Enoan
road—and that was when that dreadful dwarven wizard cast his
spell upon me," Slowin groaned.

"Merol, from the King's chamber?" Adacon asked.

"Indeed, that odd little man—his power is much greater than you'd
guess by looking at him," Slowin said, disgust in his voice.

Enthralled by the story, Adacon wasted no time in telling
his side of the separation, explaining in vivid detail how Remtall
and he were saved by the mysterious phantoms, how they had
come to Carbal Run by way of the condors, and how the jungle
had been attacked with giant fireballs. After everything that had
happened was told to Slowin, the three decided that Krem must
have been at work that day upon the Kalm, saving them from
certain doom.

"Do you think Erguile is alright?" Adacon asked, thinking
for a moment of his missing friend.

"I can't be sure, Adacon, but if any horse is
underestimated, it is Weakhoof. He was riding fast north, last I saw
him," Slowin answered.

"I hope he found some safe haven there. North is the
direction of the Dinbell Wall, and the war front, the king said.
Strangely, I am not worried about Flaer much, if at all," Adacon
said.

"That is not strange, for Flaer is no ordinary swordsman,
and teamed with the Brigun Autilus, I wouldn't be surprised to

know that the Feral Army has retreated outright at the sight of him," Slowin chuckled.

"Erguile will be fine, Adacon. I raised Weakhoof, and there is a not a braver horse in Rislind. If any creature of Darkin can carry Erguile to safety, it's old Weakhoof," Remtall comforted, and Adacon once more felt at ease in the company of his friends.

They talked late into the night, against their better judgment, as they knew the morning would come fast, and a long march would require good sleep. Adacon told Slowin about his love for Calan, though Slowin didn't quite seem to understand the same way Remtall did. Finally, the three of them had relayed every detail of their journeys since splitting up, and feeling very tired, they were all instructed by the bartender to the location of their beds. They walked down the hall together, and a dwarf guard pointed them in the direction of a house where the elven troop was staying. It was a bare rock cavern, lined with matted fur beds on cutout ledges that were stacked, one above the other. Slowin decided to sleep on the floor near the entrance, as the beds were too small for him. Remtall waddled to the first open bed and fell into it, falling fast asleep. Adacon continued down the rocky cavern, looking at all the sleeping elves, passing one that he thought was Iirevale.

"Iirevale," Adacon whispered to the sleeping elf. "Iirevale?" he whispered louder.

"Who's there!" Iirevale sparked from out of a dream, sitting upright and gripping his sword, which lay at his side.

"It's only me, Adacon."

"Ah, what is it? I'm sleeping…."

"Sorry, where's Calan?"

"I don't know—now get to bed…" Iirevale grunted, and he rolled over again and turned back to sleep. Just then a noise echoed from behind Adacon. It was Calan.

"Over here," she whispered. Adacon promptly hopped up to her ledge.

"I can't sleep," she whispered.

"It's alright, you don't have to worry now that we have Slowin with us," Adacon reassured her quietly.

"I saw him walk past with you—how strange he is. He doesn't look like any golem I've ever seen."

"He isn't. He's as strong as fifty men, and we don't need to worry as long as he's here," Adacon said, and he stroked her hair. She quieted, and together the two of them fell asleep on the cramped ledge.

*   *   *

It felt like but a minute before Adacon was awoken by the sound of a blaring horn, and soon the whole cave of beds was stirring, as elves hopped down from every corner of the rock wall. Gaiberth assembled his elves in the entrance to the main hall, and Falen sat away from the others and conversed with Slowin.

"It seems the stranger the folk, the better they get along, eh?" Remtall poked Adacon and pointed in the direction of Falen and Slowin. Adacon looked up from his preparations with an angry look on his face.

"No need to stab me," Adacon said in response to the gnome who had jabbed his ribs to get his attention.

"Sorry, I sometimes forget the weak flesh of men," replied the captain unremorsefully.

"They *are* the strangest looking ones here, might as well let them become good friends," Adacon returned in good humor, and Calan approached from behind.

"Are you two ready for a march?" she said, sounding oddly upbeat for such a perilous journey.

"When is a gnome not ready for great deeds, my beautiful druid of the forest?" Remtall flirted.

"Hah! I'm no druid, little gnome. Nonetheless, be glad I am with you, as my legs outpace any man or gnome among us," she boasted. They equipped their gear, and as they waited on King Terion's orders to depart, they walked over to Falen and Slowin.

"Ahah!" laughed Slowin.

"What's so funny, metal beast?" piped Remtall, interrupting Falen and Slowin's conversation.

"I was just telling Slowin the tale of how you so valiantly took on a Gazaran..." Falen said in his deep timbre. Slowin began to laugh hysterically once more. Remtall stomped his foot and drew his flask, filled now with dwarven rock liquor.

"I'll have you know, if it hadn't been for my heroics, this whole company of Gaiberth's would be no more," Remtall boasted, drinking merrily.

"Still with your usual breakfast I see..." Slowin remarked, noting Remtall's habit of drinking spirits first thing in the morning.

"Never mind a gnome's breakfast," Remtall said, dismissing Slowin's concern.

"Speaking of breakfast," Adacon said, smelling something delightful waft by his nose. He turned to see a group of elves feasting from what looked to be piping cauldrons of stew, each being rolled around by several dwarven guards. Adacon and Calan rushed over to eat, and Remtall stayed with Falen and Slowin.

"Well then, Falen, what do you make of this journey to the wall?" Remtall asked.

"From what I have heard, Vesleathren mounts his greatest force in the east country of Arkenshyr. It is there that he himself is commanding the Feral Brood. Rumor is that the dark mage, *Aulterion,* has been tasked with commanding the Feral army that marches south in Enoa. I have heard from the spies of the dragon kin that his evil stays the ground behind the Dinbell Wall, and while he assaults the jungles from afar with fireballs, he dually works to topple the Dinbell all the while," Falen told.

"Pah! Destroy the wall? But I saw the wall from the road, it was at least as tall as these mountains that house us now," Remtall railed in disbelief.

"Which is why our march is all the more treacherous and urgent—but you are from Rislind, correct?" Falen asked.

"Yes…" Remtall answered.

"Then surely you recall what Aulterion did to end the Five Country War—he conjured the very blast that formed…" Falen began but was cut off.

"I fought in that war, little dragon! Don't question my memories."

"Firsthand, then, you have seen the destructive power Aulterion can muster through black magic. Destroying the Dinbell Wall doesn't seem impossible for him after all, does it?" There was a silence after Falen's words, for each of them knew that the Dinbell Wall was the only thing preventing the Feral Brood from pushing directly south on the Enoan road and sacking the whole of Enoa.

"No time to be filled with fear, come and have some stew," Slowin changed the subject. Remtall and Falen followed the silver golem toward the cauldrons.

"Ah, good Slowin, you still have our best interest at heart," Remtall said with a wink. Soon they were eating alongside the rest of the group.

Once all of the elves had their fill, as well as their assorted company (a gnome, a man, a drake, and a silver golem), King Terion approached, coming down the great dwarf hall, leading a large company of armored dwarves. The army of dwarves was ten times greater than Gaiberth's force, and the elves happily welcomed the glistening strength of dwarf-built armor and axes. King Terion stood together with Gaiberth at the head of the unified legion, and Gaiberth deferred to King Terion, and Terion commanded them with orders:

"Good dwarves of Oreine, and mighty warriors of Carbal, you are assembled now to defend your homes against the invading Feral Army, held at bay by the Wall of Dinbell, defended by what's left of the Erol Drunne militia. It is frightening how fast Vesleathren's evil has come upon our fair land, and ravished its way south, already taking one of the greatest free cities of the world, Enoa—*but we go now to turn the tide*, and for the second and final time in Darkin's history, we shall thwart Vesleathren's evil! Good citizens of Enoa, this time it is no foreign cause that we go to aid, far across the mighty Kalm—it is our own country that has been invaded—it is our children and families that we go to defend. What gives rise to Vesleathren's villainy none can guess—I can only do my part to stand against it, and so you can now do yours," Terion commanded, rallying his forces, and the great army of dwarves and elves roared with the ferocity of an angry mob. "We march north, upon the open road, for all his spies to see—to Dinbell!"

"To Dinbell!" the army echoed Terion, and suddenly the great mass of warriors moved, following Terion and Gaiberth who led them out. Adacon fell in line beside his companions, walking next to Calan. Once again the bright sun of Darkin shone on him, as the great troop left the safety of the Blue-Grey Mountains, weaved its way out of Oreine and onto the Great Plain, heading toward the Enoan Road. Soon they were on the hot granite again, in a tight formation heading north, in sight of the looming Dinbell Wall, several days' march away.

"So the dwarves alone built Dinbell?" Adacon asked Calan as they marched under the silver-blue sky of cloudless sunshine.

"The dwarves will tell you that they did, but I can assure you it was a great effort of many peoples, including the elves. It is true the dwarves are most skilled at constructing monuments of stone, but it would have been an impossible effort if the great and various races of Enoa hadn't come together and helped one another," she answered.

"How old is it?" Adacon asked.

"The Dinbell has only stood since the Five Country War, and it was built in defense of the Feral Army in that time. Thankfully, it had never been needed, as Vesleathren only assaulted Arkenshyr and the eastern lands, but at the time no one was certain if his troll army would reach our northern shores," she explained.

"Amazing—the world is so rich with stories and places, and I had never before seen more than a single farm's worth of it. I see how beautiful everything is, and I am filled more than ever with a passion to fight, and defend what I can now call my home," Adacon said.

"And where would you call home?" Calan asked.

"Darkin, of course…" Adacon said.

"What I meant was, once this is all over, where will you go home to?" she prodded. Adacon looked around himself and seemed to be lost in thought at her question. He looked to his left and saw the dark green edge of the Carbal jungle, the beginnings of the Teeth Cliffs; he looked to his right, and saw the sunlit Blue-Grey Mountains, home of the curious Oreinen. He looked behind, and between rows of marching elves he saw the Great Plain stretch on and on until the mountains merged with the forest. Then he turned to look straight ahead, a granite strip running to the end of the Great Plain, where it met the towering stone-built Wall of Dinbell.

"I don't know…" Adacon finally admitted.

"I also don't know," she said. "My home is no more, my loved ones…"

"I am sorry for," Adacon began, but she interrupted him.

"It's alright, I've mourned for those Aulterion destroyed, but I know Gaigas keeps them yet, in her great spirit, and that I shall meet them again someday," she said, concealing her weeping.

"Maybe, if it's not against elven law or custom, we could find a new home together, and live together in peace and happiness," Adacon said. Calan smiled, wiping tears from her face.

"That would be my happiest ending to this, Adacon," she cried, and threw herself under his arm.

"Then you must promise me to stay well away from combat," Adacon said.

"You know I cannot do that," she answered, and Adacon understood, and he said no more—only did he hold her for a while longer as they marched north.

Two days of uneventful marching passed by, and when the times had come to do so, Terion called for the army to stop, eat, and camp for the night upon the open road. He constantly appointed sentries to protect from any possibility of a surprise attack, and the elves were used to scout farthest ahead, greatly outpacing the sturdier dwarves. Adacon noticed that Falen and Slowin had become fast friends, and Remtall had clung to them, regaling them with boastful stories whenever he found an opportunity to cut into their conversations. Even Ulpo had joined their little unit, and Remtall found that Ulpo shared his love of tobacco and liquor, and they began to get along elegantly—especially since having Ulpo around doubled Remtall's store of liquor. Adacon kept mostly with Calan throughout the days of marching, but occasionally he would fall back to talk with Slowin, asking questions whenever he had the chance. Mainly they had talked about the history of Darkin, as most of it was new to Adacon, and when they weren't discussing geography or history, talk would turn to how to properly fight the Feral trolls. Falen had been a veteran of the Five Country War, as had Remtall, so they each shared with Adacon what wisdom they had on how to fight the Feral Brood, knowing it would be useful when the time arrived.

By the third night, the Dinbell had grown much larger before them. The army of Oreine and Carbal drew near to the foundation of the wall itself, and Terion called a halt to a long day's march. The legion set about making camp for the night. It was as Adacon sat to have his dinner that he began to hear an odd, low-pitched humming noise.

"Do you hear that sound?" he asked Slowin, who sat nearby.

"Hmm," Slowin replied. He stopped eating to listen intently. "Just barely, though I cannot say what it is," Slowin said, unalarmed.

"Strange—I think I'll ask King Terion," Adacon said. He jumped up from his broth near the fire and walked through the sitting company of warriors toward the front of the army. Terion was sitting with Gaiberth, Iirevale and Merol.

"Greetings, freed slave. Adacon, isn't it?" Terion asked.

"Yes, King Terion. I am sorry to interrupt—but the noise I hear worries me…" Adacon said, voicing his concern.

"That low-pitched humming?" Iirevale asked.

"Exactly that! What is it?" Adacon asked.

"Pay it no mind! Pay it no mind…" Merol suddenly interjected.

"I had just noticed it a moment ago myself, dear Adacon," Terion commented.

"It is odd, and I have never heard such a noise before, not in all my life," Gaiberth expressed.

"I said pay it no mind—it's just the tremor of battle, coming through the ground underneath the Dinbell," Merol said.

"Is the battle raging now?" Adacon asked.

"Indeed—as the Feral Army comes against the wall, they are forced to divert their path west or east against its face—either up the Teeth Cliffs they must go, and meet the ambush of scattered militia, or down into the narrow valley of the Blue-Grey Mountains, where the last of the divided Erol Drunne force awaits them. You see, the wall funnels their evil numbers into the two tiny passages, and they can but trickle onward—that is why the last of the Erol Drunne militia still hangs on at all… though I fear we cannot count on that to continue much longer," Terion explained.

"So the wall scatters their army?" Adacon asked.

"It does, and though the Feral Army marches into the traps of our land, they are numberless, and the Erol Drunne militia will not last without our assistance. Tomorrow we march west, up the Teeth Cliffs, to its highest ridge, where we will join their force," Terion informed him.

"So I can ignore the noise then—it just sounds so unnatural," Adacon said, remembering his original concern.

"Pay it no mind!" stormed Merol, losing his temper. Suddenly, Terion turned and slapped Merol across his face.

"Mind your tongue in the company of your king, Merol," Terion scolded. Merol rose up and sulked away into the night, rubbing his cheek as he went.

"I am sorry. Merol has been in terrible spirits lately, all this has been very difficult for him—you see his family disappeared several weeks ago," Terion told.

"I am sorry to hear," Adacon replied.

"And still more strain comes to him, as he is the only Vapour of the Oreinen," informed Terion.

"He's a Vapour like Krem?" Adacon asked. Suddenly, Gaiberth, Iirevale, and the king broke into laughter.

"I wouldn't compare him to Krem, but yes, he channels magic for good intentions, and so he is a Vapour," Terion explained.

"Alright, I guess I should trust his wisdom about the noise then," Adacon said, trailing off with a noticeable trace of doubt.

"Trust *me*, if not him, Adacon. Go to rest, for I will keep our men here only as long as I deem it completely safe to do so. I'll see you in the morning when we travel west, up the Teeth Cliffs, and into battle together," Terion smiled.

"Good night," Adacon replied, and he turned to retrace his steps toward Slowin and his cooling broth.

*   *   *

The night wore on, and no one stayed up very late, as the coming day brought with it the first sure chance of combat. Adacon slept by Calan's side, and before long Falen was standing over them, blowing steam at them from his nostrils.

"Time to get up, young lovers. Today we restore the peace," Falen roared at them.

"Falen… ugh, you don't have to be so loud," Adacon moaned. Calan and he stood up, stretching under the freshly risen sun.

"The gnome put me up to it. Said if I startled you, he'd show me the secret entrance to Palailia," Falen admitted.

"Joke's on you, dear drake!" Remtall laughed from afar, and he proceeded to tell Falen that he truly knew nothing of any secret entrance to Palailia.

"I'll show you whom the joke's on," Falen playfully returned, and Falen blew a great gust of wind at Remtall. The gnome was tossed through air for a second before tumbling into some nearby elves.

"Egh, sorry about that—pay me no mind," Remtall apologized to the elves he'd bowled over. He brushed himself off and walked away, though the elves didn't seem to reciprocate the humor, and they scowled at the unkempt gnome as he went.

"The noise—it's grown louder," Adacon immediately noticed as he became fully awake.

"There's more to worry about right now than a noise, Adacon," Slowin reminded him, and Adacon tried to take his mind off the humming sound. They ate a brief breakfast then broke camp to assemble before Terion and Gaiberth once more. This time Gaiberth spoke to them in the early morning sun:

"Our scouts have given us word that the Erol Drunne militia is almost defeated. They await our numbers in the hope of renewing the fight. They tell us that they have seen no end to the line of trolls, or Gazaran—that just as each new band is destroyed, one from behind replaces it," Gaiberth relayed.

"Gaiberth means not to frighten you—he means only to prepare you for the truth of this war," Terion interjected. "Many of us will never return to our beloved city of Oreine after this war is ended—yet if we choose not to fight, there will be no such home to speak of."

To Adacon's surprise, the army cheered fearlessly in response to the grim news.

"Has anyone seen Merol? He did not return last night after receiving—discipline," the king asked while he still had everyone's attention. The whole troop silenced, looking at one another, murmuring. Many shrugged their shoulders, but none knew the whereabouts of Merol.

"It is no matter then. We march now to the Teeth Cliffs, with or without him," said Terion. He led the army up a trail that ran between the edge of the Carbal Jungle and the start of the Teeth Cliffs. At that moment, Adacon realized that the humming he had been ignoring had grown louder; the volume of the sound grew sharply, peaking in a painful cracking noise. Panicked, the entire troop covered their ears. Adacon looked up in the direction from which the cracking had sounded: to his horror, a gigantic portion of stone near the top of the Dinbell Wall was shattering. Dark lines zigzagged across the grey rock, spreading out like a spider-web. A piece came free, toppled off, rotating through the air down to where they stood.

"Run!" shouted Adacon as the first boulder landed with a thunderous tremor directly behind King Terion, who narrowly escaped being crushed to death.

"At a sprint men—sprint!" shouted the king. The whole company began running from the crumbling wall, scrambling toward the steep trail that led to the Teeth Cliffs. Many in the party panicked as they fled underneath the stone rain, and the once uniform line of the troop fragmented.

"Room for two!" said Falen amidst the frenzy, just as another piece of the great wall came crashing down nearby. "Three if one is a gnome."

"Adacon and Calan, get on him," Slowin commanded. For a moment Adacon froze, not sure what to do, hesitant to abandon the rest of the warriors. "Now!" Slowin ferociously roared. Adacon pulled Calan close and they jumped on Falen, who had bowed his back for them. Just as they hopped on, Remtall, who had been nearby, bounded on as well, slamming against Calan's back. Falen took off immediately, and with great speed they shot up into the sky. Adacon's vision leveled with the crumbling wall, and he could see hairline fractures running its length. He knew the humming noise had to have been a spell of Aulterion's, slowly working to collapse the great wall. Down below, the funneling line of elves and dwarves could be seen hurrying up the trail toward the cliffs, narrowly escaping boulders that toppled from the Dinbell.

"I can't believe they're destroying it," Calan said. Adacon continued to look out at the crumbling wall, in awe of the black throng that struggled behind it. Falen took them high above even the tip, and they could see everything on either side of the failing Dinbell; it was the most horrendous thing they had ever witnessed: on the opposite side of the wall writhed an endless army of near-black, stretching into the distance as far as could be seen. The army of trolls was a throbbing sea of arms, legs, torsos and sun-glinting armor and blades. Interspersed throughout the dark mob of trolls were shiny golden specks—warpedes—weaving through the dense Feral army, trying to force their way forward, left or right, away from where the Dinbell brought their path south to a halt. Most shocking to behold was an enormous bubble of shiny film rising as if an island in the north plain, isolated; beneath the film was a patch of green grass, stark against the frenzied black mass that surrounded it. The film of energy encased a single man, standing nearly a league from the chaos unfolding at the wall. From within the translucent blue-gold bubble, a tremendous stream of light was issuing forth in rolling waves. Adacon froze, something clicked; he placed the low humming noise as coming from the direction of the streaming light. The energy was shooting out from the man, through the shiny bubble's film, high up into the sky, then colliding into the top of the northern face of the Dinbell Wall, precisely where the wall was cracking, falling piece by piece to the earth far below.

"Aulterion!" Adacon screamed.

"Let me loose, foul drake, so that I can get down there and fight!" roared Remtall. "Quickly, before I jump!" Adacon did not doubt the gnome's threat.

"Fair enough," Falen replied. He pointed his nose toward the ground and dove, taking them toward the Erol Drunne militia who defended the cliffs. Behind the militia, Adacon saw Slowin marching forward at great speed with Terion's army, trying to reach the militia.

"Coming in fast—be ready," Falen instructed. He descended rapidly to where the Erol Drunne militia fought. Adacon reeled as the figures below enlarged. The drake spun to avoid a shower of arrows, heaved up, and then dove toward solid ground once again.

"Erguile!" Adacon shouted.

"What?" Remtall said in shock.

"Look there," Adacon pointed. Sure enough, Erguile was charging back and forth atop Weakhoof, thrusting his sword in every direction, slaying trolls wherever they approached.

"And Great Gaigas, there's Flaer!" Remtall cheered, nearly falling off the turbulent dragon. A dreadful excitement for battle filled Adacon as he trained his eyes to where Remtall pointed, and just as Erguile was below them battling, so was Flaer: he was forging a path through the Feral army using the Brigun Autilus, alone and on foot, cutting his way past endless trolls, directly toward where Aulterion stood inside his magic field of blue-gold.

"He's mad—he marches alone to Aulterion!" Adacon exclaimed. Calan watched in awe, continuously glancing backward to make sure her brother Iirevale was safe. In the distance a great burst of scarlet light exploded around Flaer, and Adacon knew that the Brigun Autilus was laying waste to all who stood in its path.

"Look!" Remtall pointed again, and Adacon saw a golden warpede barreling for Flaer. "It's coming for him." Adacon choked when he tried to yell, knowing they were too far away to help, or even shout a warning. Suddenly, Flaer turned to encounter the warpede, as if he had sensed its coming. The Gazaran attempted to clamp down on him, rising and slamming down in one motion. In a brilliant spark of light, visible even from atop Falen so far away, Adacon and Remtall witnessed the warpede go hurtling through the sky in the opposite direction of Flaer, hit the earth and roll over and over, plowing into the earth several rows of trolls that had been marching in its wake.

"One for Flaer!" Adacon cheered. Remtall withdrew his blade with a smile as Falen landed on a calm patch of the Teeth Cliffs. Adacon and Calan mimicked Remtall, drawing their swords.

"Falen, please protect her," Adacon asked.

"On my honor as a friend of Krem's," Falen replied. Adacon turned, kissed Calan.

"Come on," Remtall commanded, "No time for sentiment."

"Stay close to Falen, don't enter the fray—please—I must go aid my friends—I will return," Adacon said, embracing her quickly.

"On without you then," Remtall said, impatient. He rushed ahead to the battle that waited around the corner, where the trailhead led down to the Erol Drunne militia.

"I love you Adacon," Calan said softly, her eyes welling with tears.

"And I love you," he responded, unsure if he'd ever get the chance to say it again. Adacon leaned close, kissing her until Falen shooed him off.

"Go and fight, your friends require you. Know that Falen Firewind protects your love. Now run!" Falen commanded, and Adacon did as he was told.

"Remtall!" Adacon cried, catching up to the gnome. They were both at the fringe of the foray.

"Come lad—die or lay waste," Remtall said as he charged. Together they plunged into the heart of battle. Adacon ran alongside an Erol Drunne fighter, a human.

"Glad to have you," said the fighter as a Feral troll rushed them.

"More on the way—an army of dwarves and elves," Adacon replied, positioning his sword to help slay the incoming troll.

"Couldn't be happier to hear that…" grunted the fighter. Before the troll could reach them, Remtall jumped impossibly high, over both of them, and stood face to face with the troll.

"Sweet Gaigas," shouted the fighter as Remtall smote the troll, gouging its eye with a flurry of stabs.

"No time to be idle," Remtall chanted, and he pressed deeper into the combat, Adacon trailing him. They fought their way through several more trolls, and Adacon sensed he was fighting again as if possessed of a strange deadliness, like when he had escaped the farm. Briefly, in the heat of combat, Adacon wondered whether unseen Vapoury had aided him in battle then, and whether it still did so now. Methodically, Remtall and Adacon sliced through troll after troll, fighting along the front line of the Erol Drunne militia. Looking behind to the top of the cliff from which they had descended, Adacon saw a yellow fire swelling, heard a chorus of screams; he knew then that Falen was doing his part. Turning back, he saw a troll cut down a nearby Erol Drunne fighter. The demonic beast jumped from its prey to the next, catching Adacon off guard. The Troll's feral blade came down with a crushing blow on Adacon's left forearm. Instantly, Adacon dropped his wooden shield and his arm went limp, dangling at his side, useless from the blow. Blood trickled down and dripped from his fingers.

"Cough on my—" wailed Remtall, rushing to the aid of Adacon, "—dagger!" Remtall jumped high, and while the troll was readying its next strike, the gnome's blade thrusted deep into the troll's throat, causing it to stumble and roll down a steep incline, clearing more trolls in the process.

"You alright?" Remtall asked, frantically examining his friend in a brief lull of combat.

"Just my left arm, I'll be fine, can still use my sword," Adacon grunted, clearly in pain. His left arm remained limp at his side. He looked at a dead troll on the ground, staring lifelessly up from a pool of muck-blood, and took in its sickly features: they didn't look like trolls at all up close, or what he'd seen of trolls in books—they all looked deformed, oozing rancid pus, the same way Bulkog had atop the Ceptical Tower.

"Erguile!" Remtall shouted. Adacon looked out to see the only horse rider among the Erol Drunne forces: it was Erguile, swiping in every direction with his sword.

"Come on," Adacon rallied, taking the lead. They fought through two already-wounded trolls, coming to a Feral giant that was set to attack Erguile. The great beast looked much the same as all the other trolls, save for being larger and fitted with heavier armor. It bore a weapon in each hand, unlike the other trolls who had a single weapon each.

"We've come to help with this one," Remtall said, rushing in front of Weakhoof.

"Remtall!" Erguile rejoiced, and then he saw Adacon. "Addy!" Momentarily distracted by his old friends, Erguile was caught off-guard, struck down from Weakhoof by the troll giant. He rolled around on blood-soaked grass, Weakhoof neighing in agony as the giant prepared a death blow.

"Not Weakhoof—nor any fair horse of Rislind, foul beast!" Remtall goaded. The little gnome flew into action, preventing the giant's downward strike with a swinging dagger to the jaw, neatly placed beneath its helmet armor. Adacon quickly sliced with his still functional right arm, opening the leg of the troll behind its knee, where flesh had been exposed. The giant wailed, started to topple backwards, then fell down the hill, squashing several trolls.

"Get up," Remtall demanded. He and Adacon offered their hands to Erguile, who shot to his feet and quickly mounted Weakhoof again, unfazed.

"Am I glad to see you two," Erguile declared.

"Now is no time for catching up boy, look—they come," Remtall said, looking ahead where two warpedes fast approached. Atop each of them rode Feral trolls.

"Fight with courage, knowing you have me, greatest swordsman in the land, amongst your rank," Erguile boasted. Together they braced for the incoming warpedes.

"Second to Flaer, don't you mean?" Adacon quipped, unable to resist teasing him despite the mortal danger.

"Quiet you two—prepare to roll down the hill at the last second—we cannot take both these things alone," Remtall instructed.

"I can," said Slowin. He rushed up to his friends, leaving the dwarven ranks behind him.

"Great Gaigas, it's the silver golem of Red Forest!" Erguile rejoiced. Slowin charged past them to where the warpedes had ascended the hill, digging his feet into the earth to meet their onslaught.

"Watch for the tail strike!" Adacon warned. Both warpedes immediately swooped their jaws down toward Slowin, as if drawn by a magnet. The troll riders atop cried out in a foreign tongue, and it seemed as if they goaded their beasts into teamwork. Just as soon as the centipedes were within reach, Slowin pumped both his fists into the wide helmet armor of the warpedes. In a thunderous clap the gold helms of the centipedes caved in, forming a crater in the skull of the creatures. A high-pitched whine erupted and they bucked in unison, flinging their troll riders from their harnesses to deaths by trampling. Dazed, both warpedes writhed slowly, now with no riders harnessing them. Slowin climbed the back of one of the stunned beasts, using the edges of its gold-plated armor as a ladder. Adacon and the others watched the golem reach the warpede's head, draw from his side a dwarven dagger, then thrust it at the crater, the weak spot he'd punched into its armor. The blade ricocheted off with a metallic clang, but Slowin struck again with fury, this time piercing the gold armor. The warpede slumped to the ground. Slowin looked to the other warpede; he saw Remtall already running up its back, Erguile trailing close behind. Adacon had been assaulted by a group of trolls, but not long before the dwarves of Oreine had come down the northern trail of the Teeth Cliffs, helping to fend them off. Adacon, together with two stout dwarves, slew a handful of trolls, again feeling gripped by a surge of power, as if enchanted by Vapoury. Gaiberth and his elves broke through in time to see the second warpede crash to the earth: Remtall and Erguile mimicked Slowin, stabbing in harmony through the creature's cratered helm to bring it down.

Some of the elven fighters stayed back and fired arrows, the rest joined the mass of dwarves that swarmed the sloping hill. In the distance Adacon saw the Brigun Autilus flash brightly as it pushed toward the ominous bubble-shield of Aulterion. Erguile looked to Weakhoof from atop the slain warpede and saw a troll attempting to mount his defenseless horse.

"Adacon—help Weakhoof!" Erguile cried from afar. Adacon turned to the horse: Weakhoof bucked in madness at the oozing troll struggling to climb up on him. The troll gripped the horse's neck tightly and kicked its side in an attempt to subdue it. Weakhoof whinnied loudly in pain. Adacon rushed up from behind. The troll seemed to sense Adacon's coming, and turned to face him just in time to block the first strike. Adacon's elven sword clanged and issued a blue spark, bouncing quickly off the troll blade. The Feral mutant withdrew a second blade and began swinging wildly with both hands. In a frenzied whirlwind attack, the deformed troll charged. Adacon waited to roll out of the way at the last second. As the troll came within striking distance, Adacon attempted his roll: the right edge of one of the Feral blades cut deeply upon his foot, thwarting his escape. Lying helpless on the ground, with only his right arm for defense, Adacon looked up to his doom. Two more trolls rushed up; together the three trolls surveyed Adacon on the ground. Finally, after what seemed an eternity, the trolls made their strike, stabbing in unison. "Where is Slowin?" Adacon thought in his last moment. As if in reply to his question, three arrows whooshed by, striking each troll dead through the throat.

"Up! No time for a nap," said Calan, her arm breaking the blue sky of his vision. Adacon smiled broadly as she pulled him to his feet. There was no time to celebrate; three more trolls came raging forward. The great battle had become a fight of dwarves and elves against trolls. Adacon didn't see Slowin, Remtall or Erguile; they had been driven apart by the fierce combat. He struggled to find balance on his feet, barely able to walk with his gashed leg—the battle became foggy, a dreamlike state, and he grew faint. Despite his dizziness, he fought next to Calan, side by side with the dwarves, for what seemed like hours more.

"The wall is almost gone," said Calan. Adacon looked back to the Wall of Dinbell to see in amazement that Aulterion had almost completely wrecked the great structure, as enormous chunk after chunk was still tumbling off, spilling onto the south side of the Great Plain. The Feral trolls had started trampling one another to reach the lowest of the newly cleaved ledges of the Dinbell. Soon there were piles of dead trolls forming hills upon which the next row climbed, higher toward the top of the wall.

"Flaer is almost to him," Adacon said, fixing his gaze back upon the light of the Brigun Autilus, barely visible amidst the mass of swarming Ferals. A glint of silver caught his attention—Slowin had appeared again, farther downhill, and Adacon was relieved to see Erguile and Remtall by him, alive and fighting. Just then, King Terion ran past, charging headlong into battle, followed by Iirevale. Falen appeared next; he stopped next to Adacon and Calan and commanded them once more to ride atop him.

"It's not time to die yet young slave—your friend requires your help," Falen said. "There…" he pointed a claw toward the glowing Brigun Autilus.

"You want to fly down to Flaer?" Adacon said, only half-conscious. "I stand no chance out there, how could I help?"

"I am uncertain, but look—there," Falen instructed, and Adacon sent his gaze out over the mass of Feral army once more. Deep in the distance he saw a beam of light shining, very different from Aulterion's. Unsure if it was a hallucination, the new beam suddenly drew closer, pointed at Adacon. As quickly as he had realized the light was focused on him, it redirected itself down to the plain where Flaer struggled, almost in reach of Aulterion.

"You see, he wants you to go there," Falen said.

"Who?" Adacon asked dizzily, searching for a source to the new light. It radiated from a great height in the sky, directly above Flaer, atop what appeared to be a circling bird.

"Yarnhoot!" shouted Adacon. He strained to see what he thought was a brief reflection of purple off the rider. "Krem!"

"Get on, both of you—now," Falen commanded. This time Adacon idled no longer; he and Calan hopped on Falen's back, gripping hard to a tiny harness. Falen spread his wings to full span and started to beat them hard just as a fresh horde of trolls reached the top of the hill. Falen roared at them, opened his mouth: from his jaw rained down a stream of glowing red flame as he propelled his riders high into the air. The scorched trolls moaned in agony, curling into balls, as the drake bore his riders northwest, high above the sound of clashing steel. From above, it appeared that the dwarven army was making progress in pushing back the Feral Brood, but already a huge throng of trolls had managed to scramble over the crumbling Dinbell. The wall had all but disappeared in the very middle of its width, forming a V, standing only ten yards high at its lowest point. The trolls smothered each other in their rabid scramble, some now reaching the Enoan Road. Adacon could still spot the silver of Slowin, and the dots that were Remtall, and Erguile—who was again astride Weakhoof. They fought valiantly as a team, together with Terion, Iirevale, and Gaiberth; even Ulpo could be seen hacking a path through the vile trolls.

Falen flew on, closer and closer to Flaer, keeping enough height to outrange arrow attacks.

"Krem!" Adacon began shouting as the little Vapour came into focus atop the great condor. The old Vapour was still too far away to hear anything. Falen was closing in on Yarnhoot when a great flash of lightning overtook him, disrupting his ability to fly in a straight line. The light disappeared, and then all light, until it became as dark as a starless midnight. Frantically searching the sky, Adacon could see nothing. Suddenly the sky returned, flashing back to its midday blue, only to be followed by a chain of light, again followed by total darkness, then flashes of red. Below, Flaer had finally reached Aulterion; he was piercing right through the dark mage's bubble of energy. Each strike of the Brigun Autilus, Adacon realized, caused the blackness to overtake the sky—and each time the energy field weakened and withdrew, a great flash of red was emitted from the spot where Flaer struck at it. Taking his eyes off the battle below, Adacon leveled his gaze to see Krem was very close. Krem looked at him, pointed his staff down toward Flaer and Aulterion. Falen abruptly followed Krem's staff. The drake swooped violently down toward the flashing energy field below. Adacon wondered in confusion at how he could possibly help Flaer, who fought one of the most powerful dark mages ever to live on Darkin. Flurries of arrows whizzed by Falen as Feral archers caught sight of the descending drake. Adacon and Calan kept their eyes on Flaer, hoping they could provide some kind of help to him when Falen dropped down into the madness, but Flaer appeared to have the fight well in hand. A loud crack split the black-red sky, and the earth was torn open around the edge of the mage's bubble. Nearby trolls fell to the ground, some fell into a widening chasm ring. Both armies, good and evil, wherever they stood, shook violently. For a moment all fighting ceased except for the duel of Flaer against Aulterion. Aulterion's shield bubble had been destroyed, and the beam of light that was cracking the Dinbell started to retract, returning to its sender. Adacon watched in amazement as Aulterion began fighting with his own sword against Flaer. Adacon could not believe what he was seeing: parry after parry was traded between the powerful fighters, each thrust accompanied by a brilliant flash of light. Thunder caused the Great Plain to quake for leagues in every direction. Long red shadows spread like a god's fingers across the land, scattering the forces that were battling even high atop the Teeth Cliffs.

Adacon looked back at Krem, who smiled calmly atop Yarnhoot and flew in close behind, tracing Falen's dive toward Aulterion and Flaer.

"Here goes everything I've got!" Falen roared, struggling against the turbulent winds coming from Flaer and Aulterion. The drake landed with a thud and a bounce. Up close, Adacon could see Aulterion, recognize him: *the stranger who attacked us on the swamp road!* Adacon saw Krem land, dismount Yarnhoot. Then he saw Calan—she was trying to stand up after being thrown during the landing. Off to the side, Adacon thought he saw someone that looked familiar: *Merol!* The dwarf wizard was conjuring a blinding stream of light that poured into Aulterion, giving him strength. Everything appeared to be in slow motion. Flaer raised the sun-bright Brigun Autilus—Aulterion raised his razor-thin gunmetal blade—everything went black.

XI: EROL DRUNNE

Adacon awoke underneath heavy quilts. He was in a small, cozy room he had never seen before. A sweet aroma filtered through the room, the smell of food. Nothing came to mind except an odd dream: he and Calan had been walking through a frost-bitten meadow of flowers at dawn...

Memory came flooding back. He remembered the battle at Dinbell, the calamity of the strikes Flaer and Aulterion threw against one another. He wondered for a moment if any of it had been real. He looked to his left arm and saw a deep scar running down. There was a tiny window in the room, built sturdily with a cross frame. On its outside ledge was a high ridge of snow, the softest white he'd ever seen. Adacon rubbed his eyes in astonishment, peering out the window from the warmth of his bed, watching thick flurries of snow-crystals drift sideways. He quickly surveyed the rest of the room: there two oak cabinets and some candles burning on a table in the corner, creating a pale yellow glow. Against either wall were wooden statues of bear-like creatures and atop the only door in the room hung a worn battle axe. The walls were knotty grain wood, slightly shiny. Adacon felt relieved to become aware that he was in no slave home, not back on his farm in Arkenshyr—there were no homes there as nice as this. Suddenly the door creaked, and in walked a purple robed wizard.

"Krem…" Adacon said.

"Good to see you're finally awake lad. I thought I heard someone stirring in here," he replied with a warm smile.

"Where am I—what happened?" Adacon asked.

"Calm yourself. You are safe, and once more in the protection of my Vapoury. We are in Erol Drunne, dear Adacon."

"But—how did we get here? Last I remember…" Adacon said, trailing off, unable to express his exploding thoughts and questions.

"I had to call you down to Flaer in the final moments of his duel against Aulterion. You possess a special… power. A power you've never understood—of which no one else possesses in all of Darkin," Krem said.

"Me?" Adacon said in bewilderment.

"Without you, we would not have been able to defeat Aulterion—nor the Feral Brood in turn."

"They've been defeated? I still don't understand—how long has it been since the battle?"

"Not very long. A season," Krem answered.

"A season? I have slept for a season!?" Adacon panicked, staring out the window at the falling snow.

"Not very long, considering how much energy you spent saving Flaer," Krem replied.

"Me—save Flaer?—surely this is a dream, or the state of death," Adacon gasped in confusion. "Have you gone mad Krem? Am I?"

"Quiet boy—quiet and rest. You still need time to recover. What is important is that you are alive and well, and that Enoa has been saved. I will tell you about your power later, after you've had plenty to drink and eat, and your strength's returned."

"The war is really over?" asked Adacon, unable to fathom the suggestion to relax.

"No, not the war. The people of Arkenshyr are in grave peril. In the wake of Aulterion's utter destruction, Zesm has overthrown Vesleathren, and become more powerful than we can guess. Zesm has…" Krem stopped talking. A shadow passed over his jovial visage, but it lasted only an instant, and then the old Vapour smiled once more: "Enough—enough of talk that is serious, for now at least. There will be plenty of time, later, for that. There is a time of peace now on this side of the Kalm. We mustn't dwell on dark omens in the hour we first wake!" Just then Erguile burst into the room carrying a plate of hot pastries and a pot of tea.

"Good morning old friend, savior of us all," said Erguile, winking. "Couldn't help but overhear you finally talking again! Thought you might want something to eat—what with sleeping for months on end…" Adacon stopped trying to understand how he'd saved them; he simply surrendered to the joy of seeing his old friend:

"Erguile!" Adacon rejoiced. Erguile came over to him and they embraced. Just then, a loud argument could be heard outside, drifting in through the still open door.

"If you'll just give me a head start, I'm telling you, there's *no way* you can outswim me—no way—fat rock of a man!" shouted a familiar gnome's voice. In a moment Remtall came in through the doorway, smiling wide and holding a flask in his hand.

"What better time to perform a toast?" Remtall exclaimed. He shuffled over to Adacon and they hugged one another, giant grins spread across their faces. Adacon glimpsed Slowin standing outside the doorway, unable to fit inside.

"Slowin! Decided you'd hang around after all?" Adacon called. He attempted to get up from his bed, but Erguile restrained him.

"No you don't—not yet," Erguile said.

"I'll be here. I'm not going home just yet, friend. Very glad to see you're back with us. Oh—before I forget—Falen sends his regards—he's flown off to visit his family in the north," Slowin announced. "I think someone else is coming." As Slowin finished his last word, another familiar sound came from just outside the doorway: Calan's laughter. She rushed in, without words flinging herself onto the bed, knocking Adacon down against the quilt.

"Easy woman, he's not quite one hundred percent," Erguile warned.

"Let them be, dumb slave! Never mind the affections of an elf woman, nor the ravaging her man must pay her after many months without. Let's leave them be, how about?" Remtall said.

"We'll be just outside," Krem said, hinting for the others to leave.

"And don't be getting up for anything either, you hear?" Erguile warned. "I'll be checking up on you..." They filtered out one by one, until at last Krem stood alone in the doorway, looking at Calan and him.

"Oh, one more thing before I leave you two alone," Krem said.

Adacon nodded and smiled, waiting.

"Someone else wants to say hello," the wizard replied. Adacon stared at Krem in confusion, but soon a smile crossed his face as he realized whom Krem spoke of. Calan kissed him, and

DARKIN: A JOURNEY EAST

together they waited for the final visitor. Krem waved farewell, then scooted out the door.

Flaer stepped in.

"Flaer!" Adacon said, lighting up.

"Glad to see you're finally awake—Calan, would you mind allowing me a moment with Adacon?" said Flaer, his voice deep and gravelly. No smile formed on his face.

"Of course not," she said. After a quick peck on Adacon's cheek she bounded out of the room. Flaer quickly turned, shut the door behind her. Now alone together, Flaer moved his hands in an odd circular motion around the handle of the door. Like a wave, emerald light rolled over the door, extended to the ceiling, encompassed every wall and window in the tiny room.

"So they won't hear us," Flaer grunted in explanation.

"Hear what?"

THE END

ABOUT THE CREATOR

Joseph A. Turkot currently works as a Teacher of English in New Jersey. He graduated from Rutgers University with a B.A. in English. He has written numerous short stories and novels in the world of Darkin. The sequel to Darkin: A Journey East will be published in September 2012.

CONTACT

joeturkot@gmail.com

OFFICIAL DARKIN WEBSITE

www.novelfantasy.com

DARKIN: A JOURNEY EAST